DARK ASHES

AN ELENORA BELLO MYSTERY

JACINTHE DESSUREAULT

Demiurge
Underground

Legal deposit – Bibliothèque et Archives nationales du Québec, 2024
Legal deposit – Library and Archives Canada, 2024

ISBN 978-1-9994431-7-7 (paperback)
ISBN 978-1-9994431-8-4 (ebook)

*To my sweet Moosie,
my coffee-obsessed guardian angel
and forever love*

CHAPTER ONE

Was there a siren song playing from her refrigerator? What else could explain Elenora being lured to her fridge at 2 a.m.?

I need to stop giving in to these ridiculous cravings, she scolded herself as the bright light of the appliance blinded her. She reached for the last piece of maple sugar pie she had buried at the back of the bottom shelf so that Tom wouldn't find it. Having a tall husband could be such a blessing. And Elenora still had a few good years before she needed to upgrade her strategy to keep baby Aubrey out of her dessert stash, too.

Contorting herself, Elenora moved several jars and containers of questionable leftovers out of the way. As she thought she had reached the slice of pie, more containers seemed to appear. She let out a frustrated grunt. Hadn't she removed the pickles from the fridge twice already?

She grabbed the pickle jar. The glass container felt... squishy? She squeezed it, and it liquified through her fingers.

What the...

Oh. Right.

She was dreaming.

"Hello, my dear." An older man's voice behind her startled her. She froze. The few people she encountered in her dreams rarely addressed her so directly. Was this a premonition? And if so, why were they in her kitchen? Was someone about to die in her home?

With her senses on high alert, Elenora turned to see who had spoken to her and was relieved to recognize Albert Leclerc, an elderly man who had passed away earlier in the year. Right before his death, she visited him in a dream. He asked her to take care of his cat, Willem, and told her where he lived. Elenora relayed the information to her police detective husband, Tom, and sure enough, he and his partner, Alex Bélanger, found the retired watchmaker dead in his bed, his cat watching over him. Tom and Elenora had ended up adopting the beautiful silver-haired pet.

"Mr. Leclerc," Elenora started, unsure of what to say. It seemed rude to ask him flat-out what he was doing in her kitchen.

The friendly departed man floated near the kitchen counter, looking almost solid, though there was a ghostly softness to his appearance. "I didn't mean to surprise you. I apologize."

Elenora chuckled and pointed at the fridge. "Well, you caught me red-handed. Please don't tell my husband."

"Your secret's safe with me." He winked at her. "You must be wondering what a dead old coot is doing in your kitchen, interrupting your secret mission."

"It crossed my mind, and I'm a little concerned—the last time we spoke, things didn't end so well for you... I wish we had met sooner. I wish I could have helped prevent your death."

He shrugged. "Things happened the way they were meant to happen."

Around the time of their first encounter, Elenora had experienced disturbing premonitory dreams of fatal events. The information they gave her was always too late, preventing her from acting in time and saving the victims. These fruitless insights had been frustrating and stressful. To help Elenora cope, two of her colleagues—her medium mentor, Yukiko, and Dr. Meredith Brent, the head psychologist at the Off Path Office—had created a mental technique so Elenora's psyche could filter out the unhelpful premonitions. This gave the budding psychic a welcome mental reprieve while allowing relevant dreams to reach her.

Her mental filters had allowed the present kitchen encounter with Mr. Leclerc, telling her it could be a helpful premonition and something terrible was about to happen.

But her visitor's relaxed demeanor suggested otherwise.

Maybe this was a visitation dream, then? Elenora had only had one of them in the past, when her departed friend, Angéline—a seasoned medium herself—had summoned Elenora in her sleep.

"Besides," Mr. Leclerc said, a playful gleam in his eyes, "your husband found my earthly body before it traumatized my dear cat and the neighbors. I call that a win."

Elenora couldn't help but smile. He had a point. Her premonition had served a purpose, no matter how meager.

Still, the timing had been fatal.

Her smile vanished.

"My time was up, dear. Nothing to be done," he said

kindly, as if reading her mind. "And you took Willem in. Thank you."

"Willem's a good pet," she replied. That was mostly true. The cat had weird habits and often gave her the evil eye, but he seemed attached to Aubrey. He followed the little one everywhere, as if he had a sacred duty to guard her and took his job seriously.

Despite the feline's appreciation for her daughter, Elenora didn't wish to discuss him further—the suspense around Mr. Leclerc's presence was killing her. If there was a preventable death, the clock was ticking. "Are you here to announce an imminent casualty?"

Confusion appeared on the departed man's face before he understood the meaning of her question. "You think I'm here in a doom-and-gloom capacity?"

"Yes. That's how my premonitions seem to work."

"Ah, yes. But this isn't a premonition."

"A visitation dream?"

He nodded. "Just a good ol' visit."

Elenora would take a visitation dream over a stressful, horrific premonition any night of the week, but why would a man she barely knew choose to visit her?

"Did you want me to relay a message to a loved one on your behalf?" she asked. This would make the most sense, though this kind of request was tricky. The average person was ill-equipped to handle anything remotely supernatural, so it was best to conceal that mind-boggling reality from them.

"Oh, no! No. I was simply wondering if I could visit Willem. Would that be all right with you? I promise I'll be discreet."

A chuckle burst out of Elenora. Worrying over nothing—the story of her life. "Of course you can visit Willem. You must miss him."

He nodded. "I miss our chats."

Elenora smiled at the adorable statement while feeling sad for him. The man had returned to her plane of existence to talk to his cat. Was he lonely in his afterlife? What a heartbreaking thought.

"How are you doing, sir? How's your afterlife?"

The question took him off guard. "Dandy. Afterlife's dandy. You know, keeping busy."

His answer sounded casual and didn't suggest loneliness—this reassured Elenora, but his words puzzled her. How did one keep busy after death?

As she was about to ask him the question, she woke up, disoriented and bummed. She had so many questions about life after death! Still, what a pleasant dream, whether it had been an actual visitation or a plain old dream.

Now that she thought about it, it was probably the latter because why would a ghost seek her out to ask for her permission to see his cat?

Her stomach grumbled, and the piece of pie in the fridge crossed her mind. Dang it, she was hungry for real. Maybe her hunger had prompted the dream instead of Mr. Leclerc's spirit. That would make sense.

Elenora slipped out of bed, careful not to wake up Tom. She padded down the stairs, mindful to avoid the creaky spots. Their house was heavy on charm and original woodwork, including the staircase. The craftsmanship and history of the stairs were lovely in the light of day but less fun in the middle of the night when the home was dead quiet.

Reaching the bottom of the stairs in stealthy silence, Elenora felt victorious. But then her gaze shifted to the kitchen down the hall, and she stopped in her tracks.

An unfamiliar light glowed from the room.

Had she or Tom left a light on? They rarely did, and besides, where would this light be coming from?

She debated whether to investigate the source or wake Tom up. But what if it was something silly? Was it worth disturbing her husband's sleep? He had been working long hours.

It's probably silly.

The glowing pulsed, reminding Elenora of the first time she'd seen Angéline de Montbleu's ghost. And Mary Gallagher's.

Mary Gallagher...

Could this be Mary?

Elenora had told the local ghostly legend she would visit her but hadn't made good on her promise. She'd been busy. And sure, maybe she was in no hurry to hang out with a beheaded specter who was a little hard on the eye. Seriously —aside from ghost hunters and other paranormal enthusiasts, who would wish to have a conversation with a blood-soaked spirit holding her severed head against her hip?

Elenora grimaced at the thought. Blood was not her forte, and the mere thought of it made her queasy.

Had Mary sought her out in her own home? That was another stomach-churning thought. The last thing Elenora needed was a gory specter invading her personal space.

A man's faint voice told her it wasn't Mary.

Were they being robbed, then?

Elenora scanned the adjacent vestibule for a weapon. If

she went back upstairs, she risked alerting the intruder—intruders?—to her presence. She pondered her choices: umbrellas in the entrance closet and possibly Tom's baseball bat. But the damn closet door gave the stairs a run for their money in the creaking department. In the living room across the hall, the fire poker and other hefty metal tools stood by the fireplace, but crossing into that room might give her away, as it was visible from the kitchen.

As Elenora scrambled to figure out what to do, she noticed yesterday's newspaper in the entryway, still rolled up tightly with an elastic. Not the best weapon but better than nothing. She stepped forward to grab it, and her foot connected with a small plastic toy on wheels. It skittered across the hardwood floor in a shocking cacophony.

She stilled, sucking in a breath and swearing on the inside.

The glowing intensified in the kitchen doorway, revealing a male ghost.

"Elenora?" he whispered, as if mindful that everyone else in the house was asleep.

"Mr. Leclerc?" she whispered back.

Well, imagine that. Her dream had indeed been a genuine visitation dream, after all.

"Did I wake you up? I swear I tried to be discreet. Like I promised I would." He looked sheepish and a little nervous. "I hope you're not regretting saying yes."

"No, of course not. I just didn't expect you to visit so soon."

Willem appeared behind him and rubbed against the departed man's ethereal legs.

Huh.

Could the cat see him? Or sense his presence, perhaps?

Was she seriously wondering if her cat could see the spirit of his previous owner in her kitchen at two in the morning?

Who did that?

It dawned on Elenora that not only was there a ghost in her kitchen—and she had given him permission to be there—but her cat was even weirder than she had thought.

"I apologize for making you uncomfortable, my dear," Mr. Leclerc said.

"Oh. No, I'm... I'm just stunned that Willem is responding to you. I heard cats can sense things humans can't, but it surprises me to witness it."

Were all cats like this?

And if she died before Willem, would he expect her to visit him too?

"Willem has always been special." He bent down to pet his cat, unleashing a series of loud purrs, and lifted his eyes to hers. "I'll stop keeping you up and be on my merry way. Let me know if you change your mind about me visiting him—I wouldn't want to intrude. You have yourself a good night now."

The specter vanished before she could reply.

Willem moved toward her, brushed against her calf, and then strutted to the living room like he owned the place.

Elenora stood there, wondering if her life could get any weirder.

CHAPTER TWO

"Trust me. There's always room for weirder," Serena said, brandishing a fry at Elenora. They were having lunch at the Fish & Ship.

"It's comforting to know that," Elenora replied dryly.

Her witch friend gave her a broad smile. "Hey, if I were stuck with a ghost in my kitchen, I would choose a sweet little old man who misses his cat over most alternatives."

Yeah, be grateful it's not Mary.

Or Joseph Gill. Or Oliver Barlow.

Elenora shuddered. Memories of murderous spirits sent chills down her spine.

"I wonder if *I* have a ghost in my kitchen," Serena said matter-of-factly. "Maybe you can check the next time you—" Serena glanced past Elenora and dropped her voice, "—come over." Someone must have been heading their way.

Sure enough, Georgia—a.k.a. Curious Georgia, their server—appeared with a water pitcher. She was a good person but had the impressive hearing of a bat, a nose for gossip, and a propensity for broadcasting it. Serena had grown tired of watching their backs to keep their ghost talk from being overheard—especially by their server. She had cast a spell that warned her every time Georgia came too close to their table. Despite Elenora's inability to detect the magical warning, speaking would trigger the spell and cut her off mid-sentence, preventing sensitive information from passing her lips. The effect had been jarring the first few times, but she had quickly adapted to this quirky speech impediment and was grateful to be able to converse without censoring or watching herself.

"Still doing good, guys?" Georgia poured water and clinking ice cubes into Serena's glass. Despite the efficacy of the spell, Elenora couldn't help searching the woman's expression for signs that she knew about her kitchen ghost. The woman carried on as if she had heard nothing odd.

Elenora's gaze swept over the adjoining tables. Most of them were empty. Their favorite restaurant was quiet for a Monday lunchtime, which was a mixed blessing. When the place was packed, the service was erratic, but the collective murmur of the other patrons' conversations provided a sound blanket over their paranormal topics. With today's smaller crowd, not only did Georgia pop up at their elbows more frequently than usual, but the two friends also had to talk more quietly despite the spell and the relative privacy of their secluded table.

And with her big personality, Serena didn't do "quietly" very well.

Elenora had asked her if she could add voice-level control to the spell. The witch had replied that it could be done, but it would be too draining for her to juggle such an extra element while they talked. If Elenora had learned one thing since meeting her friend and the other witches, it was that magic was complicated.

Georgia waltzed away with her pitcher, and once she was out of earshot, Elenora asked Serena, "Wasn't your place new when you bought it?" It seemed unlikely to her that someone would have died a violent death in her friend's modern downtown condo.

"There was one owner before me."

"Did that person die?"

"He seemed pretty alive at the notary."

Then, who would have died in her home for Serena to think a spirit might haunt it?

"Was there an accident during construction?"

Elenora's question reminded her of a young construction worker named Jérémie Marsan. She had foreseen his premature death at an old house under renovation in a premonition. She had also met his peaceful spirit and helped deliver a message from him to his fiancée. The young woman had been immensely thankful to get news from beyond the veil, but her sadness had been so palpable that it still haunted Elenora. She wished she could have prevented the senseless death.

"You're looking for an answer in the wrong places, Ele. A death could have predated the construction of the condo. Who knows what happened on the land over the years before they built the tower."

Of course. Elenora gave herself a mental slap over the obvious.

"I might live right over an old burial ground, for all I know," Serena added. Her place was on the outskirts of the Griffintown neighborhood, which had witnessed plenty of history.

"You think a spirit could hang out all the way up to the fourteenth floor?" Elenora wondered how far a ghost could travel vertically.

"Why not?" Serena shrugged and dipped a fry in a crinkled paper cup of aioli before popping it into her mouth. She moaned, slid the sauce toward Elenora, and offered her a fry. "I know I say this every time, but I'm so glad they still have this."

Serena claimed the restaurant had been serving her favorite dipping sauce for over a century, and she must have known this for a fact. The witch had inherited a smidge of vampire blood, causing her and her twin sister, Claire-Lune, to age much slower than the average human being. The sisters were over two hundred years old and technically identical, but they looked different—Claire-Lune embraced her natural middle-aged looks, while Serena wore a glamour that gave her the appearance of a college kid that matched her endless energy.

"Never underestimate the magic in little things," the witch added.

"How long has this place been around?" Elenora asked despite knowing she might not get an answer. Once in a while, Serena shared snippets of her fascinating and very long past, but when pressed for details, she often changed the subject.

"For as long as I can remember." Serena dipped another fry. "I recall it closing during the First World War and being bummed about it. Back then, it had been around for a good twenty years, but it wasn't a seafood spot. The meals were simpler, and I think they originally used this sauce to cover up questionable freshness."

Elenora crinkled her nose. "Ew. Lovely."

Serena chuckled. "I'm joking. Kinda. But you know, food safety wasn't always as fancy as it is today. Oh, the things I've eaten." She made a face. "Oh yeah, they had rooms upstairs, too."

"This place was an inn?"

"A cheap-ass inn or a brothel. Nothing I had a use for. Anyway, the food was decent—that's all that mattered."

"I can only imagine what life was like back then," Elenora tried, craving more insight into her friend's past. What did it feel like to have been around for so long?

"It sucked." Serena raked a handful of fries through the sauce and shoved them inside her mouth, ending the trip down memory lane. She moaned again—exaggeratingly this time. Two women at a nearby table stared at her. Serena gave them a thumbs-up before ignoring them and returning her attention to Elenora.

"In all seriousness, it truly is the little things. There are things not only no money can buy, but no amount of magic can recreate either." She stabbed a finger at the paper cup. "And this is one of them, and it makes me happy. As silly as it sounds."

"Doesn't sound silly at all. It's beautiful to see that, as powerful as you are, you still appreciate the little things."

"Oh, don't get me wrong—I also appreciate the big things my powers give me," she retorted. "And speaking of powers... When are you gonna see Mary?"

Elenora squirmed in her seat. Way to turn the tables on her. She stole a handful of fries from her friend's plate and ate them one by one to buy herself time. Serena's eyes crinkled with humor as she recognized Elenora's delay tactic.

"Yeah, about that..." Elenora said finally.

She had told Yukiko she'd promised the repulsive ghost to visit her. Soon after, with Dr. Brent's help, the medium mentor developed a new psychic technique enabling Elenora to summon spirits by herself.

"If you don't go see her on her turf, she might seek you out on yours," Serena pointed out.

Elenora groaned at the stressful reminder. She worried that using the technique would make her even more of a lightning rod for spirits than she already was. She was also downright afraid of Mary.

While Elenora was more at ease with seeing ghosts since their victorious case at the old house on Maple Street, she didn't feel quite up to dealing with Mary yet. Her sensitivity to blood didn't help. The one time Elenora had seen her in the vacant lot she haunted, the spectral apparition had been faint and brief. The psychic's mind hadn't had the time to fully register what she'd seen. A full conversation with Mary would give her plenty of time to take in every graphic detail.

And what could the ghost possibly want from her? The question churned Elenora's stomach on a good day.

So, she avoided thinking about the visit, but kicking this can down the road only gave her temporary relief. It made her feel bad, too, and the feeling kept worsening. A mature adult would bite the bullet and make good on her word.

"What are you afraid of?" Serena asked.

"We're talking about Mary Gallagher. What am I *not* afraid of?"

"Dude! You kicked a psychotic necromancer's ass! I doubt Mrs. Gallagher is half as evil as that douche was. *If* she's evil at all. I agree she could use a makeover, but you can't judge someone by their looks. Her bestie beheaded her. Maybe her worst crime was having a shitty taste in friends."

Elenora sighed. Serena was right. Other than a rumored fiery temper, there was no proof that the murdered prostitute had been a nefarious human being or that she was out to get anyone. There was no reason for Elenora to attribute sinister intentions to the ghost and fear her.

"You're right. She was the victim."

But all that blood...

Ugh.

Serena dropped her last fries on Elenora's plate.

"Thanks."

"You want ketchup for those?" Serena teased.

Elenora made a face. "I like ketchup! Don't ruin it for me!"

"Look, as much as I enjoy teasing you, I'm only pushing you to get this done because I can tell it affects you. The sooner you do it, the sooner you can move on."

Elenora let out another sigh. "Yeah. Moving on sounds good."

"You know I'm a big fan of moving on. Let me know if you need help with Mary. I've got your back."

"I know you do, and thank you for that. She's so skittish that Yukiko thinks I'll have to approach her alone or she won't show."

"She wants you to be completely alone?" Serena frowned.

"Not completely. She and Tom will be nearby in case there's a problem. But I'm glad you're willing to help. 'Cause if things go sideways, I'd be more comfortable if you were there, too."

"You got it. Just say when."

Elenora nodded and moved a lone broccoli floret around her otherwise empty plate with her fork. "I'll make an effort to deal with Mary soon. It's just that I'm already over-whelmed—" The words *these days* died on her lips as Georgia appeared in her periphery.

"Still working on it, hon?" The server pointed at the broccoli.

Elenora stabbed it with her fork and ate it.

Georgia picked up their plates. "Coffee? Desserts?"

"Yes," Serena said.

"Do you have *pouding chômeur* today?" Elenora asked.

"How could we not?"

"Oh, hell yeah. We'll have that," Serena jumped in. "And coffee."

"Make that two?" Georgia asked them.

"Yes, please," Elenora and Serena replied in unison.

"Awesome. Be right back." The server left with the plates.

"Don't lose faith," Serena said to Elenora. "You have a lot going on. But things usually fall into place."

"There's more." Elenora reached for a sugar packet and toyed with it. "I went to see my mom yesterday."

"Okay. What's up with her?"

That was the thing. For the longest time, there had been absolutely nothing up with Muriel, Elenora's mother. The woman had been in a catatonic state—a mental coma—for years and lived in a special care facility. For over a decade, she had barely moved a muscle. However, recently, she'd had two disturbing physical reactions over Elenora's baby daugh-ter. The first time happened when Elenora and Tom announced the pregnancy. Muriel's fingers had balled into a fist, and a wild expression had flashed in her eyes.

The second time, Muriel had held baby Aubrey in a death grip with her otherwise-atrophied arms and uttered vehemently that "she was not his." This cryptic declaration had made no sense, nor had the urgency and tone behind the words. She had clutched her granddaughter so tightly that Elenora and Tom had feared she wouldn't let go of her. He ultimately convinced her to loosen her grip so the baby could nurse.

The medical staff at the residence couldn't explain what had happened. Dr. Graham was baffled, and a battery of tests yielded no results to explain the outburst.

"Pierre suggested I go alone. It had been long since it was just her and me." Elenora squeezed the sugar packet. "It felt like a mother-daughter reunion, except with a one-way conversation. There was so much silence to fill..."

Serena nodded with understanding. "And you babbled to fill it."

"I babbled to fill it."

"What'd you tell her?"

Elenora stuffed the sugar packet back into the holder. "What *didn't* I tell her?"

"You told her about your abilities?" Serena barely hid her surprise.

"Can you believe it? I told her all the crazy things happening in my life that I had kept from her in case she could understand me. I didn't want to distress her with my crazy revelations. But then, one moment, I'm filling the silence with small talk, and the next, I'm telling her how worried I am that Aubrey might be special."

Reacting to those last words, Serena looked about to interject but bit her bottom lip instead. Elenora knew her friend thought it'd be fantastic if Aubrey was special.

Georgia appeared with their dessert and coffee order.

"Freshly hot from the oven, ladies," she announced proudly, lowering two enticing pieces of cake drenched with maple syrup. The smell was divine.

The two friends dug in with gusto. The syrupy sponge melted on their tongues.

"So, you told Muriel about your concerns about Aubrey," Serena said around a mouthful once Georgia was out of earshot.

"Yeah. And then I told her all about me." Elenora lowered her voice. "The premonitions. The visions. The ghosts. I was careful not to mention the OPO, though."

She was determined to maintain the secrecy of the Off-Path Office, the shadow paranormal agency that employed Serena and her colleagues.

"I don't think you have to worry about that," the witch replied, still chewing.

"Well, they monitor the rooms. You never know who might be reading lips on a monitor."

Elenora's husband was adept at lip reading, and the skill had served him right on several occasions, both in his detective work and life in general. She knew her concern wasn't that far-fetched.

"If anyone lipread your big reveal, they'd probably think you have a few screws loose. No biggie."

Elenora nodded. "Put that way..."

"I assume Muriel took your crazy confession with her

trademark stoicism." Serena dumped a creamer into her coffee, gave it a stir, and took a sip.

"The weird thing is—"

"She reacted?" The witch leaned forward in her seat, eager to hear the details.

Elenora also leaned forward. "Well—"

"Elenora!" Detective David Demontigny, a colleague at the station, waved to her from the cash register across the restaurant. Elenora could tell he was considering coming to their table. He was a nice guy and a decent detective, except when it came to reading social cues—he was spectacularly tone-deaf in that department. And "Clingy" could have been his middle name.

"Seriously?" Serena scowled.

Crap.

Elenora had witnessed Serena magically toying with people while in a good mood. Who knew what she might do if the irritating man invaded her space. Elenora stood up and went to intercept her colleague, figuring it would be easier to get rid of him if he didn't reach their table. God forbid he would join them while waiting for his takeout order to be ready.

CHAPTER THREE

*Ville-Marie (the Nouvelle-France settlement
now known as Montréal), 1673*

"Oooohhhfff," Agnès Dumoulin groaned, draping an
arm around her protruding belly and bending over.
Her grimace told her sister, Lizzie, that she would become an
aunt soon.

The Place du Marché was busier than usual on that early
Sunday morning, teeming with merchants and buyers. Lizzie
steered Agnès to the opening of an alley so that she and her
very pregnant sister would be out of the way. "Do you want
to go home?"

Agnès puffed out a string of shallow breaths and steadied
herself before answering. "No. It will pass. It's too early. I still
have a few weeks to go." While the witch couldn't accurately
predict the time or day she'd go into labor, she had an
uncanny intuition for some things, and predicting her pregnancy had been one of them. So far, she had foreseen the
moment she conceived, the times her energy was about to

wane, and when she ought to be near a chamber pot. "And I'm not going anywhere until I have the herbs on my list."

Lizzie didn't argue. "If you change your mind, I can spare you some herbs."

As a healing witch and nurse at Miss Jeanne Mance's Hôtel-Dieu Hospital and the prison, Lizzie collected every herb she could get her hands on for her ointments and potions. She was well stocked.

Agnès nodded and winced. Her eyes closed, she rubbed the underside of her belly, not ready to go anywhere yet.

Lizzie envied her sister, whose pregnancy was obvious. She suspected that she, too, had recently become pregnant, but it was too early to announce the good news. For one thing, her intuition wasn't as sharp as her sister's, and she couldn't know for certain. But it made sense. She was strongly aware of her body and felt a transformation. Furthermore, her friend Marie-Josèphe's tea leaves had confirmed a life-altering event for her on the horizon. Of course, the leaves could have referred to something else. It was hard to tell sometimes.

But then, some of Lizzie's fellow witches at the coven had been giving her knowing looks. If they suspected something, they knew to keep the pregnancy a secret until Lizzie showed outward signs and Dr. Barthes confirmed it. In the meantime, the wait and necessary secrecy weighed on Lizzie.

A limping man appeared at Lizzie's periphery, and her gaze tracked him as he trudged hurriedly down the alley.

Marcel Godé.

She'd known him for as long as she could remember and had witnessed his saddening decline from a respectable baker to a destitute shell of a man after losing his wife and children.

The devastating loss had crippled him and made him unable to function. Despite his troubles, he remained kind, and Lizzie made it a mission to watch over him and help him whenever she could.

A moment later, the reason for Marcel's hurry became clear. Two men went around a nearby miller's cart, chasing him. Their sleek habits and stocky builds contrasted with Marcel's ragged clothes and thin frame. Their confident pace slowed as they crept toward their prey. Lizzie recognized them as members of a group of ruffians who terrorized and abused the vulnerable around the settlement. This wouldn't end well for Marcel.

Agnès's hand landed on her arm. "Do not be rash and risk revealing yourself. This is not your battle," she murmured between clenched teeth.

This is not your battle...

When Lizzie and her sister had found themselves in life-threatening situations as children, it had been no one else's battle either. Most folks had made it clear. If something rubbed her the wrong way, it certainly was turning a blind eye.

She let out an irritated sigh.

"Don't be impulsive," Agnès said, anxious.

"I know. Impulsivity will be my downfall," Lizzie grumbled with an eye roll.

Agnès grunted and attempted to steer her sister away from the alley, where the mean men were closing in on Marcel. Lizzie knew her sister was terrified of her doing something reckless. Agnès tugged on her arm to leave the alley. Lizzie relented and took a few willing steps.

But then a scream rose behind the two sisters, and Lizzie

stopped. Marcel's cry was muffled but loud enough to hear and infused with agony. It reminded Lizzie of her own abuse.

Her fingers bunched into a fist, and she saw red.

A dull thud followed by another cry made her grit her teeth.

Each blow echoed in Lizzie's soul, and she struggled not to look back and witness the beating. What were the thugs after? Marcel had less than nothing for them to take.

They must have wanted to coerce him into doing a dirty job.

Lizzie became angrier and glanced back. Marcel was balled up on the ground, trying to ward off vicious kicks from his assailants.

Agnès's grip on her sister's arm tightened. "Please," she pleaded with a strangled whisper.

Lizzie understood how high the stakes were for both her and Agnès if she exposed their nature to the good—and less good—folks of Ville-Marie. The sisters had been hunted down in their native France, and witches weren't treated any better in the New World. If Lizzie and Agnès were found out, where would they go this time?

If they could even escape again.

Torn, Lizzie spied around the alley, her mind racing. Using magic directly on the abusers was too risky, especially since Lizzie's non-healing magic was unreliable.

But what about a diversion?

The alley was narrow and empty, save for the two witches and the three men. Lizzie scanned the buildings flanking the alley, searching for something that could "accidentally" fall on the attackers, but she found no such thing in their proximity.

One man hit Marcel again. Lizzie's blood boiled hotter.

She turned her attention to the miller near the alley and his flour sacks. A sack flying down the alley to strike the aggressors would be too jarring and attract attention.

She frantically searched for something inconspicuous that could halt the abuse.

The miller's horse neighed, and Lizzie noticed its reins tied to the cart.

Marcel wailed again.

Lizzie sent an invisible wave of magic at the reins to loosen them while moving herself and her sister toward the market and out of the way. With her eyes on the horse's right ear, she let go of Agnès's arm. She brought her hands together in a silent clap and muttered, "*Tonitru, ire fera.*"

A deafening thunder stunned the people in the market and spooked the horse. Chaos ensued as the animal reared and squealed fearfully before taking off down the alley at top speed. It headed straight for Marcel's assailants, knocking one of them over and trampling the other before running past them.

Lizzie assessed the results of her intervention: one ruffian was dazed and hurt, and the other lay unconscious. Marcel was still in a ball on the ground, but the horse had fortunately spared him.

Understanding what her sister had done, Agnès blew out an exasperated breath. "Guess who will be treating those awful men. Surely, the irony isn't lost on you."

"I welcome the irony. And I'll be thrilled to be of service," Lizzie replied grimly. She was expected at the hospital in a few hours and would no doubt be treating the troublemaker who still had half his wits. As for the other one... She jutted her chin at the unconscious man. "I wouldn't bet my next meal on his chances of survival."

As the words left her lips, the healing witch felt slightly bad. She hated human suffering, but in this case, her desire for justice obscured her remorse. When she'd face the wretched coward at the hospital—if he showed up there alive—she'd have enough conscience not to give death a hand, the little nudge that would send him straight to hell. But she certainly wouldn't be bending over backward to save him.

Lizzie marched toward a shell-shocked Marcel with Agnès waddling after her. The conscious thug leaned against a building, holding his head and moaning. As for his inert friend, the closer Lizzie got to him, the gorier he appeared, confirming the truth behind her quip about his chances of survival. She grimaced. She had meant to stop the senseless beating, not kill anyone.

A pang of guilt squeezed her briefly, but seeing the extent of Marcel's beating, she chased the feeling away and decided the vile man's death would be a good thing, after all.

Good luck mistreating and murdering others now.

With rage surging inside her again, she regarded the bloodied man with contempt and came close to spitting on him but stopped herself as Agnès caught up with her.

"Thank you for your restraint," Agnès said sarcastically.

Ignoring her, Lizzie crouched by the victim, mindful not to scare him. "Marcel," she whispered. "It's Lizzie. It's over. They won't hurt you anymore." She shot a murderous glare at the other man. He looked away.

"I used to be respectable," Marcel mumbled through tears.

"You are to me," she replied softly. Putting a hand on his

upper arm, she sent a healing wave to numb his pain and soothe his soul. The comforting effect was instantaneous. Marcel looked at her with wonder.

"You're an angel, Mrs. Delacroix."

Agnès snorted. Behind her, a small crowd of onlookers was forming.

Lizzie gave her sister a smug look. "The man is entitled to his opinion."

Agnès chuckled, but then her gaze moved beyond her sister, and her expression hardened. Lizzie turned and saw the thug staggering away.

"Let him," Agnès said. "You might see him again soon enough."

Lizzie struggled to let the man get away but convinced herself she'd find a discreet way to ensure he wouldn't retaliate.

"Thank you," Marcel said to her.

She smiled and helped him to his feet.

"Let's go inspect your wounds," she said, intending to bring him to the auberge Marie-Josèphe and her husband owned. She could further heal the poor man in peace with a magic salve she carried everywhere for cuts and bruises. Also, Marcel could certainly use a meal to give him strength. Her friend's pantry was always full, which was perfect. Lizzie couldn't feed Marcel from the prison's supply of bread or her own kitchen and risk angering her warden husband. Honoré Delacroix had a formidable temper underneath his cool demeanor. He had always been fair to his young wife, and she didn't fear him, but she knew better than to provoke him.

As she helped Marcel plod down the alley, a soldier came to assist them and took on most of Marcel's weight.

"At least some justice will be served," the man said.

"How so?" Lizzie gave him a quizzical look. Had he witnessed the incident?

"A woman saw the beating from her window, and two of my confrères caught the accomplice who tried to escape. He will rot in jail if the whippings don't finish him first."

Lizzie schooled her expression to conceal her delight at the idea of the thug's retribution at the hands of her husband. Honoré corrected deserving inmates harshly but fairly.

The ruffian would soon wish the horse had trampled him to death, too.

CHAPTER FOUR

Montréal, present day

"That guy's more frustrating than an interrupted climax," Serena grumbled about Elenora's colleague who had interrupted their important conversation about Muriel.

The sticky detective had been suspiciously happy to see Elenora and probably used their encounter as an excuse to delay returning to work after receiving his order. She had tried her best to shake him off politely and quickly. Still, as suspected, Serena's patience had run out fast. The witch had asked Georgia to wrap up the rest of their order, grabbed Elenora by the arm, and dragged her out the door, away from the clueless detective.

Serena led Elenora to the park across from the Fish & Ship. It was a sunny and warm late-September day—perfect weather for eating dessert outdoors.

"So, what the hell happened with Muriel? What got her to react?" The witch steered Elenora toward a free bench.

"I mentioned the little twerp."

In dreams, Elenora often found herself at the bottom of a river, where a little blond boy appeared and bullied her. She, Serena, and their circle of friends at the OPO had tried multiple times to decipher what his unnerving presence in Elenora's psyche meant, but the kid always eluded them.

"That's what got her to react?" Serena handed Elenora her coffee and pouding chômeur from the takeout bag.

"Actually, when I first told her about him, she didn't react. But when I mentioned I had seen him when I was a child, on the night of the freak accident that took my dad's life, I thought I saw her eye twitch. But I wasn't sure. I mean, I often wish to get a reaction from her and get nothing. I thought I must've imagined it. Still, I looked closely at her face and apologized for mentioning the accident. I thought that if she had understood me, perhaps the memory was so painful that it had made her react. I didn't want to cause her pain."

"In the past, how was she when you talked about the accident?"

"We never talked about it. When I was a child, I knew it upset her, so I avoided the subject. I don't even recall talking about it in her presence."

"So, you think the painful memory made her react?"

Elenora shook her head. "Not just the memory. After I apologized, I told her I'd be careful never to mention it again and that I only did it because that was the first time I'd seen the boy. And *that* seemed to set her off. She grabbed my wrist, and I swear, she gave me the most intense look."

"She looked right at you?" Serena asked, at once skeptical and excited.

"Yes and no. Her eyes were as blank as always, but somehow, she was staring me in the eye, if that makes any sense."

"Oh, it does. I know that look. It's creepy as hell."

"It is. What does it mean?"

"It can mean many things. What d'you do?"

"I pressed the nurse's call button with my free hand, and her fingers went limp almost right away, and she let go of me."

"So, no one saw it happen."

"No one saw it happen. I told the nurse and Dr. Graham, and they both nodded politely at me. They checked the video footage to humor me, but the angle didn't show her looking at me or grabbing my wrist."

"Are they gonna do tests?"

Elenora blew out a long breath. "They said they'd be 'watching her closely.' But I think that's code for 'Tests are expensive, and it's a wild goose chase in her case, so we'll pretend to do something about it.'"

She suspected that, once again, she wouldn't get answers.

The two friends fell silent for a moment. A squirrel zigzagged past them, catching their attention. Serena unwrapped her dessert and gave Elenora a friendly elbow nudge. "Eat your chômeur before it gets cold."

The psychic dug in with a plastic spoon. "You know, I didn't use to have such a sweet tooth before I became pregnant. What's up with that?"

"If I have one piece of advice, it's don't fight the good stuff."

Elenora snorted. As tempting as it was for her to keep stress-eating desserts, the habit would catch up to her, eventually. She ought to find a more calorie-friendly coping mechanism.

"Why do you think your mom reacted to the kid? Because he's bullying you?" Serena asked.

"Maybe I did an excellent job of sharing my angst with her. I think the fact he's tormenting me in my head came across loud and clear. Talking about him riles me up. Maybe she fears for my mental health."

Serena stared in the distance, pensive. "Or maybe it's more than that."

"What do you mean?"

"Call it a hunch, but...what if she knows what the little boy means? What he represents?" Serena gave Elenora a sideways glance while taking a sip of coffee.

Hmm.

Despite the hollowness of her mother's haunting gaze, there could have been a hint of fear in it now that Elenora thought about it. Did her mom know something about the boy?

What could she possibly know?

And how?

Serena squeezed her knee. "Hey. Don't go down any rabbit holes, okay? Like I said, it's just a hunch. Don't read too much into it."

"It could make sense. And your instincts are usually on the money. But how could she possibly know about him and what?"

"Maybe you had a little jerk neighbor as a kid who pulled on your braids and made you cry, and she hated his guts and always wanted to kick his tiny ass."

Elenora considered Serena's statement. "I know some

kids are major snots, but that'd be some next-level grudge to yank yourself out of a mental coma just to react to that."

Serena chewed and swallowed a bite of cake before declaring, "In any case, I think I'm way due to meet your mom. Maybe we can find a way for her to tell us."

Elenora looked at her, conflicted over her friend's proposal. Hopeful of getting answers but afraid of what they might find. Because Serena's desire to get involved meant she suspected something otherworldly might be happening with Muriel.

The thought made Elenora shiver, even though she had already considered the possibility. She had tried to read her mother's mind once and had encountered no evil. She had concluded that nothing sinister was afoot, but her amateurish psychic attempt could have barely scraped the surface. What if there was something dark going on that she'd missed? That she hadn't been skillful enough to see back then?

Serena's hand landed on her upper back. "If you keep breathing like this, you're gonna hyperventilate."

Elenora closed her eyes in an effort to calm down.

"Look, I don't have to visit your mom, and I didn't mean to imply she was possessed or anything—"

Elenora's eyes flew open, and her heartbeat quickened again. "You think she might be possessed?"

Serena groaned. "Girl! Stop it with the doomsday scenarios!"

Elenora sucked in a long breath to calm herself.

"How about you think about it and let me know if you want me to go see her with you? And in the meantime, don't jump to conclusions. Does that work?"

"That works."

"Now, let's talk about something inoffensive so we can enjoy the rest of this fine dessert."

Elenora raised her paper cup of coffee to show she was on board and took a sip.

"How's the reno going? Is sexy Romain doing a good job?" Serena waggled her eyebrows.

"I'm sure his sexiness is doing all the heavy lifting in our powder room," Elenora deadpanned and took another sip.

Romain was an old acquaintance of Serena's, and she had been quick to recommend him when Elenora and Tom were shopping around for contractors. He was nothing but professional and excellent at his job.

"I bet Aubrey's drooling all over him." Serena chuckled.

Elenora let out a snort. Her daughter was going through another unfortunate round of teething and literally drooled over everything.

"Yeah. Big time. And woofing at him, too."

Serena became even more amused. "Woofing? Did she now?"

Elenora laughed. "Yup. He must think she's a little weirdo."

Serena shook her head. "If anything, he thinks she's a very smart and perceptive little girl."

"You lost me."

"What did he say to her woofing at him?"

"He laughed and humored her. He said, 'Not woof, cutie. Werewoof.'"

Serena's eyes danced, looking at Elenora as if there was a joke to catch and her friend was being slow.

"What?" the psychic asked.

"I think there's a prime spot at the OPO daycare with Aubrey's name on it if you want it."

"You sound as cryptic as my mother. Would you please spell this out for me?"

"Romain's a shifter."

Elenora could swear her friend had just said that the very normal-looking guy upgrading her toilet and vanity was a shifter. "A shifter? Like some of Dr. Geoff's patients?"

Their friend Rolland treated the occasional shifter as part of his work with Dr. Geoff, an OPO-associated doctor, but Elenora had never seen one in the flesh. The thought they existed blew her logical mind, and the mental leap to accept that one could be in her home was considerable.

"Yup."

"Romain can change into something?" Picturing the easy-going contractor, Elenora wasn't sure she was buying it.

"He can change into a woof. A werewoof," Serena replied, a twinkle in her eye.

Elenora smiled—she was being teased. "You're yanking my chain."

Serena finished her coffee and raised a brow at her. "Am I? Ask him. Or better yet...ask your daughter."

CHAPTER FIVE

"How's Serena?"

Pierre's question met Elenora as she slid the screen door open to join him, Aubrey, and Céleste on the back deck. Her honorary father swayed with a book on the patio swing, and the baby played in her turtle sandbox. Céleste lay on the other side of Pierre, at a safe distance from Aubrey. The German shepherd knew better than to be close to a young child with a substantial amount of sand at her disposal.

"She's good. And she thinks Aubrey belongs at the OPO's daycare," Elenora scoffed and sat next to Pierre on the swing.

Before her lunch date with her friend, she had swung by her workplace—a few blocks from the Fish & Ship—for yet another visit to the station's daycare. She had shared her concerns with Serena about sending Aubrey there. Not that there was anything wrong with the place. In fact, it was great. But Elenora was nervous about leaving her daughter in a new environment and being separated from her, even if she'd be nearby. She suspected her concerns said more about her own fears of letting go than the quality of the daycare.

Pierre chuckled. "Of course she does."

"Did you know they had a daycare?"

"No. But since they have everything you can think of, I'm not surprised."

In the later years of his police detective career, Pierre had often collaborated with the OPO. He'd been one of the few select individuals in the force privy to its existence and its colorful, powerful staff. He was a young teen when he got his first brush with the otherworldly when his friend Timothy gave him a front-row seat to what a spiritual possession looked like. Ever since then, Pierre had fine-tuned his instincts and skills to be receptive to whatever was out there. So, despite his lack of supernatural ability, he had been a terrific "civilian ally" for Serena and her colleagues.

"What do you think of Aubrey attending the OPO's daycare?" he asked Elenora.

The thought overwhelmed her. She tried to picture her daughter hanging out with little witches, vampires, shifters, and what-have-yous and had difficulty wrapping her mind around it.

"First off, we don't even know that she has abilities." Elenora turned to look at the patio screen door, mindful of her words and the volume of her voice. Romain was working inside the house. Wouldn't he have fantastic hearing if he was indeed a wolf shifter?

It sank in that not only had there been a ghost in her kitchen, but there might also be a werewolf in her bathroom.

Elenora shook her head, turned back to Pierre, and found him staring at her.

"You think she doesn't?" he asked.

I hope she doesn't.

She glanced at her daughter, happily sifting sand through her fingers, which she then ran through her hair. A bath was already on the schedule. Aubrey was a normal little girl who behaved like a normal child and was expected to get dirty from playing in the sand. She didn't move objects by looking at them. Sparks didn't fly from her fingertips. She did not salivate over raw steak. But life was fond of throwing curveballs. Elenora was living proof of that.

"Even if she doesn't have your abilities, how would that be a problem?" Pierre asked. "You're at the OPO all the time. They think the world of you. If you'd like her to attend, I'm sure that can be arranged."

"I go there now. But when I'm back at the station full-time, I won't be showing my face so much. It makes no sense to send her to the OPO when she could be down the hall from my office."

Pierre pinched his lips, as if holding himself back from saying something.

"You think there's something wrong with the station's daycare?" Elenora tried to guess.

"I didn't say that. There are few places safer for our princess than a station's daycare. Except for the OPO's, of course."

"Right. But...?"

"But *you* tell me what the but is."

"What do you mean?"

"You seem unsure about something. How many times have you visited the daycare?"

Too many times.

"I'm doing my due diligence, Pierre. You know I like to be thorough."

Pierre launched himself at Aubrey and pulled her fist full of sand out of her mouth. "Hey, sweetie, it's snack time soon. You want to leave some room."

Aubrey spat out sand and scrunched her face. Drool gushed from her lips and took care of the remaining bits.

Elenora grimaced in sympathy. "Aren't you gonna say it's good for her immune system?" she asked Pierre.

He gave her a horrified look. "Why would I say that?"

"Isn't that what people from your generation like to say?"

He chuckled. "No, I'd rather say it builds character."

Aubrey fussed, and he picked her up. "All right, little piggy. How about a ride on the swing with us?"

Pierre sat back on the swing, the baby on his lap. "What's making you uneasy?" he asked Elenora.

She unsnapped Aubrey's bib, soaked with sandy drool. The back of the cloth was relatively clean, so she used it to wipe her daughter's gritty chin.

"Honestly, I don't know what's making me uneasy. I'm trying to figure it out."

Did she have reservations about returning to work? If so, she couldn't put her finger on what they were. At first, she had thought it was a case of new-mom jitters, a sense of dread at parting with her little one after being with her full-time for nearly a year. But how could that be the problem when she knew she could see her daughter whenever she wanted to? Aubrey would be right there, a few feet away from her. Surely there was more to it than her deep-seated fear of abandonment bubbling up to the surface.

And it wasn't her job. She loved her job.

Or at least she used to.

Had that changed?

"I can only speak for myself," Pierre said, "but once I started working on paranormal cases, I found it hard to go back to the normal ones. The discoveries, the fascination, the rush of adrenaline—mostly missing. It just wasn't the same. They felt like the *same old, same old*. Whereas with the paranormal, everything felt fresh and exciting."

"And dangerous."

"And dangerous, for sure. Part of the appeal, I guess."

Elenora groaned. She was on board with the freshness and excitement. But the danger, not so much. "For *you*."

"For an adventurous single guy, sure. But think about it. If you hunt down a serial killer, and they want you gone, whether they use a gun or special powers, both can be lethal. The outcome can be the same. Evil is evil, whether or not it can sprout additional heads."

"Wow, you're really selling it," Elenora laughed. "Sure, the outcome can be the same. Except a supernatural killer on the loose who can teleport can affect more people and much faster than some psycho on foot with a knife."

"True. But this is where one with special expertise—and abilities—can make a difference. My colleagues were already adept at dealing with normal criminals. They had those crimes covered with or without me. Whereas I felt I could make a greater difference helping where maybe they couldn't."

Elenora felt a pinch of guilt. "You're telling me I shouldn't waste my abilities?"

"Love, I'm not trying to tell you what to do. I just think that, now that the curtain's been pulled back, maybe you'll find it less thrilling and rewarding to go back to regular cases. Especially when you have competent colleagues who can handle those."

Hmm.

Elenora did have competent colleagues who did just fine without her. The world hadn't stopped turning during her maternity leave. The people at the station respected Elenora, but she knew she wasn't indispensable. She was talented and a good employee, but so were the other social workers.

"You think I'm gonna be bored?" she asked. Suddenly, it seemed like a legitimate concern. How did one return to a regular job after a series of mind-blowing experiences?

What if she did find "civilian cases" boring? Would her clients feel her lack of enthusiasm? Would she care less? That would be unacceptable. She couldn't have vulnerable people thinking she'd rather be elsewhere instead of helping them.

Hmm.

Pierre had made a point worth thinking about. Elenora could only make so much of a difference while working on regular cases at the precinct. Whereas her growing, singular skills as a psychic were much more of an asset in irregular cases.

Freshness and excitement.

A frisson fluttered inside her.

Since when did her steadfast, routine-loving, quiet self crave excitement?

And she was a mom! If there ever was a bad time for such a crazy identity crisis...

Pierre patted her hand. "The OPO would love to have you, and working for them would solve your daycare conundrum. Maybe talk to Chief Costa and see what your options are."

CHAPTER SIX

Elenora tossed and turned before falling asleep. She had texted Serena to visit her mom with her the next morning to get it over with, and now she was filled with apprehension.

How would the visit go?

Would they find anything?

Elenora's mind latched onto the memory of her mother's disturbing stare when she'd mentioned the little boy and the way Muriel had grabbed her wrist. The tight grip of her mother's usually limp fingers had been as shocking as her stare.

Did I spook her into reacting by opening up to her?

Did I further scar her?

Elenora gave herself a mental kick. How could she have thought for even a second that it was a good idea to disclose her horrible and inconceivable new reality to her mother, let alone tell her everything? What had she hoped to achieve? What had she been thinking?

She hadn't been thinking. That was the problem.

Ugh.

Would tomorrow's visit make things worse?

If her mother had understood Elenora's alarming revelations, could she still be thinking about them, her daughter's words haunting her?

Was she freaking out?

Worried sick?

Elenora wished she could phone her or go see her at once to reassure her, but it was past midnight, and a visit was out of the question. She would have to wait until morning.

Will she look at me weirdly again when we visit her?

The carousel of unnerving questions spun around Elenora's mind, wearing her down. As she became drowsy with sleep and emotional exhaustion, her thoughts returned to the memory of Muriel's eerie stare. Elenora's consciousness shifted to a dream where her mother looked at her from a riverbed—the underwater place the psychic knew well from a recurring dream. The place where the bullying little twerp was bound to show up. But this was her first time seeing her mother there—or anyone she knew.

Muriel's gaze was sharp and aware, the opposite of what it had been for the longest time. Elenora hadn't seen her look this normal since childhood, except for the fact her mother sat on a purple tricycle. The bike looked familiar. Maybe Elenora had one like it as a kid.

"Mom?"

Muriel responded by throwing a tortured gaze past her daughter. Elenora turned and saw the outline of a town in the distance. She'd seen it before.

She turned back to her mother to ask her what she thought about it, but Muriel had disappeared.

Elenora looked around for her but didn't see her. Had she gone to investigate the town? An invisible pull compelled Elenora to do that—maybe her mother had felt it, too.

As Elenora approached the structures, she saw derelict buildings that reminded her of a ceramic village at the bottom of an aquarium.

An underwater ghost town?

Judging from the crooked cross on top of a crumbling steeple, the building closest to her had been a small wooden church. Its modest lines and the damaged gray planks suggested the construction was from a distant time. Windows with shattered stained glass completed the grim look.

Elenora pushed herself to move closer, but the dream abruptly segued into what felt like a premonitory dream. The water disappeared instantly, and she found herself in a community room with senior citizens sitting at tables, chatting and playing games. Right in front of her, a quartet of women played bridge. The scene was mundane compared to the tableau of Elenora's previous dream—until one player burst into flames and disintegrated into ashes within seconds.

Elenora woke up with a start and sat up in bed. The room was dark.

"Should I get dressed?" Tom mumbled sleepily next to her.

Elenora took a moment to get her bearings and figure out what was going on.

Tom's hand landed on her arm and started rubbing. "Was that a bad dream or a premonition?"

"A bit of both? One of each?"

Tom reached for his cell on his night table. "No missed calls or messages. What did you see?"

Elenora recounted her dream from beginning to end and became excited as an encouraging thought crossed her mind. "It was daytime in the rec room! Maybe this woman's death hasn't happened yet. Maybe we can prevent her from bursting into flames." She turned a hopeful gaze to her detective husband.

He rubbed the back of his neck. "Okaaaaay. How do you suggest we go about this? Did you get an address in your premonition? Or a sense of where it takes place?"

Hmm.

Elenora's hopes plummeted. "I don't think so."

After a thoughtful pause, Tom said, "How many retirement homes do you suppose there are in Montréal? Assuming this death will occur in a retirement home, not a community center. And in Montréal."

Dammit. Trying to locate the victim and the scene of the incident before it happened would be a tour de force.

Tom rechecked his phone. "Let's see if it was called in."

Elenora did breath work to slow down her racing heart and tone down her disappointment. If only her premonitions could help prevent *one* murder from happening! One! Just one! Was that so much to ask?

It was so disheartening to come so close to preventing a death but then fail from the get-go.

"I couldn't save Jérémie Marsan. I couldn't save Réginald Haché. I couldn't save Mr. Leclerc. Or anyone else. What's the frigging use?" she muttered.

Tom pulled her into a side hug while scrolling for information on his phone.

"Your premonitions couldn't prevent Jérémie Marsan's death, but you took down his murderer, and they prevented other deaths from happening at the Maple Street house. If it weren't for your gift, we wouldn't have met Angéline, and she wouldn't be with her beloved now. And think of all the trapped souls you helped free and cross over. And you saved Rolland. I'd say that's one hell of a track record."

Elenora wondered how she would manage without her husband's unwavering support, belief in her, and enthusiasm for her abilities. "Thank you for the cheerleading."

"Your premonitions are helpful, just not always where we think they can help. Please don't discount that. I know they're frustrating, but they're not as useless as you convince yourself that they are."

Elenora nodded. Tom wasn't wrong. Still, it would be nice if her premonitions could be ahead for once and give her actionable information. "Do you think there's any way to prevent this lady from bursting into flames?"

"Aside from calling every retirement home?"

"What if I went to Serena's right now and had her capture the dream? Maybe I saw the woman's face before she combusted."

Before she combusted...

What the hell had happened? Had Elenora seen the event correctly?

Had somebody out of sight set the woman on fire?

"If we review your dream, maybe we'll find a clue that will help us identify the place," Tom said, entertaining the idea. "But then... Let's say we figure out it happens at Bob's Cozy Golden Years Residence. Then what? We call them and say, 'By the way, Bernice might catch on fire today. Just a friendly heads-up to keep an eye on her, and don't let her man the grill. Good luck and have a nice day.'"

Elenora couldn't help but snort before her heart sank. "Well, when you put it that way."

"I'd love to put it a different way. That said, let's give it a shot. We can't just sit on our hands."

"I'll text Serena." Elenora grabbed her phone.

Elenora: Hey, are you awake?

Her friend was probably up. Another effect of having a trace of vampire DNA in her blood was that she required very little sleep.

Sure enough, a reply showed up seconds later.

Serena: S'up?

Elenora: Sorry to bother you at this hour. Mind if I drop by to download a premonition? Maybe we can prevent a death.

Serena: Stay put. OMW.

Twenty minutes later, Serena arrived at their home, bright-eyed and bushy-tailed. In contrast, Elenora felt like an eighteen-wheeler had hit her and thought she must have the looks to match.

At the kitchen table, Serena draped her jacket over the back of the chair next to her friend and fished her tablet out of her messenger bag as she sat.

Elenora offered Serena her hand, and the duo jumped into their premonition capture process. The witch could "download" Elenora's dreams. Eyes closed, the psychic focused on a black canvas to clear her mind and facilitate Serena's access to her memories. She stifled a yawn as the skin on her arm prickled softly with magic.

Minutes later, Elenora, Serena, and Tom watched the premonitory dream unfold on the tablet. The room with the bridge-playing ladies looked like it belonged to an upscale residence for seniors. The residents were well-dressed, and some drank tea in fine china. Other than that, there were no obvious clues as to the location, and the lady who burst into flames was in profile, so they couldn't get a clear portrait of her for facial recognition. A double bummer.

"I'll still run her image in our database and get a list of swanky retirement homes," Tom said. "And I'll ask the chief to be on the lookout for incidents in retirement homes."

Along with Tom's detective partner, Chief Manuel Costa knew about supernatural activity in his town, the OPO, and Elenora's psychic powers.

"Wouldn't she need a criminal record to show up in your database?" Serena pointed out.

"Yup. Grasping at straws. But at least we've got straws to grasp at."

"I'll send the clip to Claire-Lune so she can search in the ether, too." Serena tapped on her cell.

"Good idea. Thanks," Tom said. "I'll contact Renaud right now and give him stills of the room before the fire. Maybe he can locate the place."

Renaud was a young, brilliant colleague at the station who often gave Claire-Lune a run for her money in the research department—no small feat for a civilian. He didn't know about the paranormal or the OPO. Keeping him in the dark was a balancing act between giving him enough information to perform his non-magical magic and not tipping him off regarding the existence of something larger than his reality. He had also proven himself discreet and trustworthy and often performed tasks for Tom without asking questions—though you could tell he was itching to know more. But it was bad enough that Serena once had to perform a teeny-tiny memory wipe on him after she'd exposed him to too much truth. It was best to keep him in the dark.

"Maybe Renaud can find the woman," Elenora said.

"I'll send him her silhouette, too," Tom concurred.

"For a change, the little twerp is nowhere in sight," Serena quipped, her eyes glued to her tablet as she scrutinized the dream sequence before the premonitory bit.

"I didn't see him, actually," Elenora said.

Serena looked up from the screen. "Really? In that setting? Isn't that a first?"

It might indeed have been a first. Until now, the little boy had always appeared in Elenora's dreams taking place on the riverbed.

"I'm surprised your mom was in the dream. What do you make of that?" Serena asked.

"She was on my mind when I fell asleep."

Serena gave her an uncomfortable look. "You don't suppose she..."

Elenora frowned at her. "I don't suppose she what?"

Tom caught Serena's meaning and started dialing his phone. "If she'd passed, they would've phoned us. But I'll ask."

Elenora's heart skipped a beat. She rarely entertained the possibility of her mother's death. To her, her mother was stuck in a permanent mental coma, frozen in time in a cruel world of nonexistence.

"Thank you for confirming," Tom said before concluding the call.

"She's alive?" Serena asked.

"Yeah, nothing weird." After a pause, Tom corrected himself, "Nothing weirder."

Serena touched Elenora's arm. "I'm sorry I caused you unnecessary distress."

"It's all right. Your thinking was logical. And it has to happen someday," Elenora said. The prospect of her death unsettled her, but at least her mother would be free from her prison of flesh then.

Serena stood and gathered her stuff. "I'll let you go back to bed and see you in the morning. We can ask your mom what she was doing in your dream."

Elenora tried to fall back asleep, but her mind bounced between her mother's presence in her dream and the elderly stranger on fire. Tom had stayed up to search the precinct's database and insisted that she get more sleep. Maybe he, Claire-Lune, or Renaud would find the woman before it was too late.

Come on, guys, you got this.

Just as she convinced herself they might have a shot, her briefly soothed mind wondered yet again why she had seen her mother at the bottom of the river. What did her appearance mean? *Dream Muriel* had brought the ghost town to Elenora's attention and seemed concerned. Was she trying to tell her something?

If Elenora googled "mother tricycle riverbed ghost town dream meaning," would she find an answer?

CHAPTER SEVEN

Ville-Marie, 1673

Slicing a chunk of raw beef for the stew reminded Lizzie of the bleeding gash across Marcel's forehead. Once they had settled in Marie-Josèphe's kitchen, it was the first injury Lizzie treated. She used one of her salves to disinfect the wound and help it heal.

Lizzie's touch—no matter how delicate—had made Marcel wince, and she could tell he struggled to keep a brave face on and hide his pain.

My good man, you don't have to hide your pain from me. I wouldn't think any less of you, Lizzie wanted to tell him. She knew well what it was like to conceal pain. To hide from persecution. To lick your wounds in the shadows. She understood Marcel's predicament so viscerally it hurt.

She hoped her child would never know this kind of distress and torment. She'd do anything to make sure they wouldn't.

Lizzie sliced another chunk of beef into cubes.

"Your father will protect you," she whispered to herself. She then looked around her kitchen to ensure she was still alone and no one had overheard her. Her husband wasn't supposed to return for another hour, but she couldn't be too careful.

The room was as empty and silent as she had hoped.

Lizzie set her knife beside the cubed meat and stirred the soup, simmering over the fire in the hearth. She scooped a spoonful to taste it. It was ready. She swung the iron arm aside, moving the cauldron away from the flame to make room for a new pot for the stew.

She couldn't wait for reliable signs of her pregnancy to appear so that she could announce the good news to Honoré. Though, judging by his latest moods, she wondered how he would react. In truth, a part of her dreaded his reaction. He seemed more distant lately than usual, and she hoped the news would bring them closer. Surely, he would rejoice. How could he not? Men like him, who had married a *fille du Roy* like her, had done so to have a family.

Even though it was often hard to see why he wanted one.

On the surface, Honoré Delacroix was a hard man, but Lizzie could see past appearances. Her husband was misunderstood. She couldn't deny his brutal nature, but she chose to call it passionate. Underneath his cold exterior, a blazing fire burned. When he pulled her against him roughly, she felt his affection for her—his promise to protect her—not the brusqueness of his awkward gesture.

When Lizzie had met Honoré after getting off the boat in the Québec settlement, she had fallen for him at first sight. Beyond his good looks, he emanated confidence, respectability, and authority. Safety. Things Lizzie had lacked and craved. She had known right there and then that he would keep her safe. And in return, she'd give him a family, unconditional love, and devotion. She was content playing the docile wife under those terms. She owed him her new life and had no desire to return to her miserable past. She would do anything not to jeopardize what she had now.

Lizzie returned to cubing the rest of the beef. She was a good cook, and while Honoré was not generous with compliments, she knew he appreciated her wifely efforts.

He loves me in his own way.

So what if his love wasn't obvious? He gave her a home, freedom, and protection. And despite being ruthless with the whip toward the prisoners, he had never laid a finger on her. He allowed her to work as a nurse at the prison and Miss Mance's hospital. This mattered a lot to her.

While Lizzie preferred her work at the hospital, the prison offered her a unique opportunity to discreetly test salves, potions, and spells on the prisoners. If any of her creations needed fine-tuning and risked producing a side effect, the health and the life of her criminal test subjects already hung by a thread. Of course, she would never deliberately put anyone in danger, and this slight infringement of her healing nature and gift sometimes kept her up at night. But it was much better than hurting an innocent—the lesser of two evils.

"Is there something wrong with the stew?" Lizzie asked her husband. She was certain there was nothing wrong with the meal. In fact, she had outdone herself. But Honoré kept lifting a piercing gaze at her, the one he usually reserved to scrutinize a prisoner, and she couldn't figure out why. Warden Delacroix was known for his ability to intimidate the most hardened criminal. He never used his infamous glare on his wife. Lizzie found it uncomfortable. Thankfully, she was hard to intimidate.

Honoré took a bite and skewered Lizzie with another stare. He chewed slowly, looking unhurried to answer her question.

Two can play this game, she thought, about to return his stare. But she caught herself, remembering she was a good wife who knew her place, and diverted her gaze submissively instead.

"I heard there was excitement at the market," Honoré finally said, his gravelly voice rumbling across the room even at low volume.

Lizzie looked at him inquisitively despite knowing what he was referring to. Honoré took another bite and kept staring at her. She went to fetch the pitcher of spruce beer to refill his cup and keep up the illusion of servitude. And, more importantly, to avoid staring back.

"You must know about it." He took a long sip of his drink, watching her like a hawk.

One of his men must have seen Lizzie at the market. Honoré often had his loyal posse track her. The men were convinced she was unaware of their spying, but she could sense their presence an arpent away. If she didn't react to them, it wasn't because she was clueless but because she chose to. Just like she chose to show them only what she wanted them to see.

Fools.

"Indeed, I do," Lizzie answered cooperatively. "It was quite the scene. That poor horse being so spooked." She brought a hand to her heart for effect.

Honoré took another bite and studied her some more while chewing. He seemed to expect more from her—but what?

"I am so relieved that Agnès and I were safely out of the way when the animal madly took off," she added. "It startled us so much. I am surprised she didn't go into labor."

Honoré took a swig of beer and swallowed slowly. He narrowed his eyes at Lizzie. "Do you not find it strange that whenever there is *excitement*, you are there to witness it?"

Lizzie froze. She hadn't expected this kind of observation from him. Did he suspect her involvement in "exciting events?" Was he implying that he knew her secret?

Among Lizzie's most spectacular acts of retribution that had caused "excitement," she had magically made a soldier's fusil discharge on the crotch of a fellow soldier who had raped several young women in the settlement; she'd caused a corrupt sailor to fall to his death in the St-Laurent River from his ship; and she had made a large roof plank fall on a thief's head, killing him.

Had one of Honoré's men seen past these "accidents," made the connection, and told him? Lizzie didn't think they were observant or sharp enough to do such a thing.

Had Honoré somehow made the connection, then?

She could think of only one time when he'd been present during an incident, and his back had been turned—the very reason Lizzie had decided to act. An inmate was creeping up behind him with a shiv, and she'd seen him. Granted, the violent, instant stomachache she'd given the would-be assassin hadn't been her most subtle work, but the circumstances had limited her creativity. She had thwarted his murderous attack. That was all that had mattered.

Maybe she should have taken Honoré's witnessing of the event into account. Perhaps he had guessed her involvement in the inmate's unfortunate demise. This could explain why he was still piercing her with an unnerving stare, as if trying to search her mind and soul for the truth while drinking beer.

Lizzie recovered and gave him a sweet smile. "Such is the fate of someone who has countless errands to run and work to do around town." On top of her errands, Lizzie's work for Miss Mance often sent her outside the hospital to make house calls or attend to a scalped victim.

Honoré forked another bite of stew, his midnight black eyes maintaining a penetrating gaze on her. Giving Lizzie chills.

He suspected her...

Feeling her face paling, she turned to the *tarte à la farlouche*—her husband's favorite—she had made for him earlier and sliced him a piece. "Would you like more stew?" she asked without looking at him. "Or are you ready for dessert?"

When no reply came, she ventured a look over her shoulder and saw her husband dab his mouth with his napkin. His chair scraped back as he stood up.

"Be careful, wife..."

The warning struck Lizzie like a punch, despite a hint of genuine concern in it.

I'll do better.

Honoré headed to the entrance door of their living quarters and stopped over the threshold, his posture stiff.

"A new prisoner, Mr. Antonin Dujardin, arrives tonight." He seemed to address the wall behind Lizzie. She had never seen him avoid eye contact before.

"You will feed him from our kitchen," he added. "His health is frail. You are to give him exceptional care. Otherwise, I order you to stay away from him, and I count on your utmost discretion."

Usually, being ordered to do anything was a sure way to make Lizzie bristle and want to do the opposite, but this time, she was too intrigued to notice the order. "You know this man?"

Honoré responded with a chilling gaze. She expected him not to answer her and leave. But he stood there, gripping the door handle.

"He's valuable," he pushed the words through gritted teeth.

He's valuable.

What did that mean?

She made a sound to ask, but he interrupted her. "You are to treat him very well. That is all you need to know. He will stay in the blue room."

The blue room was on their floor, down the hall from where they lived. They used it for the occasional out-of-town guest, but mainly for storage. They had never kept a prisoner there.

Before Lizzie could ask any questions, Honoré left, ending the conversation.

CHAPTER EIGHT

Montréal, present day

S itting on the living room floor with her legs folded like a pretzel, Elenora watched Aubrey crawl after Willem, happily chasing the cat around the room.

"Don't grab his tail!" she warned the baby for the umpteenth time.

Aubrey had been hyperactive all morning, getting into as much trouble as she could. She dumped her bowl of milk-soaked cereal onto her head, prompting an unscheduled bath. Then, she unlocked the safety latch on the cabinet under the kitchen sink and spilled the contents of the garbage can all over the floor. To top it off, she pulled Willem's tail three times. It was as if she sensed Elenora's lack of sleep and apprehension over visiting her mother, and she wanted to test the limits of her nerves and thin patience.

Hopefully, Pierre would be well-rested and up to handling the mini menace when he showed up to take over.

Elenora glanced at her watch. He should be there in the next twenty minutes or so.

She looked up just in time to catch the baby sneaking up on the cat again. "Aubreeeeeeeey."

Aubrey sat up and gave her a mischievous smile. Willem licked his paw, unconcerned. Apparently, Elenora was the only one worried about their interactions. The cat always showed infinite patience with the baby, and that morning's relentless pursuits seemed no different, as he had moved from one spot to another with an unbothered, dignified air. But he was an animal, and if he were to lash out at Aubrey, no one could blame him for it. For Elenora, the constant watch of this low-speed chase between baby and cat was exhausting. She considered putting Aubrey in her playpen, but that might ruin her good mood, and Elenora didn't want to hand Pierre a cranky kid.

Elenora offered Aubrey a cardboard book, and the baby took it. Willem was now grooming his extended leg. The baby scooted closer, as if to read the book with him. Doubting the goodness of her daughter's intentions, Elenora kept a suspicious eye on her. But it soon became apparent that the two compadres were content to coexist peacefully.

A little witch and her cat.

The thought took Elenora off guard, but it didn't stun or sting her as much as it would have in the past.

Good job not freaking out.

She gave herself a mental high-five before correcting her thoughts—her daughter would certainly be more of a psychic, like herself, than a witch.

Elenora's cell phone rang, making Aubrey perk up from her book.

Tom.

"I'm afraid you were right," he said grimly. "Alex and I are now looking into the bizarre death of Ms. Eileen Robin, an elderly lady who burst into flames while playing bridge this morning at Black Chapel, an exclusive retirement home in Vieux-Montréal."

Elenora's stomach twisted.

That poor woman.

She recalled her premonition, the rec room full of seniors. Several traumatized witnesses. How horrible and devastating.

"Since you had an insight, the chief asked if you wouldn't mind tagging along," Tom added.

Elenora was about to reply, "Of course," but then wondered if she was doing the right thing. She wanted to help, but was she ready to get involved in a new paranormal case so soon after the last one? She was still processing the trauma from it.

Part of her wanted to decline and cling to her normal life, but if she was seriously considering working for the OPO, she couldn't run away from this kind of case. She couldn't cherry-pick or decide on a whim what suited her or not. Unless the OPO put her on permanent desk duty, which wasn't a real-istic expectation.

"You can always turn around if you change your mind," Tom said. "But if you sit this out, you might regret it, no?"

He knew her well. She was indeed already invested in the case emotionally and was likely to kick herself if she didn't chip in when she could have. "He wants me to read the scene?"

The silence on the line made Elenora picture Tom

rubbing the back of his neck with a sheepish expression on his face.

"The victim," he said, his voice matching her mental image of him.

The victim?

Elenora's stomach twisted again. So far, she'd only read two dead victims and had hated every second of the experience.

But hadn't this victim burned down to a pile of ashes? If so, what would there be for Elenora to read?

"How bad is she?" she asked.

"As you foresaw, she's mostly ashes—though her hands landed on the table. So you'd essentially be reading her hands."

Her hands.

How gross would it be to touch a severed body part?

Elenora grimaced.

"And the ashes, too, I guess," Tom added. "Of course, you're free to say no."

"Right."

But was she, though? Was she really free to say no?

"Okay. Count me in."

She could regret her decision later.

———

"The notion of spontaneous human combustion was more common when homes relied on open fireplaces as the main heating source," Claire-Lune's voice came from the car's speakers. Her call had come in just after Tom and Elenora had parked a block away from the Black Chapel Residence. They'd remained seated to hear what the witch had to say.

The case had changed Elenora's plans for the morning. Right after Tom's call, she had texted Serena to postpone visiting Muriel, and the witch had suggested they meet at Black Chapel so they could go see her after Elenora read the victim's remains. Serena had also offered to download the findings and help in any other capacity. Before long, her sister, Claire-Lune, was also on board, eager to share her knowledge on self-combustion with Tom and Elenora. As an ethereal librarian and researcher, the witch was a master at digging up information through the ages and out of thin air.

"Most cases were caused by a naked flame near the victim and the wick effect," Claire-Lune informed them.

"The wick effect?" Tom asked.

"In a nutshell, it's when a person's fat serves as fuel and their clothes trap it, turning them into a candle."

There's an image Elenora didn't need.

"So, there could be a non-supernatural explanation for what happened at Black Chapel?" she asked, partly relieved, partly disappointed.

"Maybe. But most cases involving the wick effect—the combustion—can take hours. People don't usually go up in flames in a few seconds. And in the present case, unless you find an explainable source of fire, I bet witchcraft was involved. Or demons—fire's their jam."

Elenora cringed at the mention of demons. She'd had a limited exposure to them but hadn't been a fan so far.

"Don't let Alex hear you—he's gonna call in sick," Tom quipped.

"Could we blame him? If demons are involved, we're not

equipped to deal with those," Elenora said. Objectively, were Tom, Alex, and Elenora equipped to deal with anything supernatural at all? What if they'd just been incredibly lucky so far? When you thought about it, the witches had done the heavy lifting.

You're getting cold feet, the devil's advocate voice in Elenora's head whispered to her.

"But Serena is. She could deal with a demon while glued to her favorite TV show," Claire-Lune reminded Elenora, her tone poised. Very little ever seemed to faze either of the twin sisters.

Serena was indeed well-versed in dealing with anything demonic. Elenora reasoned her friend would assess the situation at the senior home. Then, the OPO could take over the case if necessary.

And soon, Elenora would return to her job at the station.

Her safe, lower-stake job.

"Serena told me the Black Chapel building has been around since the Nouvelle-France era," Claire-Lune said with perceptible excitement. "I'll look into its past."

"So, unless we witness the very first natural case of instant self-combustion in human history, we should expect a supernatural element?" Tom asked.

"That's what I think. I suggest you don't poke at anything too hard until Serena shows up."

"I hear you," Tom said before thanking her and wrapping up the call.

He and Elenora exited the car and headed to a massive gray-stone building with splendid architecture.

"It might be tricky to bring in Claudia until we know

whether this case is normal or not," Tom said, glancing at his wife.

Claudia was a social worker colleague at the station. If Ms. Robin's tragic death had played out like in Elenora's premonition, the rec room would have been jam-packed with witnesses in dire need of psychological support. The residents and staff would be in shock. Since Elenora was on maternity leave, Claudia would normally take over. But if the case was paranormal, involving anyone unaware of the supernatural wasn't an option.

"Yeah. I'll fill in for her if necessary."

"Great. Though you might not have to. Perhaps there's a perfectly boring explanation for what happened."

The thought of the case turning out to be normal almost bummed Elenora.

Almost.

"You think this might be a normal case?" she asked, dubious.

"Not for one second, no."

She chuckled. "We don't do simple and easy-peasy anymore, do we?"

Tom laughed, too. "We sure don't."

"What did I miss?" Alex asked from behind Elenora.

Now that the other detective was there, it was time to find out more about the case. Part of Elenora looked forward to uncovering the truth. A good part of her, in fact. Whatever lay behind the green door called to her as loudly as the damn siren in her refrigerator.

She also sensed there would be no turning back.

CHAPTER NINE

"As you can see, Ms. Robin had expensive tastes." The young but mature-looking residence director swept a hand over a spread of brand-name beauty products on a vanity table in the victim's bedroom. With her French twist and black pantsuit, Émilie Pouliot fit right in with the opulent décor. To further prove her point, she lifted the lid of a jewelry box with the tip of her pen. The box was filled to the brim and sparkled brighter than Times Square. The room's luxury matched the rest of the apartment. Black Chapel was easily one of the most upscale senior homes in the entire province.

While they waited for Serena and the fire investigator to arrive, Tom had asked Miss Pouliot to show them Eileen Robin's room. The director didn't have to know they were stalling to avoid walking into a supernatural crime scene without a witch.

"Couldn't the same be said of your whole clientele?" Alex asked. "It must cost a pretty penny to live here."

Miss Pouliot turned her attention to him. "Actually,

detective, you'd be surprised. Many of our residents have spent their lives pinching those pennies, so a scarcity mindset is still a thing. But most have also realized that 'they can't bring it with them.' The concept of YOLO is big around here."

"Was Ms. Robin the YOLO type?" Tom asked her.

Miss Pouliot seemed to weigh her answer but didn't conceal an amused smile. "You could say she had her own brand of YOLO."

Tom answered with an amused smile of his own. "Color me intrigued. Would you care to elaborate?"

"I suspect she never met a bridge she wasn't itching to burn."

Alex snickered, and Miss Pouliot's eyes widened.

"I'm sorry, that was an inappropriate choice of words," she apologized. "Also, Ms. Robin was a relatively new resident, and I didn't know her well—maybe I'm being unfair and misjudging her character."

"It's all right. What makes you suggest that Ms. Robin was...challenging?" Tom asked.

"I'm basing myself on how she behaved toward the other residents and our staff. She moved in a few months ago and didn't seem to want to fit in. She kept to herself—nothing wrong with that, of course. Plenty of our residents are reserved..." Miss Pouliot was careful with her words again. "She didn't seem to care for friendship. People here try hard to include newcomers. I saw her sneer at the head of our welcoming committee whenever Lila tried to connect with her. Let's say she was *very independent*."

"Maybe she didn't like Lila?" Alex tried.

"Then she didn't like most people in this building, either.

Sneering seemed to be her default expression. That is, when she wasn't glaring at people, or insulting them, or issuing threats." There was an edge to Miss Pouliot's words. If Ms. Robin was as delightful as Miss Pouliot was hinting, the pool of people with a motive to see her gone could be considerable.

"So, no friends. Did she have family?" Tom asked.

"She has a daughter on the West Coast—Paulina Jackson. We were waiting for your permission before calling her."

Tom wrote the name on his notepad. "Thank you. That was considerate. We'll contact her."

"I'll give you her number."

"No other family you can think of?" Alex asked.

"I don't think so."

"Visitors?" Tom asked.

The director shook her head. "I will double-check our guest registry, but frankly, I don't recall anyone ever coming to see her. We—" She caught herself and looked away as redness crept up her neck.

"You...?"

"We, hmm—I'm not proud to say this, and I swear to you, we truly care about our clients..."

"We're not here to judge," Tom said with a friendly smile.

She took a deep breath before saying, "We had a pool going."

"On when her first guest would show up?" Alex said, struggling to keep a smirk in check.

She rubbed her neck. "Yeah. Totally professional, I know. Sometimes, we blow off steam in ways that don't involve being confrontational with our more challenging clients."

Tom gave her another reassuring smile. "Don't worry. We've heard worse."

"Had anyone guessed when she'd bite the dust? Or become dust," a female voice called from the doorway. Serena had arrived with her usual sass, and her question further flustered the director.

Alex shot her a disapproving look.

"What? You don't approve, big guy? Or you're just frustrated I said it first?" Serena winked at him. Getting Alex's goat was a favorite hobby of hers.

"Please excuse our colleague's inappropriate humor, Miss Pouliot," Alex said.

"Yeah, I apologize. Couldn't help it." Serena proffered her hand to the woman. "Serena Winston. I usually work behind the scenes—they can't take me anywhere."

The director shook hands with her. "Émilie Pouliot. Nice to meet you. Are you the expert we were waiting for?"

Tom answered for her. "She is. A fire inspector and crime scene techs will also be joining us soon."

"Should I bring you to the entertainment lounge now?" the director asked.

"Is that an expensive way to say 'rec room?'" Serena asked.

"It is."

"Before we head there, we'd like to view the security footage of the incident," Tom said.

"Of course. Right this way."

They left Eileen Robin's living quarters, and the director led them back toward the main entrance of the building. Elenora admired the stone walls lining the corridors, suspecting they were original to the building.

"If we could also get a copy of all the feeds in the residence from yesterday morning up to now, that would be appreciated," Tom said to Miss Pouliot.

"Of course, but it's going to take time. This is a big place with beefed-up security. Lots of cameras."

"Then, let's prioritize the footage from the cameras in the entertainment lounge and the surrounding areas around the time of the incident. And then the rest."

"I'll ask Eric."

"We'll also need a list of the witnesses."

"You'll get that too, detective."

After a moment of silence, Alex said, "I read this building was originally a prison. That's different."

"It was, yes," Miss Pouliot confirmed without enthusiasm. "But we don't advertise this for obvious reasons."

Alex had previously researched the building's architecture and remembered its surprising initial purpose. When they found out it was the location of Ms. Robin's death, he had been equally unsettled and fascinated. Elenora understood why he felt this way. There was something disturbing and intriguing about the place's history, especially in light of the eerie circumstances of the victim's passing.

They walked past a window in the lobby labeled "Security," and Miss Pouliot knocked on the adjacent doorframe. "Eric, you got a minute?"

A guard in his thirties and a midnight blue uniform swiveled toward them from his wall of monitors. "Yes, Miss Pouliot?" He stood up, eager, and took in the two detectives, his left eye twitching.

"Detectives, this is Eric Decker, one of our day guards. Eric, please show Detectives Madigan and Bélanger what our cameras caught of the incident," she told him before relaying Tom's footage request.

The guard sat back down and brought up the footage he'd already lined up. Tom and Alex moved inside the crammed security room and invited Elenora and Serena to squeeze in with them behind the guard. The director looked on from the doorway with a pained expression.

The image of four women playing bridge appeared on one of the bigger screens.

"This is Ms. Robin." Mr. Decker pointed at a woman in her eighties with layered, shoulder-length hair in a bottle-blond hue. While seen from a different angle, the victim, the other bridge players, and their surroundings matched Elenora's premonition. And just as the psychic had seen, the woman burst into flames and disintegrated into a pile of ashes. The footage caught up to where the premonition had ended and revealed the reaction of the other women at the table, who appeared genuinely shocked. Surely, someone couldn't fake that level of bafflement. One player let out a blood-curdling scream, the sprinklers went off, and pandemonium ensued as everyone else in the room reacted to what had just happened. Another player cried as she stared in horror at the empty seat while the last one, in a wheelchair, wheeled herself away from the table, shaking. Doing a double take, a bewildered male orderly moved closer to examine the gruesome chair as residents struggled to flee the scene. A female orderly calmly corralled everyone toward the exit.

Elenora had found the premonition dreadful, but seeing the incident play out with the elderly witnesses, she couldn't help but absorb their shock and terror, too. She looked away from the screen to regain her senses. Miss Pouliot had also averted her gaze and was staring down the hall.

A burst of grim, nervous laughter escaped from Mr. Decker. "What the fuck, right?" Another eye twitch.

"Yeah, *what the fuck* sounds about right," Serena replied.

"Would you be okay with replaying the clip in slow motion for us? Or should we watch it on our own?" Tom asked the guard.

"Sure." The guy clicked the beginning of the clip and played it at a reduced speed.

Once more, the images approached the fateful moment and clearly showed how, from one frame to the next, the unsuspecting victim went from being in top shape, pondering the cards in her hands, to becoming a human torch.

Out of the blue.

Within a few frames, her hands detached at the wrist and fell on the table, still clutching the cards.

There were no apparent clues to explain what had happened—no explosion, no incendiary device, no grenade tossed in the victim's lap.

"Could something on her have ignited?" Alex asked Tom before his eyes traveled to Serena, too, for an answer.

"You think someone might have planted something on her?" Tom replied and turned to the director. "Did Ms. Robin require help to dress herself?"

"Not usually. I believe she would have dressed herself this morning, but I'll ask Brooke if she helped her."

"We'd like to talk to Brooke," Alex said.

"Of course." She flagged down an employee walking by and asked him to fetch the orderly.

"Please replay the clip frame by frame from the top," Tom asked the guard.

Miss Pouliot bit her lip with concern. "Could we have prevented this? Did we fail her?"

"It's too early to tell. But likely not," Serena said.

"Could it happen again?"

"We'll work on ensuring it won't happen again," Tom replied kindly.

She nodded, wrapping her arms around herself. "In the meantime, what do I tell the residents? They're worried."

"I'm a social worker," Elenora jumped in. "I'll talk to them and make myself available if they need help to cope."

Perhaps I'll be able to gauge if anyone feels guilty or knows something, too.

Maybe she could even attempt to read any suspicious resident, although she had yet to pick up psychic activity from a living person—at least, one not possessed by a murderous spirit. She should ask Yukiko and Dr. Brent to look into expanding her powers in this manner. It could be helpful.

The thought caught her by surprise. Did she really just wish to expand her powers?

How bizarre.

Was she perhaps entering a midlife crisis? Is that what this was?

If so, buying a sports car would be so much more sensible.

CHAPTER TEN

Ville-Marie, 1673

"Mmm...ria... Maria. Mariaaaaa."

The labored mumbling was insistent, sometimes clear, but mostly slurred as Arthur Mondou's high fever persisted. The cold-blooded killer's body and mind had withered dramatically in the past days. Lizzie cautiously wiped the delirious prisoner's forehead with a cloth. Twisting in pain on his bed, he randomly lunged at invisible enemies. His physical strength was greatly diminished but not entirely gone. Lizzie had put a restraining spell on him but didn't trust its reliability. She also suspected the man's reflexes remembered how to be lethal on their own.

Before falling ill, Mondou was to be hung in the town square the following week. But then his execution was halted when Doctor Barthes—who was out of his depth with the convict's obscure illness—had conveniently pronounced the man demonically possessed so he wouldn't have to treat him and expose himself to his sickness. The medical poltroon had tasked Lizzie with caring for Mondou while he died in his cell. Lizzie saw through the doctor's cowardly schemes. Whether Father de la Dauversière, the doctor's comrade, also understood the game being played or he, too, lacked courage, Lizzie would never know. But the cleric had refused to attempt an exorcism, declaring the prisoner's soul too far gone to be saved, demon or not.

Lizzie didn't think the prisoner was possessed, but for her own safety, she had snuck her coven sister Félicie into the prison to assess Mondou. The witch could sense evil in a person. She confirmed that the man's soul was rotten, but no demon plagued him.

"Mariiiiiiaaaaaaaa," the dying prisoner rasped.

His empty gaze traveled to Lizzie's face, making her uneasy. He had been vicious to most people during his lifetime, taking several lives, but Lizzie had never been on the receiving end of his cruelty. Maybe because she had always seen fit to send a clumsy restraining spell his way whenever he was in her vicinity—there was no sense in tempting fate. But these past few days, witnessing his intense suffering stirred mixed feelings inside of her. He deserved to pay dearly—she didn't question that fact. But did anyone, no matter how guilty, deserve to agonize like this in their mortal envelope on their way to being judged? Wasn't it for God or the devil to confront his spirit and decide his punishment?

"For...for...ggg..." Arthur struggled.

Forgive me, Maria.

Lizzie's heart squeezed. She had heard his plea countless times, and the repentant words touched her every time, for they couldn't be disingenuous. The brink of death was a more powerful truth serum than any she or her coven sisters could ever concoct.

Begging for forgiveness. A pure glimmer of good amidst the darkest of darkness.

What had Mondou done to this Maria woman to beg for her forgiveness so ardently? Had she been a scorned lover? Had he taken the life of a loved one? Had he terrorized her?

If Maria were here, would she forgive him?

Lizzie put herself in the mystery woman's shoes. If given the chance to face those who had persecuted her, would she forgive them?

She didn't think she could ever bring herself to do that, no matter how loudly they implored.

The man before her groaned and writhed. Lizzie reached for a blue vial she had set on the floor. She pulled the cork out, poured a spoonful of the remedy made of willow bark and a sedation spell, and brought it to the man's trembling lips.

Mondou's agitation had worsened since his last intake of medicine, and she struggled to get the liquid inside his mouth. Most of it dribbled out. Lizzie poured more elixir on the spoon and tried again, with a similar result. Short of physically restraining him and forcing the liquid down his throat —which would require the guard's help—it was a lost battle.

Lizzie gave up. She couldn't risk someone witnessing the magical efficacy of her unconventional remedy and exposing herself.

She sighed and shoved the cork back on the bottle. She had high hopes that this new concoction would ease the man's pain, but she had no choice but to let him suffer.

Lizzie picked up her bag and the lantern she'd set next to

the bed and called to the prison guard waiting on the other side of the heavy wooden door.

"You done?" he asked her.

"For now."

Lizzie had to get going. She was expected at Miss Mance's Hospital and had one last prisoner to see first.

With a pang of sorrow, she glanced at her dying patient one last time before leaving the cell, wondering if her next visit would be too late. The guard locked the door behind her.

"Madam." He nodded at her and began to leave.

"Wait. I'd like to see Paul Mason."

The guard frowned. "Mason?"

"Yes."

"Why? He's about to receive the last rites."

Last rites?

Of course.

Lizzie struggled to keep an eye roll to herself. She should have known that Dr. Barthes would jump the gun. After all, he had declared Mason's case irreversible and ordered Lizzie not to bother with the prisoner. This had not sat well with her. Sure, the wounds were gnarly and puss-oozing, and the patient looked like he was at death's door. But had her superior even tried to heal him? She suspected he hadn't because Mason wasn't worth his time. Undeterred, Lizzie had ignored his order, choosing to give the convict a chance. And now, she was eager to see if her clandestine care had made a difference.

The guard studied her with narrowed eyes, hesitant. Finally, he shook his head and escorted Lizzie down a long, dank corridor. The tang of blood from whippings permeated the air and clung to the stones and mortar of the walls. The basement brought Lizzie painful memories of her and Agnès as children when they hid in the Tombe-Issoire quarries to save themselves from being killed. To this day, she spent much time and energy trying to forget those horrific years of her life. Here, at the prison, there was no escaping the frequent reminders.

You are safe here. Your mind is playing tricks on you. You are safe here.

Lizzie always reasoned herself, but it didn't stop her from wishing there were no cells for her to visit in this gloomy part of the building. Many inmates were kept in the basement to add to their discomfort and mental distress. Lizzie could only imagine the devastating effect it would have on her if she were imprisoned here.

If she were caught and accused of witchcraft.

She shivered.

If she were caught and accused of witchcraft, she wouldn't stay in this dungeon very long. They'd burn her at a stake on the square as fast as they could build the fire.

The metallic clanking of a key unfastening a lock cut through Lizzie's thoughts. She prepared herself to see the prisoner with hopeful expectation.

As she entered the cell, the convict lifted his eyes to her, a gleam of relief and gratitude in them. A sense of pride and purpose filled Lizzie. Paul Mason looked much better than the night before—his skin tone was almost no longer frightening. "Let me see those wounds, sir," she chirped.

He struggled to sit in bed while Lizzie moved the ratty, itchy blanket aside to get access to his multiple bandages.

She asked the guard to come into the cell and shed light on the wounds as she inspected them. He complied while keeping a cautious eye on the prisoner. Paul Mason was a giant and a formidable brawler, but Lizzie knew he wouldn't try anything funny with her. There was kindness in his eyes, and she sensed good in him. While he was the physical opposite of Marcel, he reminded her of him. She presumed he was in for a crime that didn't fit the harshness of his sentence.

Lizzie removed the bandage covering the worst wound on the prisoner's calf. A putrid smell hit her nostrils, and she saw the guard flinch at her periphery. The odor was milder than it had been, as was the color of the puss. While there was room for improvement, she was pleased with what she saw. The healing had begun, and Mason had a chance of recovery. She reapplied a spruce sap ointment on the injury and secured a fresh bandage over it.

"What is the meaning of this?" an obnoxious voice boomed.

Lizzie looked over her shoulder and saw Dr. Barthes giving her the evil eye from the doorway. Father de la Dauversière stood behind him, perplexed.

Bracing herself, Lizzie moved aside to show off the miraculous new condition of the patient. Barthes took in Paul Mason with a baffled scowl.

He looked at Lizzie again, and his scowl deepened.

Lizzie's heart sank. She could do no good. In fact, the hotheaded doctor had made no secret that he only tolerated her because she was the warden's wife and Honoré wanted her there.

"Is this the correct prisoner?" the clergyman asked.

Barthes's face reddened. He didn't answer the priest and crept closer to the prisoner instead. He turned an accusing glare on Lizzie. "What did you do, woman?"

"Let me show you." She reached for her bag, prepared to show him the ointment and poultices she had used to treat Mason. The doctor wouldn't see the dash of magic she'd added, and since he had attempted no treatments, he would have no grounds to challenge the efficacy of her natural products.

"Don't you dare talk back to me!" he thundered, more redness creeping around his collar. He must have been reacting to her tone.

It was always the tone.

Lizzie bit back a retort and sighed inwardly. Her blood boiled a little. The man was an unpleasant and arrogant fool, and she frequently fantasized about ways for him to get what he deserved someday. It would have to be subtle and undetectable. Preferably permanent. But then a wave of guilt would hit her and make her feel contrite.

Until the next time he was an arse to her and impeding the care of a prisoner.

For show, she diverted her gaze and forced a contrite expression. "I apologize," she whispered.

Doctor Barthes pursed his lips and stormed out of the cell. Father de la Dauversière offered Lizzie a dark look and mouthed the word *witch* at her before following the doctor. Lizzie stiffened at the unspoken word, careful to conceal how rattled she was to the guard.

Never let anyone think it's true.

Was she giving herself away by healing prisoners?

Was it worth it for her to risk her life for them?

Lizzie forced a pleasant smile and finished inspecting the prisoner's other wounds. "Everything looks promising," she told him once done. Their eyes met. She read concern in his.

She stiffened again. Had he caught the "w" word on the cleric's lips? She put on a cheerful air. "I will let you rest now."

She put away her supplies, her gaze fastened on her bag to avoid looking at either man in the room.

"Thank you, ma'am," Paul Mason said with sincerity.

She nodded, headed out, and almost crashed into another guard outside the cell.

"Mrs. Delacroix, you are needed in the blue room," he said.

The blue room. Her husband's mystery guest prisoner—whom she was to serve hand and foot—had either arrived or soon would.

Lizzie cheered up for real. She was about to find out what her husband's cryptic demeanor had been about.

CHAPTER ELEVEN

Montréal, present day

Elenora's apprehension grew as they neared the rec room—the *entertainment lounge*. So far, dealing with intact cadavers had made her queasy and taken all the courage she could muster. She never had to touch detached limbs before and dreaded doing so.

And then, the expected stench of burned flesh would add a nice touch to an already morbid situation.

Gah.

"D'you have menthol on you?" she asked Tom. The two times she'd gone to the morgue, her husband had given her menthol to smear above her upper lip to mute unsavory smells. She should have foreseen this. Why didn't she think of bringing some? A fine psychic she was.

Tom retrieved a stick of menthol and a mask from his inside jacket pocket and handed them to his wife. She took them, relieved. "You're a lifesaver."

"Saving you is my mission in life," he whispered to her.

"Miss Pouliot, you wanted to see me?" a forty-something female orderly heading their way asked the director. Elenora recognized her from the footage—the woman who had calmly gotten folks out of the lounge after the incident.

"Yes. Detectives Madigan and Bélanger would like to ask you a few questions about Ms. Robin." She turned to Tom and Alex. "Detectives, this is Brooke Gélinas. She was assigned to Ms. Robin's wing this morning."

"Ms. Gélinas, how would you describe your interactions with Ms. Robin this morning?" Tom asked her.

The orderly made eye contact with him as she spoke. "Normal. I went to her room around eight. She was watching the news, as usual. I placed her medication and a glass of water on the side table beside her. I surveyed the room, asked her if she needed anything, and left."

"Did anything seem off? Different?"

She shook her head. "No. Nothing out of the ordinary."

"What did you talk about?"

She scoffed softly. "Absolutely nothing. She pretended I wasn't there. Like always."

"She often ignored you?"

"All the time. Either she ignored me, or she was openly hostile. Depending on her mood. But that's how she behaved with most of us—most of the staff."

"She had a beef with everyone?" Alex asked.

"She had enough beef to open a butcher shop."

"Did she ever say what her problem was with you?" Tom asked.

"She never spelled it out, but rumor had it she thought I was giving the male residents too much attention. But that's my job, and that kind of accusation seems too innocuous considering the threats she made to me. That she'd find out where I lived and that matches are cheap. She told my husband she caught me having sex with a coworker, which is a bewildering lie. But the worst, she said that not only would she get me fired, but maybe she'd find an even more atrocious way of getting rid of me. That I'd better watch my back."

"She sounds like a grade-A biatch," Serena murmured to Elenora.

The victim did sound like a manipulative piece of work. This bummed Elenora. It was hard to feel empathy for a victim who had made life hell for others.

"I understand many of our residents are frustrated to be aging and losing autonomy," Brooke went on. "Most of them would rather live in their own home. I understand that and try my best to give them empathetic care. Treat them as I'd like to be treated if I'm ever in their position. I can assure you I always treated her the best I could, despite her mean attitude. I don't understand why I was the target of such vileness."

The orderly was composed, but a slight tremor in her voice betrayed how upset she was. As far as Elenora could tell, Brooke Gélinas seemed neither cold and calculating nor to be raging inside. It was reasonable to be shaken after suffering from relentless bullying.

"Did you report her to management?" Tom asked her before glancing at Miss Pouliot.

"She did, and we documented her case, as well as the others," the director answered. "We would have alerted the authorities if things had gotten out of hand, but Ms. Robin seemed to be all talk."

"I knew that Émilie—Miss Pouliot—had my back, and I

wouldn't get fired," Brooke said. "They understood how manipulative she was. Most of us did. But her vague threat of harm... That was unsettling. And exhausting."

"She didn't hint at what she'd do?" Alex asked.

"Other than suggesting arson? No. I wish. Then I could've watched my back for something specific. Maybe her vagueness was deliberate to keep me on my toes."

Serena shook her head. "What are little old ladies coming to?"

"Not all bullies age gracefully," Tom pointed out. "Mrs. Gélinas, were her issues with any of your coworkers known?"

The woman glanced at the director, as if seeking permission to speak. Miss Pouliot nodded for her to go ahead.

"She accused Bernard of spitting in her food and said she would report him. She accused Adélaïde of stealing a ring from her, and again, she threatened to report her. Petty things that were probably lies. Those are off the top of my head. You should ask them."

"We will."

"Brooke?" a frail man called, his head peeking in the doorway of a nearby room. "I need help with a jar."

"I'll be right with you, Mr. Brady."

Tom gave the orderly his card. "Thank you for your time. Gimme a call if you think of anything."

"Will do." She pocketed the card and went to the senior waiting for her.

Miss Pouliot led the team to the lounge, her key ring jiggling as she searched for the right one to unlock the double doors.

"Do you need me in there?" she asked Tom, wrinkling her nose.

"No, we'll take it from here, thank you. Please let our fire investigator and the techs know where to find us when they show up."

She nodded with visible relief. "Just holler if you need anything. I'll go work on the list of witnesses." She left in a restrained hurry, maybe in case Tom reconsidered needing her presence in the lounge.

Alex glanced at his watch. "Do you know what's keeping Steve?"

"Actually, the chief said he was sending someone else, but that's all I know," Tom replied.

"He's sending a new guy on the weirdest fire case we've got in ages?" Alex blew out a breath. "We don't have time for green."

Tom gave his partner a *whatcha gonna do* shrug.

"Reena!" a deep voice called from the end of the hallway.

A pleased grin appeared on Serena's face. "Oh, this guy is the total opposite of green."

CHAPTER TWELVE

A jovial, balding man walked in their direction. Serena greeted him with open arms. "Günther! It's been ages!"

"It has, hasn't it? We've been visiting Liv-Unni's family. Just got back last week."

Tom and Alex assessed the stranger, who looked in his late fifties. Why had the chief sent him?

"Cool! How's Norway this time of year?" Serena inquired.

"Splendid as always. What's up with you, girl?" Günther asked.

Serena shrugged. "Meh. Same old, same old. Too much work, not enough life." She turned to Tom, Alex, and Elenora. "Guys, this is Günther. Your fire investigator."

"Mr. Günther. Detective Tom Madigan," Tom greeted him with a proffered hand.

Alex and Elenora followed suit, and they received a firm handshake.

"You're the insightful one," Günther said to Elenora.

"That's a generous way to put it," she answered.

Tom was still eyeing the man with interest. "You know Serena from work?"

"That's right. OPO."

"Did Chief Costa ask for you?"

"Yeah. He calls me in from time to time."

That figured. While this was the first time the chief had sent them someone from the Off-Path Office, it made sense. An OPO fire investigator had to have supernatural skills, and this man seemed confident.

"Are you a warlock?" Alex's voice dropped on the word *warlock*.

"I wish, but no. I'm half-phoenix on my mother's side. And half-demon on my dad's, though we don't shout that fun fact from the rooftops."

The word *demon* disconcerted Tom, Alex, and Elenora.

"I also trained as a firefighter as a young man," Günther went on. He tapped his sizable abdomen. "But then the donuts caught up to me. So now, I investigate instead." He laughed.

His joke fell flat, as his audience hadn't recovered from his shocking announcement.

The OPO works with demons?

Elenora needed a moment to wrap her head around the idea.

She knew the agency worked with folks on Satan's payroll at the Gray Court when absolutely necessary. But as collaborators? Elenora thought of Stefan, the clerk, and Thelonious, the custodian, and couldn't picture a harmonious partnership with either of them. Maybe because they were full demons instead of half?

Were they even demons?

Elenora wasn't sure what they were and would have to ask. But whether or not they were demons, they had a vicious vibe going.

"Guys. He's cool," Serena jumped in. "I assure you, in his case, nurture won over nature—big time. And you're gonna get answers."

Tom was the first to recover. He looked around to make sure nobody was eavesdropping. "What about the M.E.? How's that gonna work?"

"The techs coming in are in the know," Günther said, not seeming to mind the trio's guarded reaction to him.

"They're OPO too?" Alex asked.

"Not quite. They're both relatives of OPO members. We've worked together many times. Your wise chief thought of everything a while back and put a well-oiled machine in place."

"Are the techs Gonzalez and Sauvé?" Tom guessed.

"Bingo," Günther confirmed.

The detective grinned. "Of course the chief thought of this. He can see everything miles ahead. Might even be a little psychic, now that I think of it." He sent Elenora a questioning look.

Was their boss psychic? Now, that would be a twist.

Serena patted Tom on the shoulder. "He's not."

"When you say well-oiled machine... Was there a surge of *special* arson in the past? Is there a surge now?" Alex asked.

"I don't think there was a surge, but I don't know the details—that was before I came on board. And as far as I can tell, it's not raining cases now, if that's what you're worried about."

"Fun fact: the collaboration with the OPO got set up decades ago, when Chief Costa was young," Serena said. "That's the best time—when they're young. They're more receptive and open-minded. And you'll be happy to know that Pierre was a key player in putting everything in place." She beamed a proud smile at Elenora.

The news that Pierre had helped set up the collaboration filled Elenora with pride, too. "That sounds like something he would do."

"It does, and I have so many questions for him," Tom chuckled before gesturing at the doors to the rec room. "All right, ladies and gents, shall we?"

As Alex reached to open one of the doors, Elenora adjusted her mask. The menthol helped but didn't fully cover the eye-watering, acrid smell that wafted from the room, as if the space had recently hosted a convention of garlic-bread-eating chain-smokers. She held on to that image—it was better to associate the assaulting aroma with smoking garlic aficionados rather than charred flesh.

"Reena, would you handle the security cams?" Günther asked Serena. Neither seemed bothered by the toe-curling smells.

"Sure thing." The witch flicked her fingers behind her back. After a moment, she said, "All good."

"Thank you." The fire investigator surveyed the room before walking to the table with the burnt chair, his sneakers squelching against the waterlogged carpet. The sprinklers had rained on every inch of floor and furniture.

Alex sidled up to Serena. "What's your woo-woo doing to the cameras?"

She gave him a blank look.

"Please?" Alex added.

"It's gonna hide any magic that might occur in this room. Should something irregular manifest, the spell will fill in the footage with innocuous images of us working."

Alex pondered her words. "Cool."

"Damn right. And now I'm gonna go check for demonic presence or remnants," she said, starting to wander around the room.

Alex joined Elenora and Tom, who watched Günther inspect what remained of the victim. As expected, a pile of ashes stood where Eileen Robin had sat, and her hands lay on the table, gripping soaked playing cards.

Elenora dragged her stare back to the fire investigator. There was no need to let the surreal sight of the hands freak her out ahead of time.

"Brutal. Such a good hand, too," Günther said about the victim's cards.

"You play bridge?" Serena asked him.

"I learned before I could even light a candle," he joked and looked up at the ceiling, which showed no fire damage. In Elenora's premonition and on the security footage, the flames had shot up but not high enough to reach the ceiling.

The half-demon then crouched to check the floor. Tom, Alex, and Elenora imitated him. They searched underneath the victim's chair and the table for anything that could have ignited the fire. They found no apparent cause.

Moving closer to the chair, Günther brought his hands

gently over the ashes, mindful not to disturb them. Elenora wondered if he had reading abilities like hers. She watched him with interest, hoping to learn from him if that was the case.

Günther's hands remained still over the ashes for a minute. Then he shook his head. "A priori, I'm not picking up anything, but I will analyze the ashes more deeply after Elenora does her thing."

"To be honest, if you're not picking up anything, I doubt I will," she replied.

"Stop selling yourself short, Ele!" Serena called from across the room.

"I'm not selling myself short! I'm just being realistic," Elenora called back before asking Günther, "Were you reading the ashes?"

"Not quite. I was scanning them but not psychically. In my case, it's mostly a vibe, an instinct, if you will."

"And when you analyze them?"

"In a nutshell, I will test the ashes with magic. But I don't want to disturb them before you take a shot at them."

Tom offered Elenora a pair of gloves. She put them on, her eyes traveling to the victim's hands.

Gah.

"How about you start with the ashes?" Serena suggested. "Maybe you'll get something from them, and that'll be enough."

Elenora needed no convincing and focused on the pile of damp ashes. Before proceeding, she reminded herself to factor in the latex gloves' muffling effect when reading the remains and then wondered how the gloves would interact with them.

"Won't the ashes stick to the gloves? Won't I mess up the evidence?" she asked Günther.

"Don't worry about that. We won't be looking for prints on the ashes, and there are more than enough to analyze, anyway. And honestly, I doubt we're dealing with a natural scenario. We'll probably find our answers beyond what's left of Ms. Robin here."

Elenora glanced at Serena.

"I got your back," the witch said.

Elenora's hands hovered over the ashes and then lowered slowly to touch them. She stilled, closed her eyes, and pushed her anxiety aside to clear her mind. She concentrated on her breath to force herself to relax as nothing came.

After a moment of sensory blankness, she turned her mental dial, scanning for something.

Anything.

But the ashes refused to speak to her.

Dammit.

She opened her eyes and took a deep breath to squash the dread rising inside her, but the atrocious smell caught in her throat and made her regret that she even breathed. She moved to the victim's hands, eager to be done.

It's okay. You're wearing gloves.

Elenora brought her fingers over the victim's hands, steering clear of the wrists and keeping her touch light, and closed her eyes. In the past, she'd feared being hit with a vision, bracing herself for horrific images to flood her mind. Right now, she'd give anything to get a quick insight.

But no such luck. Eileen Robin's hands were as silent as her cremains.

Hmm.

Elenora opened her eyes again and let go of the hands.

Serena was looking at her with a sympathetic expression. "Want to go around the room and see if you have better luck? I'll go with you."

"I might as well."

For the next fifteen minutes, they wandered through the room. Elenora ran her hands over damp surfaces. The only thing they got was exercise.

"Would you like to try summoning her?" Serena asked the psychic.

Hmm.

Elenora had noticed no shimmering in the entertainment lounge—a sign of a spirit beckoning to her. But since she knew the victim's name and what she looked like, maybe that'd be enough to coax Ms. Robin's spirit into the room using her new summoning technique.

"See it as an opportunity to practice," Serena said.

It was indeed an opportunity for Elenora to practice the technique—a good one with low risks that didn't include searching for haunted places or going to cemeteries to find friendly ghosts willing to help her gain experience. Then again, she could try on Mr. Leclerc in the comfort of her home. She'd bet he'd be amenable.

"Sure. Why not."

Elenora returned to the burnt chair. Staring at it, she recalled the victim's face from the security footage. She added her mental dial in an overlay and tweaked it slowly while watching for the telltale shimmering.

"Ms. Eileen Robin, I respectfully summon you. Please show yourself."

No signs of a spiritual presence manifested. Elenora

moved her mental dial again, but she wasn't feeling it. Maybe the spirit wasn't around or had already crossed.

She gave up. "Hopefully, we'll have better luck talking with the witnesses."

"Let's go have chats while Günther does his magic," Tom agreed.

"I'll stick around," Serena said. "I'd like to try a few more spells."

"Sounds like a plan. Text me if you find anything."

CHAPTER THIRTEEN

Ville-Marie, 1673

"A fellow book lover, I see," the stranger said as Lizzie entered the blue room. He stood by the window, leafing through one of her books, his back to her. Either he was psychic, or he'd been expecting her.

"Mr. Dujardin, I presume," she said, getting closer to him while keeping a safe distance. While he was an acquaintance of her husband's, Antonin Dujardin was still a prisoner. There was usually a reason for being one. Not always—as Lizzie knew—but most of the time. Until she knew more about him, she would err on the side of caution.

"You presume correctly, but call me Antonin." He turned and showed her the book—a florilegium from England she knew well. Honoré had given it to her. Her husband knew how much botany books meant to her and tracked them down to please her. She loved that about him—the little things he did to make her happy.

"Then please call me Lizzie."

He scoffed playfully. "I doubt our dear Honoré would approve of me doing such a thing. How improper that would be, Mrs. Delacroix. I will refrain from familiarity to save you from gossip." He winked at her and smiled. It reached his eyes, but his grin had a wolfish quality.

Our dear Honoré.

Antonin Dujardin was a puzzling man.

"As you wish, Antonin," she said lightly. Better play along and not let him see she was appraising him.

"Have you read *Canadensium Plantarum*?" he asked.

Lizzie's eyebrows rose to her hairline in surprise, and he seemed to delight in her reaction.

"Have you?" she asked. "I've never seen it, only heard of it. How did you know about it?"

The book's author, Jacques Philippe Cornut, was a French doctor who had never set foot on the New Continent but had collected plant specimens from Nouvelle-France sent to him. The opus was a prized reference, and Lizzie was dying to get her hands on it.

"I read it in Paris. Shortly before I came here."

"How is it?"

Antonin shrugged. "From what I hear, your knowledge of the colony's native plants might surpass Cornut's."

Lizzie's heart soared at the compliment.

"I will see if I can get you a copy. Would you like some tea?" He gestured at a tea set on top of a chest of drawers, the only piece of furniture in the room beside the bed.

"Certainly," Lizzie accepted before her mind caught on that she'd accepted tea from a prisoner. A beverage she hadn't seen prepared. Which could be laced with anything. What was wrong with her?

Being blinded by flattery.

Antonin Dujardin was a word magician. She had let his sweet rhetoric bring her guard down and had missed his deft sleight of hand.

You may be clever, sir, but I dare you to outmagic a bona fide witch.

"Oh! I must decline your kind offer, after all. Miss Mance is expecting me at the hospital. But before I go, do you have medical needs?"

Antonin looked unfazed by Lizzie changing her mind. "I do." He finished pouring himself tea, brought the cup to his lips, and took a long sip, almost mockingly. As if to show her he knew she had reservations about the tea.

A skilled manipulator.

That explained the wolfish grin.

Her gut told her he thrived on playing games. Games and manipulation. Maybe this was the extent of his dangerousness.

When Honoré had announced Antonin Dujardin's impending arrival, Lizzie had wondered what kind of crime the man had committed and imagined a variety of barbaric acts. She had pictured a tall and burly man of great strength—the opposite of the stranger before her, who was slender and meek-looking, his power seemingly in his silver tongue. Maybe his crime was related to politics. A plausible possibility. If he posed little physical threat, that could be why Honoré had put him in the blue room.

Furthermore, Lizzie's husband had insisted that she attend to the newcomer with great care. If he deemed the man worthy of such courtesy, how dangerous could he be? If he were, they'd keep him in a dingy cell with a double lock, not in their relatively comfortable guest room.

It dawned on Lizzie that the door to the blue room only locked from the inside. Antonin Dujardin was free to roam around the prison. That was surprising. But Honoré must have had his reasons to allow this. Maybe he trusted that the guards' surveillance of their "guest" sufficed to keep him in custody.

The more she thought about it, the more the political scenario for the man's imprisonment made sense. She felt silly for overreacting.

Antonin put down his cup of tea and rolled up a sleeve, unveiling a considerable rash for Lizzie to inspect. The man's arm was predominantly red with patches that neared burgundy, peppered with oozing pustules. The sad state of his skin clashed with his overall elegance.

"They refused to treat it. A deliberate form of torture, if you ask me." He tried to sound unaffected, but a veneer of vulnerability coated his tone.

"It's not only on this arm, is it?" Lizzie suspected there was more.

He shook his head. "My back is even worse." His eyes shifted to hers, and he whispered, "Would you work your magic on me, Lizzie?"

She bristled at his choice of words, but the pleading look in his eyes suggested the phrasing of his question had been innocent. At that moment, he appeared humble. Honest. After all, Lizzie's reputation as an excellent caregiver often preceded her.

She forced herself to chuckle. "I don't know about magic, but let's see..." She opened her bag and selected an ointment she had created. She swept a finger in the little clay pot and scooped up a fair amount. "This will sting at first but then soothe your skin. And the healing will begin."

Antonin nodded and looked away as she gently spread the ointment over the infected rash on his arm. He tightened his jaw and swallowed a grunt.

Mitescere eum, Lizzie thought, careful not to mouth the words. The spell might be less effective this way, but this patient seemed observant and shrewd. She couldn't risk tipping him off.

"Were you born here?" he asked through clenched teeth, perhaps making small talk to distract himself.

"No. In France. I arrived here two years ago."

"A *fille du Roy*?"

"Indeed."

"This is how you met Honoré?"

She nodded and smiled. "Indeed, again. He was looking for a quiet wife. And I was...quiet enough." She laughed, and he laughed too before hissing—she'd rubbed ointment in a deeply infected area.

"A quiet force," he mumbled before skewering her with a knowing stare that destabilized her. Here it was again, what seemed like a taunt. A game. An attempt at manipulation. A confusing interaction for sure. Lizzie felt the urge to rub the ointment with more pressure to strike back at him but restrained herself. Antonin Dujardin made her feel naked. As if he knew her deepest secrets—and if not, had the means to unearth them.

The intensity of his gaze changed again, welcoming a persuasive warmth. How did he do that?

"You trained as a nurse in the old country before you

came over?" he asked with sincere interest—a new, benevolent friend who wanted to know everything about her.

A charming friend.

"I did," she replied, careful not to elaborate or show he affected her.

"Who taught you?" he fished.

Lizzie could swear she caught a glimmer of malice in his eyes. This encounter was maddening.

"More good people than I could count." She forced a smile. This man—this *convict*, she reminded herself—didn't need to know how she had become a nurse in France without a formal education. That her apprenticeships had been unorthodox. And that when you had magic at your fingertips, it was child's play to falsify papers.

Lizzie liked to think there was no deceit in calling herself a nurse—she felt more qualified as a healer than most healers without supernatural abilities. And as a fast learner, she has always soaked up the knowledge she has encountered.

As for the false papers that had allowed her and her sister to board a boat to Nouvelle-France as *filles du Roy*, that was a different story, but Lizzie had made peace with their deceit. They had chosen life over death. Could anyone blame them?

While the sisters hadn't been orphans sent by the king to help populate the new colony, the orphan part was genuine. And they both had been keen on starting a new life and a family in a new land. It wasn't their fault if the members of their coven had been hunted down and forced to scatter. It wasn't their fault if their mother had been burned at the stake and their father murdered. It wasn't their fault if they'd had to steal food to survive, living in the shadows to evade those who had unfairly made them outcasts.

The sisters' scheme to escape to Nouvelle-France had been a life-or-death decision. Lizzie refused to feel guilty about it. But even now, a part of her still felt like an outsider who would never belong. An imposter. She was used to playing a part.

"And these days, working under Miss Mance teaches me so much," she said to Antonin Dujardin, hoping to satisfy his curiosity and end his uncomfortable line of questioning.

"I bet you were a natural," he insisted. Knowingly.

A change of topic was badly needed. "What about you, Antonin? What brought you here?"

He answered with an enigmatic smile. "I must have toyed with the wrong people."

Then he laughed, as if his situation was delightfully hilarious and he had not a care in the world. Like trouble slid off him like water off a duck's back.

Lizzie found his demeanor deeply unsettling. And in a twisted way, fascinating. She was usually good at reading people, but this... She didn't know what to make of him.

Antonin's laughter proved contagious, and Lizzie laughed along nervously.

A loud throat clearing caught their attention. Honoré stood in the doorway, a scowl deepening as he took in the duo's merriment, his dark eyes growing cold. An odd behavior even for him.

Before Lizzie could ask him what was wrong, he left abruptly, slamming the door behind him.

CHAPTER FOURTEEN

Montréal, present day

"It's horrible she passed away like that. Now she's gonna haunt this damn place, and we'll never get rid of her," Myriam Blackwell grumbled. The senior was one of the three ladies who had been playing bridge with Eileen Robin when she died. She lifted her eyes to the ceiling and shouted, "I'm not moving out on your account, Eileen!"

Alex cringed and crouched next to the tiny woman engulfed in a velvet-upholstered recliner to be at eye level with her. "You were playing cards with her," he said. "Was she really that awful?"

Ms. Blackwell skewered him with a sharp gaze, and her reply was just as biting. "She wasn't awful—she was *impossible!* And we only let her play with us this morning because Susan wasn't feeling well."

"Couldn't you have played without her?" The question earned Alex another death stare.

"How are you supposed to play bridge with three players,

young man?" she snapped, as if thinking he'd been dropped on his head as a child.

Maybe it's the trauma talking, Elenora told herself, suspecting it wasn't the trauma talking.

Armed with the list of residents and staff members who had witnessed the incident, Tom, Alex, and Elenora had begun the individual interviews with the bridge players. Ms. Blackwell was the third person they'd talked to, and the other two ladies, while less aggressive, had also given the clear impression there was no love lost between them and the victim—a loud recurring theme.

"To your knowledge, was anyone antagonizing Ms. Robin?" Tom asked her.

The dainty senior snorted a snort that spoke volumes. "She didn't need anyone antagonizing her to be a supreme bitch. She was a natural."

"We heard she had her eyes on some of the men—" Tom said before the woman cut him off.

"She was a shameless harlot! She wanted all the men for herself. I told her countless times to stay away from my Bernard. But did she listen? Did she?" Her gaze shot up to the ceiling again. "Maybe if you had listened, you wouldn't be where you are now, Eileen! Serves you right!"

Alex cringed again and took hold of the woman's arm. The tight expression on his face said, *Lady, stop taunting the mean, dead woman's spirit.* "Yo. She probably can't hear you."

Elenora noticed Alex's choice of words. Before they started working on paranormal cases, he would have told the witness that "the victim *can't* hear them." Not "*probably can't.*" Her formerly non-believer colleague had come a long way.

"Oh, don't let her fool you. Her hearing is just fine," Ms. Blackwell spat.

It occurred to Elenora that Eileen Robin's spirit might be eavesdropping on their conversation. If she was, would she go poltergeist and retaliate against Ms. Blackwell to put her in her place? Was this something they now had to worry about, departed folks getting back at those who spoke against them? Or even spilled the beans about them?

Don't speak ill of the dead.

Maybe the saying was more than an expression inviting people to be kind toward the departed. Maybe it was a warning to the living.

"Ms. Blackwell," Tom said, "what do you mean—"

"Which part?"

"You implied the accident served Eileen Robin right because she didn't listen. Could someone have had enough of her not listening and decided to take matters into their own hands?" Tom kept his voice calm, careful not to accuse the elderly woman. But despite his tact, his question still ruffled her feathers.

"How would I know? I abhor gossip. I am simply speaking the truth. I'm sure many of us wished she had gotten her comeuppance sooner. Do you know the ratio of men to women our age, detective?" she asked him in a snooty tone.

"I don't have a figure, but I know women tend to live longer."

"Exactly."

Tom waited for her to go on and make her point, but she didn't.

"Who was upset that she was eyeing the men?" Alex prompted the senior.

"I never said someone was upset. Aside from my Bernie, have you seen our pool of men here? Ugh." She glanced at her watch. "Son of a gun, I'm missing my show."

She reached for the remote control and turned on the television, ignoring them. Tom and Elenora exchanged an amused look while Alex pinched the bridge of his nose.

They'd been dismissed.

"Thank you for your time, Ms. Blackwell." Tom put a business card on her end table. "Please let me know if you think of anything."

They moved on to the next witness on their list, Mabel Grammond, whose studio apartment was three doors down. She looked delighted to have visitors.

"I was doing a puzzle by myself. I'm very hard of hearing, and the kerfuffle happened behind me, so I was slow to respond. It's the sprinklers that took me away from my birds." She offered them a sad smile. "My granddaughter gave me that puzzle. Now it's ruined."

"I'll look for it in the lounge. Maybe it can be replaced," Elenora told her.

The lady turned a hopeful eye on her. "Would you? You'd be a dear."

"It's my pleasure." Elenora texted Serena, asking her to snap a picture of the puzzle box if it was still there.

Tom moved in front of the lady to get her attention. "Ms. Grammond, how would you describe your interactions with Ms. Robin?"

"Hmm?" She tilted her head, prompting him to repeat his question.

"How were your interactions with Ms. Robin?" Tom enunciated each syllable.

A wry smile appeared on her face. "She steered clear of me. It irritated the bejesus out of her to have to repeat herself to me. Nothing deflates a threat like having to say it multiple times."

Alex laughed. "Well played, ma'am."

The rest of the conversation revealed nothing new. While Ms. Grammond had avoided most of Eileen Robin's nastiness, she'd witnessed the woman's bullying of the staff and residents. And she, too, confirmed the victim had been men hungry.

Their next chat was with a male resident.

"Mr. Tardif, how would you describe Ms. Robin?" Tom asked a man with a physique so youthful he seemed almost out of place. He no doubt was a regular at the residence's gym.

Pondering Tom's question, he looked away and stared into the distance, as if remembering a fond memory. "Oh, she was a sweetheart."

Tom, Alex, and Elenora did a double take at his words.

Maybe he's thinking of someone else.

The man chuckled. "You should see your faces. I got you good, didn't I?" He grinned wide, proud of himself, and slapped his thigh.

Tom played along. "You sure did, sir. You sure did. How would you describe her then?"

"How about high-maintenance, dramatic, malicious, overbearing? To put it nicely," he replied. "Oh, and I almost forgot conniving. Her chief talent."

Every interviewee had been allergic to the victim. The trio got little information aside from ample confirmation that Eileen Robin had been a miserable, insufferable human being who harassed fellow residents and the staff.

The female residents considered her bitchy, offensive, territorial, and after the men. Ms. Robin's bold advances had flattered a few male residents, while they admitted she'd been a toxic flirt and her personality, not her strongest suit. The other men had suspected her from the get-go, keeping their distance from her. A handful of them thought she had stalked them and viewed them as a mark. Some had even considered moving to a different home to get away from her.

When Tom asked the interviewees if the victim had friends, he received blank expressions, snickers, or barked laughter.

To say the least, Eileen Robin hadn't been up for a resident-of-the-year award.

Beyond their shared dislike of Ms. Robin, most witnesses feared suffering the same grim fate as the victim and bursting into flames themselves. While they manifested their anxiety in different ways, deep down, they were panicking.

This was no surprise, and Elenora had expected their worries about the mysterious, deadly threat. However, she hadn't expected her unease to grow with every interview, as she grasped the severity and uncertainty of the situation, which could affect not only more residents but also her team.

Were they sitting ducks?

Could they, too, burst into flames out of the blue?

When they'd arrived at Black Chapel, Elenora had hoped

that either she or Serena would quickly find a clue to get the ball rolling on eliminating the threat—or at least containing it—and protect everyone at Black Chapel. But things were playing out differently.

Upon her arrival, Serena had cast an alarm spell over the residence that would detect and potentially slow down any new fiery manifestation, allowing her to react. She had tethered the spell to Claire-Lune, too, for good measure. But as she'd explained, it was a blanket spell with limitations. Until they knew what had caused the seemingly spontaneous fire, she could not tailor her magic efficiently against the mystery threat. But she had a feeling that they—as outsiders—wouldn't be targeted since the death looked personal.

Serena's gut is usually spot on, Elenora tried to reason. Still, her stress was through the roof. How did members of the OPO withstand this kind of pressure day in and day out?

Tom did his best to reassure the people they spoke to, and Elenora admired his cool while struggling with her anxiety. She wondered if any of the seniors noticed her forced smile, but they seemed too busy giving Tom dubious stares, not fooled by the lack of tangible answers to explain what had happened in the entertainment lounge.

Elenora gave everyone her business card, insisting they call her if needed. She'd be happy to talk or come back for a visit.

And then she hoped they wouldn't reach out to her until she was in a better position to truly help them.

CHAPTER FIFTEEN

"Good work, Renaud. Keep digging," Tom said into his cell before hanging up. He, Elenora, and Alex had been on their way back to the entertainment lounge when their colleague called.

"I gather he found better info than my useless dream gave us," Elenora said matter-of-factly. She had no desire to compete with Renaud.

"He found information your premonition would have struggled to convey," Tom replied. "Like the fact our dear Ms. Robin survived three husbands."

"A three-time widow, huh?" Alex said. "Given her loving nature, this doesn't raise any red flags..."

"Renaud will check their causes of death and their financials."

"You think she might have been a black widow?" Elenora asked.

Alex chuckled. "I bet that'd be a popular opinion around here. And if she'd been, the folks we spoke to made it sound like she was still in business."

Eileen Robin's luxurious possessions came to Elenora's mind. "She was already loaded. I guess some people never have enough."

"That, or she went through money like shit through a goose and needed to find another purse to pay her rent here." Alex's gaze traveled around their exquisite surroundings, lingering on the woodwork. "This crown molding isn't cheap."

"Or maybe she liked the thrills of the hunt," Tom suggested.

"Did Renaud find anything about this place? The old prison?" Alex asked.

"Not much. A few riots over the years. Several deaths. But nothing fire related. Which doesn't mean much. The prison was built in the sixteen hundreds—was it?"

"1666," Alex answered.

"Yeah, so a lot of its past predates the police archives. But he's gonna phone museums."

They turned a corner, and the double doors to the lounge came into view. They hadn't heard from Serena or Günther, but Elenora still hoped they'd found something.

The trio entered the room, and Olivier Gonzales and Marc-André Sauvé—the two OPO-aware crime scene techs—greeted them before returning their attention to the victim's chair.

Elenora questioned Serena with an expectant gaze. Had they found anything?

Serena shook her head.

Dammit.

The witch gave her a small smile and jutted her chin at a table with a pile of soaked cardboard. "I found the puzzle, ordered a replacement, and got her another one with a very Zen country setting. Lots of pretty flowers."

Serena's kind gesture tempered Elenora's disappointment. "You're awesome."

The witch shrugged. "It's nothing. I figured an extra puzzle might help soften her trauma."

Elenora brightened. Serena was onto something. "Actually, it's far from nothing. She will appreciate the gesture, and the puzzle might help rewire her brain from the trauma."

Serena reached for her phone. "Then I'll place a mass order."

This was a fantastic initiative.

"I'll chip in a fifty," Alex told Serena, his gruff voice clashing with his generous spirit.

"We'll help too," Tom said, his eyes intent on what Günther was doing. Elenora went to investigate the source of her husband's fascination. The fire investigator leaned over a small pile of ashes on a silver tray. Tendrils of blue fire danced from his fingertips.

Some kind of fire magic?

Elenora didn't dare ask for fear of breaking the half-demon's concentration. It looked like a delicate maneuver.

Once the blue flames disappeared and he seemed done, Tom asked him, "Got anything?"

Günther ran a hand through his comb-over, disturbing the little hair he had left. "We will conduct a thorough analysis, of course, but we have found no traces of paranormal activity yet. I still don't see this as a civilian case. It's just that nothing obvious has popped up yet."

"So, not a straightforward case." Alex blew out a long

breath. He must have been clinging to his last shred of hope that they would find a quick and rational explanation.

"Likely not straightforward, yeah."

"Serena? Nothing at all, eh?" Tom asked the witch.

She shook her head. "I've scanned the room thoroughly more than once and found nothing demonic or out of the ordinary." She turned a teasing grin on her OPO colleague. "Other than Günther."

He stuck his tongue out at her. "There's nothing ordinary about you either, Reena."

"Damn right," she retorted and then told Tom, "I also suspect this isn't a natural scenario. Maybe Juniper would have better luck finding something. D'you want me to ask her to swing by when she can?"

Juniper was a healing witch with telekinetic powers. She could grasp things at an atomic level. She might find remnants of paranormal activity around the room that neither Serena nor Günther had perceived.

Tom nodded. "Yes. Please do."

"Consider it done. In the meantime, if we could look around the building, maybe we'll find something. If evil was careful in here, maybe it was less so after it left the room. Demons, in particular, can be sloppy." She slapped a hand on Günther's shoulder. "No offense, man."

"You'll need to up your game if you hope to rile me up, love."

"On it."

"You think whatever did this went around the residence?" Alex frowned at Serena.

"Depends what it is. It could have appeared straight here

from wherever the hell it came. Or it could have walked in through the front door. Maybe even literally."

"Lovely," he muttered.

"All right. We'll let you guys work in peace and go check out the rest of the building." Tom gave Günther his card. The fire investigator took it and handed Tom a fancy embossed card with shiny gold lettering.

Alex let out a whistle of mock admiration. "Something tells me the OPO has a healthier budget than our precinct."

Serena elbowed Elenora teasingly. "If you join us, you can get pretty, shiny cards too."

CHAPTER SIXTEEN

"Let's start with the top floor and work our way down." Left eye twitching, Eric Decker led them down the main hall and up two flights of stairs. Stuck on a conference call, Miss Pouliot had asked the guard to give them a tour of the residence.

Covertly looking for clues, Elenora and Serena trailed a few steps behind the men. The psychic's senses were wide open as she glided a gloved hand over the stair's polished banister, hoping to trigger a vision or detect something.

Serena's elegant fingers emitted discreet particles of magic in search of anything otherworldly. Tom adjusted his pace to give them a chance without alerting the guard. Alex also helped their snail's pace by showing interest in every architectural detail they encountered.

"Such a gorgeous place. Must be pleasant working here," Tom told Mr. Decker, interested in getting the guard's impressions away from his employer.

"I sure could do worse," the man replied.

"Been here long?"

Once at the top of the stairs, they headed down a long corridor of senior apartments like the ones Elenora, Tom, and Alex had already seen when they had done the interviews.

Being out in the open complicated Elenora's mission. She was used to more privacy when practicing her skills and felt exposed in the hallway. Unlike Serena, who could perform her magic subtly, Elenora couldn't escape the scrutiny of the security cameras or passing residents or the guard. Tom and Alex were distracting Mr. Decker, but the outsider's presence made it difficult for her to focus. She wasn't used to juggling this much at once, watching for both a vision and a paranormal manifestation. The two maneuvers were at odds with each other. She found it easier to access a vision when her eyes were closed, but she had to keep them open to notice a shimmering.

Maybe one eye closed and the other open?

Way to act natural.

Elenora remembered she could still feel warm chills—another telltale of a ghost wanting to talk to her—with her eyes closed. A spirit could still get her attention while she wasn't looking. She brightened up.

But if anyone or the cameras caught her walking around with her eyes closed...

She let out a soft groan.

"Stop fretting. This is just due diligence. Look at it as a long shot," Serena told her softly, her intent gaze scrutinizing every inch of the corridor.

"I know. But I'd really like to find something."

"You and me both. But don't beat yourself up." The witch grinned at Elenora and elbowed her playfully. "I know you want to."

Elenora chuckled. True, she wasn't one to miss an opportunity to beat herself up.

"What did you think of Ms. Robin?" Elenora heard Tom ask Mr. Decker several feet ahead.

The man in the dark uniform laughed. "She was a nasty piece of work, if you don't mind me saying."

"I don't mind you saying," Tom encouraged him.

"Honestly, I'm glad I rarely had to deal with her. Aside from breaking up her catfights."

"Catfights? She got physical with other residents?" Alex stopped walking as he asked, prompting everyone else to do the same.

Elenora jumped on the opportunity to be still. Feeling pressured to act quickly, she turned to face away from them and closed her eyes—cameras be damned—and hoped to muffle the guard's distracting presence and his talk of high-class senior citizens engaging in catfights.

Though it was hard not to be curious about that.

Focus! Block the gossip. Clear your mind. Picture a black canvas.

"Not quite, but close," Mr. Decker's nasal voice cut through Elenora's self-talk. "The old biddy liked to invade people's personal space, but I've never seen her hit anyone. She got in their faces real good, though. She was a pro at that. And I'm sure she was a scrappy fighter if she ever had to defend herself." He laughed. "That woman was like a wet cat."

The image of a wet cat popped into Elenora's mind.

Come on. Black square. Radio dial.

"A wet cat that threatened people," Tom pointed out.

The image of the cat lingered next to the radio dial.

Can you guys stop it with the damn cat?

"Sounds about right," the guard said.

A beat of glorious silence ensued. Elenora ignored the insistent feline and moved the radio dial in her mind, mentally sweeping airwaves.

"How did she threaten you?" Alex's question broke Elenora's fragile concentration once more. Why was she being so sensitive to other people's presence? In the past, she'd had visions and perceived paranormal activity while others had bustled around her.

Other people she knew and trusted. No strangers.

If she were to work with the OPO, there wouldn't always be optimal conditions for her to use her gift. She'd have to work on this performance anxiety in the presence of strangers until it became second nature.

Like Serena.

Who had centuries of practice under her belt.

Right.

"She didn't really threaten me," Mr. Decker answered Alex. "I mean, nothing serious. Just empty threats. Nothing I couldn't handle."

"Empty threats. Like what?" Tom pressed.

Elenora felt a nudge on her arm, encouraging her to walk backward. No doubt Serena. She opened her eyes and turned around. The group had resumed walking, and the guard was gesticulating.

"Like, whenever I'd *gently* pull her away from someone, she'd accuse me of brutality or sexual harassment. She'd threaten to report me. But there were always witnesses." He pointed at a camera nestled in a corner near the ceiling. "And the security cameras. And management knew her little game. She would never have had a leg to stand on."

Elenora drifted closer to the wall. While her gaze kept a general view of the corridor for shimmering, she skated a hand over an ornate handrail, aware of her fingertips.

Like everything else, the handrail was smooth and perfect and seemed to hold no secrets.

The nearest door wasn't for another twenty feet, so Elenora took a chance and closed her eyes again. If caught, she could say she had a headache. She kept a good pace and turned her mental dial slowly.

She saw nothing but darkness.

"D'you hear she tried to have Brooke fired?" the guard asked.

"I did. Do you know why?"

"Jealousy?" the nasal voice replied.

Frustrated, Elenora reopened her eyes. The building had witnessed centuries of unsavory characters and surely its fair share of violent deaths. How could it be so unresponsive?

Should she try a blanket summons even if the odds of it working were quasi-inexistent?

No. Too risky, especially in front of the guard. And if a random psychopathic ghost showed up and toyed with them, that could muddle the case.

"Jealousy?" Tom repeated the guard's guess and played dumb. "What do you mean?"

"I think she saw Brooke as a competitor with the male crowd."

"Do you know if Ms. Robin had her eyes on someone?"

The guard chuckled. "Anyone with a dick."

"Including you?" Alex jumped in.

"Me? Nah. I'm just some poor schmuck. The only booty she was interested in didn't involve sex, if you catch my drift."

"You think she wanted more money than she already had?" Tom asked.

The guard considered Tom's question before shrugging. "Who knows why some people do the things they do, right?" His left eye twitched up a storm.

A nervous tick?

Innocent people were often nervous in the presence of cops, but the guard worked in security. For him to be anxious was odd.

Was he hiding something?

Could he be involved in Eileen Robin's death?

Elenora turned to Serena, who kept scanning the hallway diligently. Judging by her bored expression, she was not picking up on anything. Elenora leaned close to her and whispered, "Could our guide be...*special?*"

"Other than a dorky civilian? I don't think so," the witch muttered.

As if to prove her point, the guard burst into a series of ungraceful snorts, presumably laughing at his own joke. Serena rolled her eyes.

Elenora felt a matching eye roll on the inside. "Any chance you could put me in a bubble of silence?"

Her friend chuckled. "You mean nerve-grating laughter and dick talk aren't conducive to visions?"

"To be fair, everything seems not conducive to visions right now."

"Sorry, babe. No can do. That would require too much juice. Some other time."

"Okay. Just thought I'd ask."

"Why don't you focus on shimmering? You don't need peace and quiet for that."

"Yeah," Elenora replied half-heartedly. Giving up on visions felt like admitting defeat.

They turned down an adjacent corridor similar to the previous one.

"We never know how things will progress. We can always come back," Serena said. "And there's often more than one way to skin a cat."

Another cat. And a gruesome image to boot. There was no way Elenora could clear her mind now. "Where did that horrible idiom come from, anyway? Did people use to do that?"

If so, did she really want to know?

"No idea, but it's been around a long time."

Mr. Decker led them to a stairwell and headed down.

"Wait? Isn't there an attic?" Serena's question stopped him in his tracks. He gave her a bewildered look, his eyes in full blinking mode.

"Huh... There is an attic, yes." His words were careful.

"Then, shouldn't we be going up?"

He appeared uneasy. "You want to see the attic?"

"Yes."

He shifted his weight. "Do you *need* to see the attic?"

A flashback of the attic in the old house on Maple overcame Elenora. The intense horror of her experience over there was still vivid in her mind. She was in no hurry to set foot in another creepy attic space ever again. Surely, whatever was underneath Black Chapel's roof would not disappoint.

Elenora was with Mr. Decker on that one. Did they *need* to see the attic?

They probably did.

In fact, *she* probably did.

Ugh.

"Of course we *need* to see the attic. What's wrong with that?" Serena stared blankly at the guard, as if she couldn't begin to see why requesting to visit the centuries-old attic of a building with a grim history could possibly be a problem.

"Okaaaaaay," the guard drawled, scrambling. He gave Tom and Alex a pleading look, hoping they would have a different opinion and tell him the attic was of no interest. But neither let him off the hook, even if Alex didn't seem thrilled by the prospect either.

Serena gave Elenora's arm a supportive squeeze and whispered to her, "You've worked wonders in attics before."

Elenora was afraid of that, but even so, a sense of pride and power swelled inside her as the haunting memories of the old attic on Maple made way for a victorious recollection of helping a house full of spirits recover from trauma and move on. What if the Black Chapel attic was another opportunity for her to do good?

"All right," the guard capitulated with a heavy sigh. "Let me see... If I'm not mistaken, the main access to the attic on this wing has been condemned." He pivoted, his gaze studying the high ceiling at the end of the hallway, where a narrow trap door was expertly concealed. "I think we'd need a ladder to—no, wait. Maybe we could use the stairs at the end of the south wing. But I can't guarantee we'll even be able to open the door. It's been years since anyone's been up there."

"Worth a try." Serena gave him an attractive smile, flustering him even more.

"Sure... Right this way, then." He led them down the corridor at a brisk pace.

Elenora guessed he was eager to be done with the unpleasant request. A part of her was, too, while a greater part now looked forward to discovering what was up there. Out of the blue, going up there suddenly felt right.

Serena hooked her arm with hers. "I'll have your back, but even if you feel something, you don't have to interact. We can come back with reinforcements."

Elenora nodded.

You got this.

Ville-Marie, 1673

I*f only this were a mind-reading spell or a working truth serum. I could test it on Honoré and understand his odd behavior of late,* Lizzie thought as she analyzed a concoction from Diandra, one of her coven sisters.

Although Diandra knew the basics of magical healing, her remarkable talent was influencing the thoughts and emotions of others. Her creation in Lizzie's hands—a truth serum—was a longtime project dear to her, a way to right wrongs and avenge one of her cousins who had burned at the stake in the Trois-Rivières settlement. Early on, she had asked Lizzie to help perfect the serum. Lizzie had agreed in a heartbeat—not only was Diandra a quiet and quirky force of nature, but Lizzie also recognized the potential of using the serum on the prisoners to assess their guilt and level of threat.

Combining native plants and magic, the mixture had come a long way since its inception and yielded encouraging results. But it was still unstable and riddled with side effects.

Lizzie looked forward to doing another round of tests on chosen prisoners. However, the serum needed time to ferment after each tweak to its formula.

The truth would have to wait.

As would getting straight answers from Honoré.

His recent reactions to Lizzie affected her. Yesterday, he had shown up in the blue room while she tended to Antonin Dujardin's wounds. Later, in their private quarters, he lashed out at her for being too close to the prisoner. He had seen her change bandages on other men's naked backs countless times and no differently. The outburst had been uncharacteristic of him—his anger with her was usually calm and calculated.

Then, at dinner, he gave her a glacial lecture about impropriety and decorum. She asked him how he would like her to tend to the prisoner's wounds so she wouldn't offend him. Should Dr. Barthes take over?

Honoré had turned red and growled that Lizzie was to take good care of Antonin and keep the doctor away from him.

Lizzie had gone to bed hurt by her husband's demeanor and bewildered by his contradictory orders.

A bird thumped against the window in front of Lizzie, startling her.

"Oh, little one!" she exclaimed.

As the bird fluttered around in a daze, Lizzie held her breath. Thankfully, it recovered its wits and flew away, seemingly unscathed. The positive outcome of this close call made her happy. Whenever a bird broke its neck against the glass, it always tugged at her heart. Such an unfair loss of life.

Using her index finger, Lizzie scooped up a bit of serum and tasted it to check the flavor. Bitter notes still lingered.

She reached for the bottle of maple water to further sweeten the mixture. It wouldn't enhance the serum's effectiveness but make it more palatable and less noticeable to the subject.

Despite the small dose, Lizzie's tongue tingled, and she knew the potent serum had some effect on her. Thankfully, she was alone, and its efficacy would wane quickly. She needed to perfect it, and this slight risk was worth taking. Besides, what were the odds of a witch-hunting mob showing up at her doorstep in the middle of this sunny afternoon?

Honoré could show up unannounced, though.

And then she might speak her mind about his attitude.

The thought mortified her, but would it be so bad? It would certainly be uncomfortable, but far worse things had happened in her life than angry looks and biting words.

As Lizzie stirred the maple water into the serum, she realized it was more than Honoré's angry looks and biting words over her interactions with Antonin Dujardin that bothered her—he had grown distant from her lately. Starting about the time the prisoner had arrived. But why?

Could he be jealous of them?

Was he worried about losing her to his acquaintance?

Antonin was a handsome and charming man—this much was true—but it would take so much more than good looks and smooth words to put a spell on her. To make her stray from her savior. She had eyes only for Honoré. And she was carrying his child!

But then, her husband didn't know that. She needed to assuage his concerns and watch herself even more around Antonin Dujardin.

Their charming guest.

Something about him was unsettling, but she couldn't pinpoint what.

Yet.

Maybe it was the sly glint in his eyes that made her believe he was always one step ahead of her. The feeling of being observed. Appraised. Quietly judged.

And when she felt like returning the favor, he'd disarm her with his amiable disposition. Making her feel like the most important person in his world and silly for even thinking there was anything strange about him. She almost wanted to apologize to him for being unfair.

It was obvious Antonin Dujardin was well-learned. He held his own in conversations on a broad variety of topics. Lizzie had overheard him explain a complex military strategy to a guard. His knowledge of botany was also impressive, and she couldn't help but appreciate the information he shared with her. He respected her intellect, a rare thing coming from a man.

Why did he have to display such a perplexing character?

How much more pleasant it would be if he were a simple and kind individual.

Lizzie reached for a bottle of ground birch and knocked the serum bowl off the table with her elbow. Instinctively, she threw a spell at the vessel to slow its descent—she couldn't have it spill its precious contents.

She crouched to pick the bowl up from the floor.

"Is gravity a mere suggestion in this room?" a male voice asked behind her, its tone dripping with honey.

Lizzie's shackles rose. This couldn't be happening.

"Or is the magic all yours?" More honey. And a hint of malice.

Lizzie had a pretty good idea whose voice this was.

She composed herself and chanced a look over her shoulder.

Sure enough. Antonin Dujardin stood in the doorway with a cocky smirk on his beautiful face.

CHAPTER EIGHTEEN

Eric Decker hadn't lied. The door to the attic was buried at the back of a utility closet filled to the brim with stuff. It barely budged once they'd cleared a path and attempted to open it.

"Let's move more shit out of the way so I can give it a good try," Alex said, lifting an old vacuum cleaner.

Once the detective had better access to the door, he gave the black metal handle a forceful tug.

The door remained stuck. Alex massaged his upper arm.

"Too bad you don't have a sledgehammer or a baseball bat," Tom said, shooting Serena a knowing look.

How would a sledgehammer or a baseball bat help Alex open the door?

It took Elenora a second to understand Tom's reference. He must have been alluding to the time his detective partner had benefitted from magical help to punch a necessary hole in a wall with a sledgehammer. A paranormal resistance had hindered Alex's powerful baseball swing. Until Juniper had pushed back on the interference, helping him strike a forceful blow.

Alex caught Tom's meaning, and he, too, glanced at the witch. "You like baseball, Serena?" His question dripped with a hidden request.

Elenora could hardly believe that he, of all people, would ask for magical help.

Serena also caught his drift. "Juniper's more of a fan, really," she replied carefully, giving him a pointed look before her eyes started roaming the cramped room, as if assessing the space and potential risks.

Elenora rarely saw her friend doubt her abilities, but the more time she spent with the witchy crowd, the more she understood there were myriads of nuances and gray areas. While some basic spells and magic seemed accessible to most witches, there were talents and specialties, and some spells were trickier to perform than others, even if they appeared simple. Alex's request must have been one of those.

"I like baseball," Eric Decker interjected, unsure of where the conversation was going.

"But you're...athletic," Alex argued to Serena. His insistence was unexpected. Perhaps he thought a door-opening spell was benign or he was desperate to get things going. Maybe both.

"Fine. Suit yourself," the witch mumbled and shrugged.

There was a hint of a *please sign this release form* warning in that shrug. A flicker of doubt appeared in Alex's eyes. But then his back stiffened. He raised his chin and crossed his arms defensively over his chest, his resolve returning out of sheer will to not let Serena get to him. "Great. Bring it on."

Eric Decker's head swiveled between the detective and the witch, confused by their cryptic interaction.

"Alex, you're gonna try the door again? Or should I?" Tom stepped in, maybe to give his stubborn partner an out or highjack the guard's attention from the magic about to happen.

"I'm gonna try a trick a friend showed me." Alex gave Serena a questioning look. "I got this, right?"

She gave him a curt nod. "Of course you do, hun."

Alex bristled at the term of endearment and faced the door. "I'm gonna go on three."

The witch discreetly raised her hand in his direction.

"One..." Alex swallowed hard as his hand landed on the door handle. "Two..."

Serena's fingers wiggled. Elenora felt the air crackle. The door didn't stand a chance.

"Thr—" Just as Alex was about to pull, the door swung open. He jumped back just in time to avoid being hit in the face. A cloud of dust spread across the closet, coating him and the surrounding space with grimy particles.

"Jesus! That better not be asbestos!" Alex barked between coughing fits. He pulled a handkerchief from the inside pocket of his jacket and wiped his face while shooting daggers at Serena.

She gave him an exasperated look. "I hear there's no crying in baseball."

"It's dust," the guard mumbled into his sleeve, his eyes watering. "When they converted the building into a retirement home, they cleaned it up pretty good—hazmat suits and all. A lawsuit from a deep-pocketed client was the last thing they wanted."

As the dust settled, Tom pointed to the steep staircase that disappeared into darkness. "Shall we?"

Mr. Decker took a step back. "Why don't you folks go ahead?"

Alex looked at Serena again and made a gesture toward the stairs. "Ladies first."

The guard's eyes widened, and he raised a hand, as if to object.

Serena patted him on the shoulder. "All good, man. Not my first time around this block." She flicked on her cell's flashlight and took the lead, climbing up the creaky wooden stairs.

"You good?" Tom whispered to his wife.

Elenora had butterflies, but they had a supernatural pyromaniac force to stop. "Let's go get answers," she declared before losing her nerves and followed Serena.

"There should be a light switch on your right!" the guard called from behind.

Serena found the switch, and a series of overhead lamps turned on, shedding light over the vast, empty space. Small windows near the floor allowed some natural light in. Sizable wood beams crisscrossed overhead underneath the roof. Enormous gray stones and aged mortar adorned the walls. The attic was less grim than Elenora had expected. If anything, it was architecturally stunning.

Alex cleared his throat and asked the guard, "Do you know if they ever hanged prisoners from these beams?"

Mr. Decker's left eye twitched in rapid succession. "I don't, and frankly, I'd rather not think about that. But I think in the early days of the prison, they mostly used the public square for hangings."

"'Cause who doesn't love a good spectacle?" Serena mumbled loudly enough for Elenora's benefit.

The scowl on the witch's face suggested she was familiar with such gruesome events. Elenora sometimes forgot her upbeat friend had witnessed atrocities over the centuries.

But she's also witnessed marvelous things that no one else ever would in a single lifetime. This thought usually followed. There was comfort in thinking she hadn't only experienced trauma but also great things.

"Anything?" Serena whisper-asked Elenora.

Elenora let herself feel the room. Save for the dust, the air felt normal.

"I'll let you all explore," the guard said, heading down the stairs. His discomfort about the attic was welcome. It would allow Elenora to roam and close her eyes without worrying about him. She followed Serena, already walking the perimeter with her hands outstretched. Elenora noticed Tom and Alex were not far behind her. Tom gave her a smile and a thumbs-up. She smiled back, closed her eyes, and prepared herself for anything. Hopeful.

Elenora went around the entire space and felt deflated as she came full circle and empty-handed at the top of the stairs. She shook her head.

"It was worth a try," Serena told her as they descended the stairs.

Elenora was about to agree when the back of her neck tingled, as if she were being watched. She halted and hazarded a look over her shoulder.

"What is it?" Serena spun around and lifted her hands, prepared to wield magic.

Elenora assessed the space before answering. The brief tingling was gone, and there were no signs of ghosts or vision. "I thought I felt something, but..." Her gaze swept the attic one last time.

"Do you want to look around again?" Tom asked.

"No. It must have been my imagination. Or my subconscious reminding me never to turn my back on an attic space."

"Your subconscious is wise," Alex said, disappearing down the stairs.

The guard waited for them in the utility closet, looking relieved they were done. "Found anything?"

"Just lovely craftsmanship," Alex responded.

"Other than the fire in the entertainment lounge, do you know of any other fires in the residence or prison over the years?" Tom asked Mr. Decker.

"There were a few, as you can imagine." The guard endeavored to close the finicky door to the attic. "Back in the day, with so much wood, buildings went up in flames easily." He grunted, battling against the recalcitrant hinges.

"Allow me." Alex gestured to the door, and the guard let him take over. The door slammed shut before he even tried to close it.

He glared at Serena. She batted her eyelashes at him.

"Impressive," the guard said to Alex as he led them out of the closet. "Do you lift?"

"I don't. My strength is fueled by bottled-up annoyance."

The guard frowned at the detective's bizarre retort but didn't comment.

"Do you know where those fires happened?" Tom steered them back to the topic at hand as they went down another stairwell.

"The old prison kitchen, not surprisingly, and parts of the third floor, I believe. A section of the roof had to be redone. The chapel—where we're heading—had a few fires. At least, that's the rumor."

Tom exchanged a glance with Alex, and Serena with Elenora.

"Any fires in the lounge before today?" Serena asked.

"Not that I know of, but don't take my word for."

"Do you know what part of the prison was, originally, where the current lounge is?" Tom asked.

Interested in the question, Mr. Decker thought hard. "I'll have to check the old floor plans, but I believe it was some kind of administrative wing. So, possibly the warden's quarters or the infirmary?"

"Could we please get a copy of those floor plans?"

"I'll ask Miss Pouliot." He stopped before a large wooden door, next to which an antique plaque stated, "Black Chapel, est. 1666." He reached for the wrought-iron door handle. "Ladies and gentlemen, the most famous room on our tour. The chapel after which the residence is named."

He opened the door with a dramatic hand flourish, unveiling an ancient and very brown room with a cruciform layout and a cathedral ceiling.

As Elenora passed the threshold, an eerie sense of foreboding struck her.

Something in there didn't feel right.

Elenora took in the old chapel, searching for what could have triggered her feeling of doom and gloom. A quick visual appraisal gave her no clue. The space's mood and appearance were modest and solemn, as one would expect based on its function and history.

What about the air?

She focused her senses on the atmosphere. It didn't appear any denser than usual, but maybe there was something different about it. Was there? Elenora was unsure. Something nagged at her in the back of her mind. A perplexing sense of dread vibrated inside her.

Tom gave her a questioning look before he asked the guard, "Mr. Decker, you said several fires occurred in this room. Do you happen to know where in the room?"

"Might just be a rumor. But there is one spot..." The guard headed down the aisle, and they followed him. "They've done a great job restoring the floor. Unless you know what to look for, you can't tell."

He halted near the middle of the room next to a long wooden bench identical to the others.

As Elenora got closer to Mr. Decker, conflicting gut feelings warred inside her, at once beckoning her to come closer and warning her to stay away. A vision awaited her—she just knew it. This sense of certainty was a new thing for her. She'd never sensed an impending insight so clearly—as if it were waiting for her, and she could choose when to access it.

An odd but welcome sense of control.

"Right here. Look at that. Amazing, huh?" The guard pointed at the floor near the bench, beaming with pride, like he had done the restoration himself.

Alex crouched to examine the repair. "I see what you mean. That's top-notch craftsmanship."

Elenora studied the special spot from a safe distance, itching to read it, but mindful of the guard's presence. How could she go around him? If only she could assess the floor discreetly, but that notion was a wild card—she could never predict how she'd react to a vision. It was one thing to sweep for clues in a hallway with gloves on when the security guy was busy chatting with Tom and Alex and the chances of finding something were low. It was another for her to risk acting like she was possessed right under the stranger's nose when her gut knew something powerful awaited her. So far, she'd had a variety of unpredictable physical reactions to insights, including being thrown across the room by an invisible force. Usually, though, she would remain in place, but her eyes' gray irises sometimes paled and turned nearly white. Either of these manifestations would be hard to explain.

And then the security cameras... She looked up, and sure enough, there was a recording device above the altar.

"So, one fire happened right here, and there might have been other ones in this room," Tom recapped to the guard.

"Again, maybe just a rumor. But that's what the old guards like to tell the newbies. We'll never know for sure if it's true. But let me tell you, one night round in here by yourself will make you believe some weird shit happened."

"I bet," Tom said. "There's something about this room."

"There's something about this room, indeed," Elenora said, sounding as if she was merely agreeing. But her detective husband caught what she really meant.

He offered his hand to the guard. "My kind sir, you've been a great help. Thank you for showing us around. We won't keep you any further. We'll see ourselves out."

A flicker of disappointment passed over Mr. Decker's face. "Are you sure? You haven't seen—"

"Before you go," Serena interrupted him and pointed at the camera Elenora had noticed. "Is this the only security camera in here?"

"It is. Would you like the footage?"

"Yes, please," Tom said. "Let me walk you out." He gave the guard his card as they went to the door.

"You got something?" Serena asked Elenora quietly. Alex was all ears.

"I feel I'm about to get something."

Alex gave her a light frown while Serena smiled wide. "Your instincts are sharpening?"

Were they?

"Maybe?"

But what if her gut feeling was wrong and they got rid of the guard prematurely? Elenora made a face.

Serena drew her into a side hug. "Trust your gut, girlfriend. It's your best ally."

Tom came back to join them. "Can you put some kind of lock on the door?" he asked Serena.

"Good idea. Gimme a sec. I'll deal with the camera first."

While the witch took care of the security device and the door, Elenora prepared herself for the brewing vision. Her gut twisted with a horrible thought, and she turned a worried gaze on Serena.

"Serena?"

"Yeah?" The witch returned from locking the door.

"Even with the spell you put on the residence to slow down ignition, could I still catch on fire by accessing this vision?"

"You wonder if the vision will elude the spell?" Serena asked.

At the same time, Tom said, "You think the spell won't cover where the vision brings you?"

"Yeah. Both. I don't know if my mind ever travels out of a room—concretely—but what if it kinda does?"

Serena rubbed her chin.

"How about I cast an extra fire-retardant spell specifically covering your mind, just in case?" she proposed. "And I'll also have my eyes on you. We'll pull the plug at any sign of trouble."

Elenora considered the plan. She trusted Serena with her life, but she'd also seen spells going wrong or being counteracted in spectacular ways before, so she knew there was always a risk.

A powerful tug from the spot grabbed her attention, as if the vision was getting impatient.

Elenora had to see this through. But could it be a trap?

"Actually, let me consult with Wren to ensure I have the best approach to this." Serena reached for her cell.

Wren answered the phone on the first ring and helped her colleague tailor the spell for Elenora. In no time, the psychic had a green light, though Wren insisted on staying on the line to help should anything go sideways.

Elenora felt at peace with the precautions in place and her decision to proceed. Furthermore, while the two witches had conferred, the pull from the vision had gotten even more insistent. She was now eager to experience it.

She reached for Serena's hand for extra security.

"Oh, good idea! Let me grab my tablet," Serena said, interpreting the handholding differently. Trying to capture the vision in real time was indeed a good idea.

Once the tablet was in the witch's other hand, Elenora stepped over the restored section of the floor, and as predicted, her consciousness went down a psychic rabbit hole. She found herself surrounded by smoke. Radiant heat warmed her skin as a circle of flames danced around her. An overwhelming sense of grief and despair threatened to crush her. She fell to her knees and heard herself mumbling something—a feverish prayer? Rage and bitterness intensified her sensory landscape.

Focus. What's going on?

Elenora willed herself to look around through the thick smoke.

Were these human silhouettes?

She observed one of them—a man, who suddenly burst

into flames. Was he burning alive? His piercing scream confirmed her gruesome guess.

Five more male silhouettes ignited. They, too, howled in pain.

Elenora struggled to make sense of the vision. She could still hear a voice coming from her, but it wasn't hers.

I'm inside someone.

The prayer intensified, and another man went up in flames.

The prayer...

What am I saying?

She tried to decipher the muttered words, her task complicated by the wails of the burning men and the panic and chaos in the room. The little she caught of the murmured words sounded like gibberish to her.

Wait, not gibberish. Latin?

And then she saw him: the little boy from her dreams was among the burning men. Watching her. Smirking.

Smoke snaked into Elenora's airways, stinging her lungs. She noticed her clothes were on fire.

I'm on fire!

She panicked.

Intolerable heat seared her skin, and she felt woozy.

Fresh air hit Elenora's face. She gasped for air.

Disoriented, she swatted her clothes manically to put out nonexistent flames.

Strong arms embraced her from behind—Tom's. "It's okay, Ele, we've got you. You're okay."

She was back to reality in the old chapel of the residence. Alex and Serena stood in front of her with concerned expressions.

"Reena, is she okay?" The fear in Wren's voice came out clearly through the phone's speaker.

"I'm okay," Elenora croaked to reassure everyone before checking that she truly was. A quick look at her clothes told her they were fine. Her bare arms showed no burn marks. Her heart thumped frantically from the adrenaline rush, but that was normal, considering what she had experienced in the vision.

"How about you sit?" Tom steered her to the closest bench.

Plopping down on the hard seat, she collected herself.

"Wren, I'm gonna go now. I'll let you know if we need more help. Thanks again." Serena ended the call.

"Did it work?" Alex pointed at Serena's tablet.

The witch checked her device. "Looks like it! Let's see what we got. Is that okay with you, Ele? Or do you need a moment?"

In the safety of the present, Elenora was keen to revisit the vision with her friends. "I'm good. Go for it."

They gathered over Serena's tablet. Smoke filled the screen in the video, depicting what Elenora had seen.

"I felt like I was burning," the psychic said once the clip ended. "And I was so angry and distressed."

"I'm sorry you had to go through this." Tom rubbed her back.

She released a chuckle. "Just taking one for the team. Like you guys often do."

And then Elenora remembered muttering words in the vision. "I was mumbling something, but I have no idea what. We didn't hear that, did we?"

"Crank up the volume?" Alex asked Serena.

They rewatched the images, but the sound was muffled and distorted. Barely audible murmurs came across as an unclear, guttural rumbling. On top of that, the roaring fire and commotion in the chapel spiked and distorted the soundtrack.

Serena tapped around on her tablet. "I'll send the clip to Wren for analysis. Maybe she'll get some info out of it."

Elenora was about to say that she hoped the other witch would also get details on the little boy when she realized that, once again, his likeness hadn't been captured. She groaned.

"What is it?" Alex asked.

"The little boy made an appearance in the vision. I'm sure I saw him, but he's not in the video."

"You saw him in the vision?" Serena perked up.

Until now, Elenora had mostly seen the little pest in premonitory dreams—and twice in real life, but these occurrences could have been hallucinations or her tired mind playing tricks on her. This was the first time he'd appeared in a vision while she was awake.

"In the vision, yes. Clear as day. And hard to miss. While the other male figures were burning, he had his hands in his pockets, unaffected. In fact, I think he was enjoying the show." Her mouth twisted. Such sadism seemed on-brand for her mental bully.

"Little asshole," Serena muttered under her breath. "One day, I swear, I'm gonna kick his tiny little ass."

"Question is: why was he there now?" Alex pondered.

"Why is he ever there?" Serena replied, frustrated. "And why can't he just get a damn life instead of picking on her?"

"I don't disagree," Alex said. "And trust me, I'll be the

next in line to kick his ass after you're done. I'm just wondering what his connection to this case is."

Serena nodded. "I hope we'll find the connection. But I've encountered enough evil losers with no purpose in life other than tormenting others. Sometimes, there's no rhyme or reason."

Tom surveyed the room and then pointed at the floor where the fire had occurred. "Ele, assuming the burning person in your vision stood right here—"

"I think it was a woman," Alex interrupted him. "The fabric in front of Elenora that caught on fire looked like a skirt. Does that seem right?" he asked his psychic colleague.

"I think it does." She tried to recollect her burning garments. "It could have been a skirt, yes."

"Please replay the clip," Tom said to Serena.

They watched it again. When the person at the center of the vision kneeled, a pile of green fabric resembling a skirt appeared amidst the fire and smoke.

"Good catch," Serena said to Alex. He looked unsure of what to do with her compliment.

Elenora chuckled inside. These two sure kept each other on their respective toes.

"So, assuming the burning woman stood right here, then," Tom made a sweeping gesture with his hand, "the men who burst into flames would have been around there, judging from where the crucifix is."

"You saw the crucifix in the clip? Where?" Serena played the clip again in search of the religious symbol. She stopped the video, leaned closer to the screen, and zoomed in on the still image with two fingers. "Wow. Who's your optometrist?"

Tom laughed.

"Okay, so, assuming the crucifix hasn't moved since then, one of the men on fire would have been standing around here?" Alex crouched to inspect the floor a few feet down the aisle.

Tom studied the distance between where the vision had occurred and Alex's position. "Looks about right."

"Hmm. Hard to tell, but these planks might have been replaced." Alex looked at Elenora. "Ele, would you mind checking out the floor over here?"

Elenora went to Alex, and he stepped aside to give her room. Serena joined her and slipped her hand into hers.

Elenora moved around the presumed area, hoping she could see the burning woman from that vantage. If they could identify her, they might have a breakthrough.

Unfortunately, nothing came to her this time. She moved around, dragging Serena along. Since they were guessing, maybe she wasn't in the right spot.

The sense of dread and the beckoning from the vision she'd felt earlier when entering the chapel didn't return. Maybe she'd seen all there was to be revealed in the room. But Elenora wasn't ready to give up yet.

"Where would you say the other burning men would have been?" She looked around and moved a few feet to her left. "Around here?"

Tom nodded. "Yeah..."

Once again, she moved around, trying to get an insight. Nothing.

"Try over there," Alex suggested. Elenora moved to yet another spot with Serena in tow. Still nothing.

Elenora dropped her friend's hand and returned to the vision's location while Serena performed a magical sweep of the chapel for demonic remnants. This time, the psychic tried to feel a spiritual presence and looked for a telltale heaviness in the air, but aside from the stuffiness typical of an old environment, the air wasn't notably thick.

She felt no chills either.

She pivoted and scanned the room. She saw no shimmering, no sign that a spirit wanted to talk to her. The only thing she noticed was a ringing in her ears, like a mild case of tinnitus. Barely perceptible. And totally unrelated.

Getting old sucks.

Then again, at forty-one, Elenora was still a spring chicken compared to the residents of Black Chapel—not to mention some of her friends. "That's pretty much it for me," she announced.

Tom smiled at her. "And that's already a lot."

"Yeah. Awesome as always," Serena said.

"Anything on your end?" Tom asked the witch, and she shook her head. "No, but Günther's wrapping up in the rec room."

"Okay. Tell him we'll be there in a minute."

"Found anything?" Tom asked the fire inspector as he gently tipped the tray of ashes he'd been testing to pour them into a small black container.

"No, but we will." His reply came with a cryptic smile.

Alex narrowed his eyes, not liking the sound of it. "Care to expand?"

"I suggest we find that Ms. Robin's cell phone battery malfunctioned and set her on fire. And we will argue the wick effect, even though the victim was slimmer than a toothpick."

Alex's eyes seemed to narrow even further. "You found a cell? Where?"

"No, we didn't find a cell. In fact, we don't even know that she had a cell—though I think it's relatively safe to assume she did." Günther was still grinning, enjoying himself. He pulled a clear baggie containing a charred hunk of metal out of his tool bag.

"A burnt cell?" Tom said.

"Yup. A recent popular model, too."

"But you just said— Wait. You're gonna plant evidence?" Alex's voice reached an unprecedented amount of annoyed gruffness.

"As a last resort only, to buy ourselves time. But unless one of us pulls a rabbit out of our hats or asses pronto, we're gonna have to go there." To stop Alex from launching into a major objection, Günther added, "Unless you have a better idea or don't mind admitting to the world that an unidentified supernatural force grilled a random, innocent woman. Good luck maintaining law and order after that. And I bet this is already all over social media."

Alex swore.

Serena checked her phone. "Hashtag 'Old Folks BBQ' is trending. Jeez, people are dark these days," she tsked.

Alex's face fell. "You gotta be joking!"

"Actually, I am. But it's only a matter of time before it spreads like wildfire on the interwebs."

Alex mumbled something about rotary phones and the good old days.

Tom asked Günther in a voice of reason, "How will the

assigned M.E. buy the cell phone theory? Assuming they won't be knowledgeable about the OPO and their field of expertise."

"We can use gentle persuasion to make them buy it if needed."

Alex let out a loud snort of disbelief.

"Nothing drastic," Günther added good-naturedly. "Surely you can appreciate the bigger picture here, detectives. I recommend acting for the common good until we figure out what's going on. It's much easier to adjust reports later than to contain and de-escalate mass hysteria. Wouldn't you agree?"

Alex groaned his displeasure.

Tom nodded reluctantly. "Sounds like you've been there. Do what's best for now. I'll inform Chief Costa. And let's do all we can to solve this case and make things as right as possible."

"Excellent. We'll proceed as such for the time being." Günther's gaze slid to Serena. "And until we get an answer, maybe we can get someone from the OPO to stand guard over here. That would at least reassure the residents and the administration."

"Good idea. I could also cast a suggestion spell so they would remember Ms. Robin having a heart attack instead of witnessing her going up in flames."

"You mean alter their memory," Alex pointed out.

Serena shrugged. "The brain already tends to do that with trauma to protect itself. I can give the collective memory a little nudge in the right direction to ease everyone's anxiety. Unless you think they can benefit from the trauma." She shot him a defiant look.

"But how would you explain the sprinklers and water damage?" Alex countered smugly.

"Sprinklers can malfunction."

"And the coincidence with the death?"

"What coincidence? The sprinklers went off and shocked Eileen Robin into a heart attack."

Alex answered her with a blank look. "If she died of a sprinkler-induced heart attack, then we don't need to plant a cell phone."

"I still need something for the M.E. to explain the ashes," Günther said. "They're unlikely to buy the sprinkler-heart-attack-spontaneous-combustion theory, even with a dash of magical persuasion."

"How about we limit our truth-stretching to the planted cell phone for now so we don't need a spreadsheet?" Tom said.

After a thoughtful silence, Serena said, "Tom, I appreciate the need to keep things simple, but how about a mild spell to dissuade people from sharing the news outside these walls? Nothing drastic nor memory-altering."

"Like the spell Claire-Lune puts on classified cases?" Elenora asked.

Claire-Lune had a "spell of disinterest" for supernatural cases involving civilians. Once they'd been solved and before they were archived, she'd cast the spell over them to discourage people from looking at the files.

"Similar, yeah."

Tom gave the idea some thought. "Sold."

CHAPTER TWENTY

After their work at Black Chapel, Elenora and Serena grabbed a late lunch at a nondescript sandwich place near the residence, the only not-tourist-trappy eatery in sight. They planned to visit Muriel while Tom and Alex analyzed the footage and determined the next course of action. Serena had instructed the two detectives to look out for blurs, static, and other visual disturbances when viewing the clips, as they could be signs of a demonic or other supernatural manifestation.

On their way to Serena's car, the witch's cell rang with a famous circus tune. She groaned.

"You changed your ringer?"

"No. That's a Kévun-specific ringer."

"The guy from accounting has his own ringer?"

The song "Entry of the Gladiators" kept playing.

"The ding-dong from accounting, yeah. And if I don't answer him, he's gonna hit speed dial every twenty seconds."

Elenora bit back a smile. "Your job is full of hazards and hardships."

Serena snorted before muttering, "Cell B16 in my time sheet is probably the wrong shade of gray. Let me get rid of the barnacle." She answered her phone in an exasperated voice. "Yeah!"

While Serena paced, Elenora looked around. She rarely came to this part of Vieux-Montréal. She took in the charming boutiques and cafés.

And then a sense of uneasiness prickled her skin. Was she being watched again?

Elenora's gaze switched from the historical buildings to the pedestrians on her side of the sidewalk and across the street. Everyone seemed busy and minding their own business.

But the feeling became even more unpleasant.

Her eyes caught a poster inside a nearby bus shelter of a little blond boy eating an ice cream cone.

Elenora's uneasiness morphed into full-on dread.

She cautiously moved closer for a better look. She recognized those eyes staring at her over the top of the ice cream cone.

The little twerp from her dreams.

The printed image shifted—the boy lowered the cone to reveal a disturbing smirk.

I must be hallucinating.

She blinked hard, hoping to reset reality.

The image shifted again. The boy's eyes were now devoid of malice. He did bear some resemblance to her night-time harasser, but he was a different kid.

Elenora was about to dismiss the experience and blame it on stress and poor sleep when she noticed her reflection in the dirt-coated plexiglass panel of the bus shelter. Next to her, a man's face appeared, as if he were standing right behind her, watching her with mocking malevolence.

Elenora gasped.

Don't stare at him! her gut screamed at her.

If she stared and slipped into a trance, she might invite him onto her side of reality. She'd already learned this the hard way once when she'd involuntarily hypnotized herself in her bathroom mirror and a pair of murderous hands came at her from the other side of the glass and almost choked her to death.

With a forceful *thunk*, a hand landed on the plexiglass panel next to her reflection, and magic particles skated across it.

The stranger's reflection froze.

Serena struggled and strained. "Come on, asshole," she commanded.

The image of the unsettling stranger vanished as the witch lost her hold on it. "Dammit!" she yelled.

A young, sketchy-looking dude walking by shot her a look.

"Keep walking!" she snapped at him before asking her friend, "Are you okay?" while scanning the shelter with hawkish eyes. She blasted another shot of magic at it.

"You saw him?" Elenora asked incredulously.

"No. But I recognized that look on your face and got a feeling. And then I felt a presence. I swear I had him there for a moment. Was it the little jerk?"

Elenora told Serena what had happened and then said, "Let's try a download. How far are you parked?"

They rushed to the car. Once again, the download didn't

capture the elusive underaged bully. However, a faded image of the man did appear.

The two women sucked in a breath in unison.

But the older jerk had turned away, offering them the back of his head instead of his face. The vision was altered and didn't match what Elenora had seen.

They watched the stranger walk away, taunting them.

"Seriously? What the fuck!" Serena barked.

"Wait. D'you see that?" Elenora pointed at the tablet screen, which had faded to black. "Play it again."

Serena replayed the brief clip, and Elenora pointed out the man's clothes: he wore a cassock.

"Some kind of priest."

"A Jesuit." Serena frowned at the screen, pensive. "You have a kid barely out of diapers and a Jesuit tormenting you..." She turned a puzzled expression on Elenora. A slight teasing smile appeared on her lips. "What the hell did you do, girl?"

Elenora shook her head, taking in the absurdity of her situation. "Your guess is as good as mine. Maybe it's karma for a previous life. Do you think Claire-Lune can get anything out of this?"

"I'll send it to her, but she might have better luck getting blood from a stone. It's not like the Jesuits were in the habit of posing with their backs turned to cameras."

"But the garment itself, maybe it will give her a clue?"

"Yeah, maybe." Serena didn't look convinced. Her face darkened. "I think your little jerk might be escalating, and I don't like it. And now this creepy guy. I don't know how we're gonna get them, but I won't give up. Whether they're a real threat or bullying your psyche for shits and giggles, this isn't cool, and it's been going on for too long. Consider this official OPO business."

She yelled at her tablet, "You're messing with the wrong people!"

"Do you want to postpone visiting my mom?" Elenora suggested. "She's likely to send our frustrations through the roof after this."

Serena's eyes softened. "Nah. I'll take a chill pill. Trying to understand what's up with your mom is very important. In fact, I should have gone to see her sooner."

The first thing Serena did was rule out the possibility of Muriel hosting an "evil guest." She dragged a chair in front of the senior crumpled in her recliner, sat, and leaned forward close to her. She laid her hands on the frail arms before her, and with magic, she controlled the woman's eyes into meeting hers—a maneuver Elenora had seen Serena do on Rolland when he'd been possessed. Muriel's blank gaze didn't fight the witch.

Remembering how the spirit of Oliver Barlow, a British serial killer from the early 19th century, had put up a fight through Rolland while possessing him, Elenora whispered, "It's a good sign she's not fighting you, no?"

"It is, but I've encountered conniving spirits that cooperated only to deceive me better," Serena replied, further examining her subject. "How about you try giving her a read?"

Elenora approached her mother and attempted to look into her mind like she had tried with her once and had done with Rolland.

Neither woman sensed evil in Muriel.

Some good news.

But...

"How can her mind be so blank?" Elenora asked. "If her brain no longer functions, how could she have had verbal reactions recently?"

"The EEGs have always shown some brain activity, no?"

"Yes, but..."

But what? Elenora was tired of not knowing what to think.

"Maybe it's a spell. Or a curse," Serena mused.

"A curse? Why would my mother be cursed?" Of all the baffling theories Elenora had entertained, this one had never entered her mind. "She was a stay-at-home mom!"

Serena shrugged. "Hell if I know, but it's worth considering. Let me try a few things."

She skimmed a hand down Muriel's arm, creating a trail of magic dust, her eyes watching for a reaction. The senior remained unresponsive.

The witch performed more magical tests—all ineffective.

"Hmm." Serena tapped her chin. "What else..."

Elenora reached for her purse. "Maybe we've got all the answers we were supposed to get for the day. And it's not like my mom's going anywhere."

"Right. I can come back anytime. Just let me know if you want me to." Serena grabbed her messenger bag and was about to follow Elenora out when she said, "Wait. Don't open that door yet." She let go of her bag and crouched in front of the senior. "Do you know why we're here, Muriel? We're here because Elenora saw you in a dream with a little boy at the bottom of a river. Does that ring a bell?"

Serena's gaze was locked on Muriel's eyes. She took her hands. "If it does, speak up. Because the little fucker's been harassing your daughter for months. And on our way here, she saw him again in a bus shelter poster. And she saw a Jesuit priest lurking in a reflection. I think they want to hurt her. So, if you know anything about any of this, it'd be really dandy if you could tell us."

Elenora held her breath, alert for even the slightest sign from her mother.

But they might as well have tried to provoke a stop sign.

Serena let out a disappointed sigh and slung the strap of her messenger bag over her shoulder. "All right. Better luck next time."

"Thanks for trying," Elenora told her. At least her mother wasn't possessed.

As they crossed the room's threshold, a strangled rasp came from behind them.

They both whipped around and found Muriel frozen in her usual statue-like pose, staring into space.

"Okay, come on. We did *not* imagine that," Serena declared.

CHAPTER TWENTY-ONE

Ville-Marie, 1673

He wouldn't dare.

    He's a convict.

It would be his word against mine.

Lizzie's thoughts circled in her brain, her mind stuck on Antonin Dujardin witnessing her doing magic. While under the influence of a truth serum.

Her stomach knotted up as she walked. She was early for her coven meeting, so she meandered around the settlement. Being on the move usually calmed her. Except now—being alone with her thoughts stoked her anxiety. The snaky prisoner's unspoken threat had occupied her mind all day, and she was exhausted. But what else could she do other than roam the streets, killing time away from home?

He wouldn't dare. He's a convict. It would be his word against mine.

My secret is safe.

Lizzie had fled home after dinner as soon as she could

without raising her husband's suspicions. Being under his scrutiny while her mind kept returning to Dujardin had been a balancing act. She'd already given herself away in front of the prisoner—she couldn't afford to reveal herself to her husband, too.

He wouldn't dare. He's a convict. It would be his word against mine. My secret is safe.

Serving Honoré his meal had been difficult. Artfully avoiding eye contact without appearing shifty. Making just enough small talk with a voice steady enough that didn't reveal her agitation. She couldn't wait to leave for what the warden thought was her weekly handicrafts guild meeting.

The guild's membership was limited to the coven sistren, and it was a necessary pretense for them to get together. Lizzie lacked skills in most handicrafts, but embroidery interested her. Not only did it give her credence as a guild member in her husband's eyes, but it also fed her creatively.

He's a convict. It would be his word against mine. My secret is safe.

Lizzie hoped embroidering at the meeting might distract her mind from obsessing over her imprudence. Talking to Agnès might help, too. Indeed, she should tell her sister what happened. Agnès would know what to do. And Lizzie trusted her judgment.

She would tell Agnès everything after the coven meeting. And she would insist that she didn't confirm to Dujardin that she had magic. That she was a witch.

But you didn't deny it either, said a little voice inside her head.

The truth serum prevented me from doing so! she wanted to scream back at it.

I danced around the truth without lying—a nearly impossible feat. That has to count for something.

After Lizzie had softened the bowl's fall and prevented it from spilling the truth serum, Dujardin had asked her "if the magic was all hers." With that stupid smirk of his.

She had taken a moment to collect herself before reacting. She was proud of that moment of self-control.

"What do you mean?" She turned to face him and cocked her head, trying to pretend confusion, but the serum forbade her facial muscles from fulfilling her intended deception.

Lizzie had no clue what muddled expression she gave Dujardin, but he called her bluff, still amused. "Do you want me to say that you used magic to save the bowl? Then let me say it. You used magic to save the bowl."

She tried to narrow her eyes at him, but the serum fought her again. "A bowl has no soul." She stalled with an unrelated —but true—philosophical statement.

He gave her a blank look. "You used magic. And we both know what that makes you."

Heat crept up from Lizzie's neck to her hairline as she felt cornered.

Dujardin gave her a satisfied smirk. He knew he had her —the snake coiling around his prey.

But Lizzie refused to be an easy prey. If only she could lie, she could escape this predicament more easily.

She cursed her momentary inability to lie.

Find a different weapon then, as Agnès was fond of saying.

If Lizzie couldn't lie, then maybe she could keep skirting the issue with random truths.

"Magic?" she asked. Not a lie. Just a question.

"Yes."

"What is magic when you think about it?" Again, not a lie —another mere philosophical question. "Being alive is magical, if you ask me."

"We are talking about the bowl."

"Hmm. You, sir, are talking about the bowl."

He stared at her, a hint of irritation making his smirk waver.

The tables have been turned. Now, don't push your luck.

"How may I help you, Mr. Dujardin?"

He had opened his mouth to speak before closing it in a soft scowl.

Reaching the wharf, Lizzie turned around, savoring the memory of Dujardin's annoyed expression.

Until her intrusive thoughts returned.

He's a convict. He wouldn't dare. It would be his word against mine.

No matter how clever her response had been, Dujardin hadn't bought a speck of her innocence. She hadn't fooled him. And she knew he would not drop the issue. He would out her as a witch.

His word against mine.

But he's a man. And he would speak the truth.

Lizzie felt deflated. Even if he lied about her, he'd be believed.

She'd have to appeal to Honoré and be more convincing than Dujardin. She could argue that the *convict* was mistaken about what he'd seen. After all, claiming that she had magically altered gravity was a laughable notion. And why believe the word of a criminal?

The man was obviously delusional.

Lizzie could also claim he had been feverish. She was worried about his state.

Maybe she should share her concerns with Honoré before Dujardin had a chance to say something.

Yes. That's good.

Lizzie felt slightly better. Her pace decreased, and her body relaxed. A soothing breeze coming from the St-Laurent River caressed her face.

She looked forward to her sister's opinion on speaking to Honoré and exposing Dujardin.

Agnès would give her flack for being so careless, but she was loving and understanding. She'd comfort Lizzie and help her rectify the situation.

But this wasn't about her comfort. If the secret got out, it would make her and her sister vulnerable. Her sister's soon-to-be-born baby. And Lizzie's. Maybe put her coven at risk, too.

Lizzie struggled to breathe.

Calm down. Agnès will think of something.

Or maybe a fellow witch could craft a spell or a potion to silence Dujardin.

About to cross the street, Lizzie stopped. A man she knew to be fond of liquors was riding her way at a fast trot. She let him pass.

"Mrs. Delacroix." He tipped his hat at her, making him shift on his seat and almost fall off his horse.

"Mr. Grant."

Mr. Grant was a friend of her coven sister Henriette's husband, who was sick and in considerable pain. Lizzie had promised to give her a mint potion to make him feel better. But in her haste to leave home, she had forgotten to bring it.

She debated whether to return to the prison infirmary to fetch it or apologize instead.

But you promised Henriette you'd bring it.

The prospect of returning home caused Lizzie great distress. But it would be unfair to punish Henriette and her husband because of her cowardice. And Lizzie couldn't avoid home indefinitely.

She headed back to the prison, planning to go straight to the infirmary from the north entrance to avoid her living quarters and the blue room.

Her plan worked out, and she was relieved to reach the infirmary without encountering another soul. She opened the door quietly and snuck inside.

A string of grunts caught her attention, and she stilled. Two silhouettes moved in tandem over the bed. Two men, it seemed. It took her a second to realize what they were doing, but a long moan clarified the picture for her.

Oh!

Lizzie looked away and took a step back to leave the room.

The floor creaked under her foot.

Her eyes shot toward the men. They kept rocking, but the one in front was staring squarely at her. A smirk familiar to Lizzie appeared.

Abashed, she made another move to escape the room.

The man draped over Dujardin looked up, and his gaze met Lizzie's.

Honoré.

CHAPTER TWENTY-TWO

"Seems like the day's theme," Serena said, glancing in the rearview mirror. "A lack of paranormal activity at the Black Chapel residence when the case is obviously not normal. Same with your mom."

After Muriel's baffling manifestation, the witch and Elenora had spent the rest of the afternoon conducting more tests on her, only to find nothing wrong.

Even though there clearly was.

Serena blew out a frustrated breath and added, "And then, the unwelcome appearance of that creepy asshole kid and some creepy older asshole—like we have time for their stupid shit."

A blue sports car swerved in front of them. Serena leaned on the horn like her life depended on it. "Self-entitled asswipes!"

"Who? The people in that car? Or the kid and the stranger at the bus shelter?"

"All of them."

"Yeah, I could have done without the freaky thing at the bus shelter *and* my mom's reaction. Just when I think she's gone and I make peace with it, she does something freaky."

"It's hard when things are off, and there is no tangible proof. I hate it when that happens."

Elenora nodded. Her nerves were frayed, and she felt gloomy and drained by the day's events, but at least she was grateful her friend understood.

"We got Claire-Lune in our corner," Serena said. "She'll scrutinize what you got from the bus stop and look into your mom's situation. You know how brilliant she is—she might find something. And Wren can help, too. And just about everyone at the OPO. As I said earlier, I will bring your harassment case to the agency. It's lasted too long, and that little fucker has to learn there are limits and repercussions. We'll figure everything out."

"Thanks for being such a good friend."

Elenora's phone chimed with a text.

Pierre: I'm roasting chicken to give you and Tom a break and feed Alex, too. Is Serena with you?

Elenora smiled. Not everything was wrong with the world, after all.

"Hey, you want to come over for dinner? Pierre's roasting chicken."

"That'd be cool. I haven't seen him in a while. Is he making his potato salad?"

Elenora texted back.

Elenora: Yes and she wants to know if there will be potato salad.

Pierre: Can one legally eat roasted chicken without potato salad?

Elenora read his reply out loud.

Serena answered with a big smile. "I'm all there, then. I keep telling him he should mass-produce it. He'd have a bright future as a chef if that whole retirement thing doesn't pan out."

Elenora laughed. "Aubrey and I keep him too busy to consider another job."

"And I'm sure he wouldn't change a thing."

The car's Bluetooth picked up an incoming call from Claire-Lune, and Serena pressed a button to answer it.

"Loonie! What d'you got?"

"To start, I got Tom and Alex on the line with us."

"Awesome. Ele's with me."

"Hey, Elenora."

"Hi, Claire-Lune."

"All right. Here's what I got." Claire-Lune said. "I found eight combustion deaths on September 30th, 1673, in the prison. Considering the number of deaths on that single day, this is likely what Elenora saw in her vision. And then five more combustion deaths happened over time—individually."

Tom's voice came on. "In the chapel?"

"I could not find a tangible confirmation of the location of any deaths. Only a sense that they occurred in the prison."

"When did the other deaths happen?"

"Um... 1730. 1742. 1800. 1834. 1923. I will look for a correlation between the dates and see if I can find a pattern or tie them to external events. There were also other deaths around the prison, but they didn't seem related. I won't dismiss them, but they're on the back burner for now."

"Those weren't caused by fire?"

"Correct. Several were from whippings. Others from an illness or suicide."

"Other than her vision in the chapel, Elenora didn't feel any presence around the residence," Alex said. "Given the number of violent deaths, doesn't that seem odd?"

After a moment of thoughtful silence, Claire-Lune asked, "Did you guys go to the basement? They might have kept the worst inmates down there."

"Crap! No." Serena looked ready to bang her forehead against the steering wheel.

"We stopped at the chapel because of the vision and since the rest of the building yielded nothing," Alex said.

"Still a rookie move. I should have known better," Serena berated herself.

"We'll go back," Tom said.

"Maybe Yukiko could try summons in the chapel and the basement," Elenora suggested. "And perhaps she'd have better luck with Ms. Robin, too."

"Great idea, and I'm sure Yukiko will be on board," Claire-Lune said. "I'll try to find victims' names related to the 1673 fire to facilitate the summoning process."

While Yukiko could reach a departed person without knowing their identity, the more she knew, the easier it was for her medium mentor to establish a connection, and the better the chances of success.

"That sounds like a plan," Tom said, sounding upbeat. "Anything else of note?"

"Nope, that's all I got."

"Excellent. Great work. Alex and I will go back to squinting at the footage."

CHAPTER TWENTY-THREE

Céleste greeted them at the door with a wagging tail. Serena gave the dog a good pat before looking for Aubrey. She liked to call herself her *witchy godmother*, and her enthusiasm for the baby rivaled Pierre's. To her disappointment, the little one was napping.

Pierre offered her a glass of pinot grigio. "She'll be up soon."

Elenora grabbed a can of sparkling lemonade from the fridge as Aubrey peeped in the baby monitor.

"Oooh! I'm it!" Serena squeaked with excitement. She put her wineglass on the kitchen counter and bolted toward the staircase with Céleste in tow.

"Need some help?" Elenora asked Pierre about the dinner preparations.

"I've got this. Why don't you go catch up?" He jutted his chin toward the dining room, Tom and Alex's makeshift office.

Elenora went to join the two detectives glued to their

laptops on the formal dining table. Her husband was leaning ridiculously close to his screen.

"You're doing the eye equivalent of gritting your teeth in your sleep, dear," Elenora told him, her free hand squeezing his shoulder. She thought his posture wasn't healthy either, but she held her tongue on that one. She had to pace her nagging if she wanted it to have an impact.

Tom leaned back in his chair. Clasping a hand over hers, he turned to look at her, squinting exaggeratedly on purpose. "What?" he asked jokingly.

She laughed.

Alex stretched. "Ele, you got a point. I'm cross-eyed from searching for demons in the pixels. Time for a break." He stood and pointed at her drink. "Got any more of those?"

"In the fridge. Go ahead."

Alex headed to the kitchen as Serena came down the stairs holding the baby, with Willem on her heels and Céleste a few steps behind.

"If you're gonna trip me, Dingbat, at least wait until I'm not holding precious cargo," the witch scalded the cat as they reached the bottom of the stairs.

As if understanding her, Willem gave her a wider berth and glared at her defiantly. She noticed and entered a staring match with him.

Aubrey squealed, getting Serena's attention.

The witch answered her in a bright tone, "I know, right? There's something not right about your cat, love."

Elenora chuckled. "Cats are special."

Willem flicked his tail at her, lifted his chin disdainfully, and sashayed to the kitchen without looking back.

"We're on to you, Fluffy!" Serena called after him.

The cat shot her one last murderous stare over his shoulder.

The witch arched a brow and smirked. "Prove my point, why don't you?"

"You're like Céleste," Elenora said. "She spends every minute keeping a close watch on Willem, and she doesn't know what to make of him."

"So, how did it go with Muriel?" Tom inquired.

Elenora recounted their bizarre and unsuccessful visit to Muriel and the just-as-bizarre incident at the bus shelter. Tom listened with wide eyes.

"I don't like the sound of that," he said.

"Neither do we. Serena is bringing the issue to the OPO. She thinks it's time to end this maddening charade."

"Damn right," the witch said, bouncing Aubrey on her lap. Alex returned to the room with a lemonade drink and Serena's glass of wine. He put her drink on the table at a safe distance from the baby's grabby fingers.

"Thanks," she said.

"What did I miss?"

Serena gave him the Cliff's Notes version of what had happened at the bus shelter.

"Jesus," he bristled.

"I don't know if Jesus is involved, but Creepy Dude pretends to be a follower of his teachings," Serena retorted.

"What do you mean?"

"He wore a cassock."

"What in the fresh hell?" Alex shook his head with a scowl.

"My thoughts exactly."

"They definitely crossed a line," Tom said. "It's bad

enough that Elenora is bullied in her sleep, but this feels like something bigger than a sleep issue."

"I think the OPO will agree and be keen to get involved." Serena took a sip of wine.

"Thank you for bringing this to your agency's attention," he added.

"Don't mention it. I'm eager to make sure that appropriate retribution is given. It'll be like Christmas." She took another sip. "I gather you guys have found nothing exciting yet."

"You gather correctly," he replied. "Nothing that suggests paranormal activity."

Elenora sensed Tom's disappointment with the footage not shedding light on the victim's death. "Maybe Ms. Robin knows who killed her and a summons will get us that answer."

"Not to rain on your parade, Ele, but if she killed even just one of her husbands, she might have gone straight to hell. Might be hard to summon her," Serena pointed out.

"Why does crime solving have to involve hell now?" Alex groaned.

"Because it makes life more exciting." Serena faked an enthusiastic smile.

Hmm.

They might not be able to reach Eileen Robin if she had indeed committed murder, and maybe this was why Elenora's summoning attempt had failed. But sometimes, circumstances weren't black and white. Working with gray areas and understanding the bigger picture was part of her job.

"What if—" she started.

"—she circumvented going to hell because she was abused as a child?" Serena raised an eyebrow at her.

Elenora smiled at her friend seeing her coming. "Yeah. Among other things."

"My dear friend, you see too much good in people too easily. Trust me, there's a healthy dose of evil out there to balance things out."

Elenora sighed. Serena wasn't wrong. "Yeah, but sometimes... We saved Rolland."

Most people would have considered their friend Rolland beyond redemption when Barlow's evil spirit possessed him.

"We did because he had a strong conscience, and it was intact. He was salvable. But Barlow sure as all hell wasn't. And neither was Gill. You can't save a soul when there isn't one. And our dear Ms. Robin sounds a little challenged in that department."

"Let's assume she deserved to have gone to hell. But let's play devil's advocate for a minute," Alex said.

Serena snorted. "You mean literally?"

The witch and her colleagues at the OPO occasionally conducted business with the Gray Court, a so-called judicial system operated by literal devil's advocates.

Alex grinned. "Yup. Could someone at the Gray Court grant us access to her, even if she went to hell?"

Serena's expression soured. "That would require asking for a mighty favor from someone you don't want to owe a favor to."

"Before we think of involving the Gray Court, let's start with the summons," Tom said.

"I agree, but we know from Elenora's vision that Eileen

Robin was staring at her cards when she died. It's not like she saw the killer coming at her," Serena argued.

"But maybe she knew who was out there to get her," Alex argued back. "Maybe they threatened her."

Tom nodded. "All good points. The odds of Eileen Robin knowing who killed her might be very slim. But let's start with Yukiko giving it a try if she agrees, and let's keep our expectations low."

After the call with Claire-Lune on the drive home, Serena had left Yukiko a voicemail explaining the situation and requesting her help. While Elenora had failed at summoning the victim, her experienced mentor might have better luck. She looked forward to a new summoning attempt and was eager for them to hear back from Yukiko.

"So, the footage gave you nothing?" Serena asked Tom and Alex. "Nothing at all seemed remotely off, even if it didn't scream paranormal?"

"Well..." Tom replied, unsure of what to say. "Nothing obvious. However, I think we can rule out Brooke Gélinas. But please tell us if you see something we're missing."

He brought up a clip of the orderly who had visited Eileen Robin before her death while Alex, Elenora, and Serena—with Aubrey balanced on her hip—gathered behind him.

The laptop screen filled with a security camera view of a hallway with several doors—some closed, some open—Brooke Gélinas appeared relaxed as she walked into view and knocked on a door.

Tom paused the clip and turned to Serena. "Does she look possessed to you?"

The demon expert leaned closer to the screen. "Play it again?"

Tom replayed the clip, starting seconds earlier, and paused it as Mrs. Gélinas opened the door.

"If she is, she's hiding it well. Can we see what happens next?" Serena asked.

Tom clicked play and said, "She enters Eileen Robin's room, and then we can't see the rest because there are no cameras in there. But when she leaves, she doesn't look like someone who just got the ball rolling on an impending murder, if you ask me."

He skipped the clip forward and showed the once-again peaceful woman coming out of the resident's quarters.

"Still...could she have placed something in the woman's pocket that could have accidentally or intentionally ignited?" Pierre stood behind them, holding up a wooden spoon.

"Anything is possible," Alex replied.

"Anything is possible, sure, but Günther and the techs would probably have found it if it were the case," Serena said. "He might seem easygoing, but he didn't suggest planting that cell lightly. Trust me, he's conscientious and talented, and I've never seen him wrong."

"Good to know," Tom said.

Aubrey waved her arms at Pierre.

"Let me take this little bag of potatoes from you," Pierre said to Serena before taking the baby from her. "Who's a bag of potatoes?" he asked the baby, pretending to drop her, making her giggle. "Who's a *heavy* bag of potatoes?" He lowered her again, causing more giggles.

"It smells great, Pierre." Elenora gave him a grateful smile.

"Thanks. Dinner in five. I'll go settle little Miss Potato in her high chair," he said as he started retreating to the kitchen with the baby.

"Do I have time to show them the chapel clip?" Tom asked him.

"Go for it."

"What happened in the chapel?" Serena's excitement rose.

"Not much. In fact, it's so far-fetched that I'm almost embarrassed to mention it. But it's also too much of a coincidence to ignore." Tom brought up another clip. "All right. Here we go. Meet Lucien Villemure and his friend Chuck Leyner. Two more residents I'd like to have a chat with."

An overview of the chapel caught from the single camera in the room appeared on the laptop. The place was empty, save for two men: one in a wheelchair near the row of benches in the middle of the room and the other sitting near him on a bench.

"They look pretty close to where the burning woman in my vision was," Elenora said. "Especially the man in the wheelchair."

"Exactly. Eerily so," Tom agreed. "And weirder even, look at the timestamp."

The timestamp matched the time Eileen Robin had caught on fire.

Elenora studied the man in the wheelchair, willing herself to find a clue. His eyes were shut, and his forehead creased in a frown. His lips moved, as if in deep prayer. But then he opened his eyes and spoke—nothing unusual given the context.

"Play it again, but from a minute or two before Eileen Robin became a torch," Serena asked.

Tom did as she requested, and they watched the images unfold.

Once again, the senior in the wheelchair had his eyes closed and prayed. The man next to him looked like he was dozing off. The timer on the microwave beeped as they reached the fateful timestamp.

"Well, that wasn't anticlimactic at all," Serena deadpanned. "The good news is, they don't look like power-hungry warlocks about to unleash a deadly spell. Thank God for small mercies."

Under normal circumstances, Serena's words might have sounded absurd. But they had recently dealt with a power-hungry, deadly warlock, and Elenora was grateful this wasn't a déjà vu.

"I guess this gives them an alibi," Elenora said.

"Technically, yes," Tom said. "But someone could have tampered with the timestamp to provide a fake alibi."

"A guard would have done this?"

"It's possible. Though it's hard to see why. Unless..."

Elenora tried to follow what her detective husband was saying. What could a guard gain from giving the two men a fake alibi?

"Someone is trying to cover up a supernatural murder and pin it on these two by placing them at that suspicious spot in the chapel at the time of the murder," Serena said matter-of-factly, as if doing this was commonplace.

"That's what I'm thinking," Tom said.

"Kids! Dinner!" Pierre called from the kitchen.

Tom stood up. "Anyway, let's have a chat with Mr. Villemure and Mr. Leyner tomorrow."

They followed the tempting aromas wafting from the other room.

"Mind if I tag along when you have a word with them?" Serena asked Tom as they lined up to grab a plate. "I detected nothing weird in the feed, but I could tell better in person whether they have magic or a 'guest.'"

Tom gave her a big grin. "I was hoping you'd be interested."

"Do you know what they did before they went to the chapel?" Elenora inquired.

"Nothing suspicious, unfortunately," Alex answered her. "I tracked most of their movements around the home—outside their apartments. Lucien Villemure wheeled around the residence. He had positive interactions with a few people. He joked with the janitor. He seems likable. Chuck Leyner was at his place until Villemure knocked on his door to go to the chapel with him about fifteen minutes before the time of death."

Serena made a beeline for the potato salad. "You saw nothing suspicious in either man's demeanor?"

Alex shook his head. "No, but I've set those clips aside if you don't mind giving them a look after dinner."

CHAPTER TWENTY-FOUR

As Tom fetched peach gelato from the freezer, his cell phone rang. "It's Renaud," he announced to the room.

"Put him on speaker," Alex said, collecting empty dishes from the table.

"Hey, Renaud. I'm putting you on speaker." Tom placed the gelato container and his cell down on the counter. "What d'you got?" he asked, retrieving bowls from the cupboard.

"Eileen Robin's three late husbands were loaded, and every cause of death is listed as cardiac arrest," said their colleague on the phone.

Alex snickered. "What are the odds she found a 'natural' way to get these cardiac arrests without raising suspicions?"

"This crossed my mind, too. I'm working on warrants for their medical records."

Serena whispered to Elenora, "Sounds like the chances of a successful summons just went down."

"Yeah," Elenora whispered back. Logically, she knew they would likely waste their time trying to summon the woman again, but she believed in the principle of innocence until proven guilty. She also wanted to believe in coincidences. Maybe none of the deaths had been the woman's fault. "But it's still worth a shot."

Serena shook her head at her teasingly. "Ever the kindhearted optimist."

Tom had gotten off the phone and was distributing gelato bowls around the table.

"Does the daughter have an opinion on how her dad and step-dads croaked?" Pierre asked, taking a bowl from Tom.

"I spoke to her," Alex replied. "She was a baby when her dad died and a young teen when the second husband died. By the time husband number three came around, she'd been estranged from her mother for a good decade. She said she moved out at midnight on her eighteenth birthday. She couldn't get away from mommy dearest fast enough."

"I take it the news of her toxic mother's death devastated her," Serena deadpanned.

Alex snorted. "Yeah..."

"What did you tell her happened?" Elenora asked.

"I told her the cause of death hadn't been determined yet."

Tom lifted his gelato. "Mind if we all take these to the dining room?"

"Good idea. I'll review Alex's clips." Serena said.

She managed to scrutinize the footage of Lucien Villemure and Chuck Leyner before the OPO called her in on another case. Her keen eyes didn't pick up demonic clues—that part was comforting.

She stood up with her empty bowl.

"Leave it," Pierre told her.

"The least I can do is bring it to the sink. It's bad enough I won't be able to chip in with the dishes," she retorted.

"You chip in plenty where it matters most," Tom said, gesturing to his laptop. "Thanks for all the help on this. And with Muriel."

"Don't mention it." Serena disappeared into the kitchen. When she returned, her messenger bag slung over her shoulder, she crouched in front of Aubrey, who sat on Elenora's lap.

"You keep an eye out for the bad guys while I'm gone, okay?"

The baby responded with a drooly smile.

Serena kissed the fluff on top of Aubrey's head. The dark hair she'd been born with kept getting lighter. Elenora often wondered if it would ever turn white, like in her vision of her daughter when she got pregnant—a notion she still found profoundly strange. How many kids had hair devoid of pigment? Would it mean she had a rare disorder? A quick internet search had revealed that early graying hair was usually hereditary, but Elenora couldn't see the source of this in her and Tom's combined family tree.

After Serena's departure, Elenora sat Aubrey on her play mat by the patio door and loaded the dishwasher. Willem parked himself near the baby, and Céleste joined them, lying down beside the high chair and watching them—a familiar tableau.

"Want me to take over?" Pierre asked Elenora. "You've had quite the day."

"So did you."

"She was an absolute angel."

Elenora glanced at Aubrey, who was quietly playing. "I'm glad to hear it."

Pierre grabbed a dish towel. "Wash or dry?"

"I'll wash." She wedged the last plate into the dishwasher. A tightness in her neck and shoulders made her aware of how wound up she was. Mindful of that, she focused on Pierre's calming presence to unwind.

"What's on your mind?" he asked.

"What's on my mind?" she repeated, trying to sort out the countless thoughts vying for her tired mind's attention. She laughed. "What isn't on my mind?"

"Then what's the most harrowing thing?"

So much had happened that day. But the thing that screamed the loudest was the unknown.

"My mother being weird, and that there's a murderous, unidentified supernatural force out there, on the loose, that neither an experienced witch nor a half-demon could identify."

"You fear it might strike again?"

"Yeah." Elenora rinsed the suds off a pot and put it on the dish towel spread on the counter. "And I fear we've been exposed to it, and it might come after us next."

Pierre picked up the pot and cocked his head at her. "You mean like catching a virus?"

"I dunno. Maybe? We don't know what this thing is. How it operates. Why it targeted Eileen Robin. What if it clung to our clothes, and we brought it home, and it's just a matter of time before one of us bursts into flames, too?"

Elenora could hear herself and knew her spiraling

thoughts were likely irrational. But she couldn't help working herself into a lather as thick as the soapy water in the sink.

Pierre stopped drying, choosing his words.

"Well, first, given how abrasive the victim was, I can give you several reasons for targeting her that don't apply to you. Second, while some paranormal events remain unsolved, there's usually a method to the madness. Some evil forces are unhinged—that's not impossible. But I'd argue that's not the norm. There's laziness in their world, too, you know. Unmotivated actions are rare."

"So, you think I'm worried about something that probably won't happen? Especially since Serena put spells over the residence and us all?"

Elenora felt her anxiety melt with her own words. Spelling out her irrationality made her fears more concrete and easier to deal with. Maybe she was being silly. Why did her mind always have to think the worst?

"She put one on this place, too," Pierre added.

"She did?"

"Yeah. She cast a protective spell on your house on her way out. She said it was overkill but didn't want to gamble."

"Oh. I missed that. That's awesome."

Elenora felt herself further loosen up. A protective spell on her home was reassuring.

"Of course, feel free to fret over an unlikely hypothetical anytime," Pierre teased her.

She cracked a smile. "Yeah, like I'd ever do that."

He chuckled.

She gave a pot one last scrub and rinsed it.

"It's normal to be uneasy at the unknown," Pierre said, taking the pot from her. "God knows I popped my fair share of antacids during my career. But you know what helped me?"

She looked at him expectantly.

"Focusing on the good bits going right. The progress, no matter how small."

"But we're stuck."

"It might feel like you're stuck, but look at the evidence. You have two new people to investigate. It's hard to believe they just happened to be in the very spot where you had your vision at the very time Eileen Robin died and are somehow not connected to what happened. That sounds like a piece of the puzzle. Even if it's hard to figure out where it fits, you might still have part of the work done."

Elenora nodded as she scoured the rotisserie pan.

"And more importantly, you had a vision," Pierre went on. "It was captured for us to see—that part still blows my mind. You and Serena are a serious force to be reckoned with."

The comment pleased Elenora. Not long ago, she would have cringed, but now, she embraced the compliment, and it felt good.

No, it didn't feel good—it felt damn good.

"Yeah. It blows my mind, too. But should I remind you that my vision yielded nothing much?"

"Did it, though? Claire-Lune's analyzing it. We both know better than to underestimate her. Who knows what she might find. And even if she finds nothing, maybe your summons with Yukiko will."

Elenora dislodged a tenacious bit of caramelized chicken skin from the pan with satisfaction—another small win for the day.

"I'm proud of you." Pierre had always been proud of her and never stingy saying so. Still, the praise echoed deeply this time. Elenora felt proud of herself, too. Like as if she'd taken an important step in the right direction today.

"Thank you. I am *starting* to recognize that my abilities are an asset. Even if they still pain me and I'd rather not have them in the first place."

Was this still entirely true, though? Elenora had cursed and wished away her newfound powers in the past—because, really, who needed such stress and horror in their lives? But she had recently recognized a few times that she no longer quite wished them away.

She still felt a healthy dose of ambivalence but no longer hated her abilities.

Not as much, anyway.

Come on, stop lying to yourself. You feel special.

Did she?

Maybe she did.

Yeah, she did. And it was okay to feel special.

Her powers seemed to be there for good, so why not enjoy them?

"It would be convenient if I could provoke visions about specific things," she said, wishing her powers could confirm that she, her family, and the people at Black Chapel were not in danger.

"Like what?"

"Like tell me that what happened to Eileen Robin was a one-off. That whatever did this won't strike again at Black Chapel, despite the protection spell."

"If it does strike, Moss is stationed at the residence tonight, and Tom's two suspects are on his radar. I worked with him a few times before he left town. He's hard to read but as competent as they come."

From what Elenora understood, this Moss guy was a young warlock working with the OPO who had moved back to Montréal from the Calgary branch earlier in the year. She hadn't met him yet but had heard about his legendary stoicism. Supernatural agencies weren't above water-cooler gossip.

"When was that? I thought he was a younger guy."

"He *looks* young. I worked with him in the seventies."

"Does he wear a glamour like Serena?" It seemed odd that a warlock would feel strongly enough about his looks to choose to mask his age with magic.

You're being sexist. And judgmental.

"Rumor has it he was born on February 29th," Pierre replied.

Elenora couldn't tell whether he was serious or joking. "For real?"

He gave her an amused shrug. "No idea. But we've seen weirder, no?"

Once Pierre left, Elenora gave Aubrey a quick bath before bed. Drawing water and splashing sounds often reminded her of the night of the accident—the family car plunging into icy waters—that had caused her father's death and her mother's mind to slip into nothingness.

Muriel's audible reaction from earlier that day came to Elenora's mind.

As the psychic was about to, once more, search for meaning, analyze everything to death, and torture herself over her lack of answers, Pierre's wise words about focusing on progress cut through her thoughts,

and she talked herself off the ledge of that bottomless
rabbit hole.

Fretting doesn't help. Focus on the things that go right.
Serena is on the case. The puzzle will reveal itself in time.
Things will fall into place.

They usually did.

Right?

CHAPTER TWENTY-FIVE

Ville-Marie, 1673

"I added the spell to the grimoire," a perky young witch named Oliva announced to the Ville-Marie coven members in the attic of Marie-Josèphe's auberge, where the guild met every Tuesday night.

"We need a spell to help contain eye rolls," Agnès whispered to Lizzie.

On any other day, Lizzie would have snickered at her sister's jibe. Oliva's excessive pride over her silly spell to remove lumps in flour—better than a sieve!—was indeed painfully embarrassing to witness. You'd think she had created a magic formula to cure every ailment known to man. Her overblown enthusiasm warranted a snicker. But the horrid anxiety tightening Lizzie's core prevented her from caring.

She shouldn't have come to the meeting.

She had considered not showing up, but her absence would have raised her sistren's suspicions, especially Agnès's.

Lizzie didn't want to talk about walking in on her husband and Antonin Dujardin and had hoped that pretending nothing was wrong would buy her time. But things weren't going according to plan. Agnès had already asked her twice if she was fine. The first time, Lizzie had replied that she was tired. The second time, that she was not feeling all that well.

She gave her sister a tight smile while Oliva blathered about her exploit.

Not fooled one bit, Agnès frowned at Lizzie.

"I practiced my penmanship before I dared to touch our sacred book," Oliva said. "I think we should all do that." She danced with excitement.

Lizzie almost rolled her eyes but caught herself in time. Now was not the time to attract attention.

"I agree. An eye-roll containment spell would be most useful," she whispered back to Agnès.

"You will find it indispensable in your everyday life," Oliva droned on. "I urge you to try it. Let me know if you need guidance."

"A *sedatus* spell would be useful, too," Lizzie added to Agnès.

Agnès snorted. "For her or us?"

"Both."

Lizzie could use a calming spell to dull the pain. What she'd seen in the infirmary an hour earlier had eclipsed her worries about Dujardin revealing her secret to the world.

What she *thought* she had seen, she corrected herself. Her eyes could have deceived her. She hung on to that hope.

The room had been dark. Maybe it hadn't been Honoré that she saw. Maybe it hadn't been Dujardin.

Maybe Lizzie hadn't caught the two men in bed.

But no matter how much she questioned herself and her recollection of the brief incident, she knew the heart-wrenching truth.

After she'd made eye contact with her husband, Lizzie had fled the prison, expecting him to go after her.

She expected him to catch up to her, grab her arm, and confront her.

Yell at her, maybe. Probably.

Threaten to destroy her if she said as much as one word of what she thought she'd seen.

She wouldn't have said anything to anyone, of course. She was too loyal to him.

As Lizzie fled across the courtyard, she expected to hear the prison door bang open and close behind her.

But only silence followed her.

She ventured a look over her shoulder, still expecting to see Honoré. But he wasn't there.

Did he not care about her?

Lizzie slowed her pace. He must have been delayed. Of course. He'd have to make himself decent before going after her. He couldn't have pursued her down the hall while naked.

She stopped to catch her breath, her heart and legs screaming in pain.

What had happened in there?

Her mind could barely make sense of what she'd seen.

Honoré loved her.

He would never do something like this.

Would he?

Minutes passed, and it became clear that he was not

coming to confront her. Lizzie didn't know how to feel about him ignoring her.

He would wait for her to return to confront her. Surely, this was his plan.

With her mind swirling and her feelings numb, Lizzie walked away from the prison, roaming the streets again.

Maybe her eyes had deceived her. They must have. Maybe she hadn't walked in on her husband in bed with another man when he thought she was gone to her guild meeting.

The meeting.

It would soon start, and she debated going. What was the use, especially since she'd failed to get the mint potion for Henriette in the infirmary?

But I'd better go, even if that's the last thing I want to do.

Lizzie had resumed walking, dragging with her a heavy feeling of betrayal as she headed to her friend's auberge.

An elbow poked her under the ribs, and the sharp nudge brought Lizzie back to the present. Diandra stood by her, looking at her expectantly while Oliva still rattled on in the background.

"Hmm?" Lizzie asked Diandra.

"I said I had a breakthrough with the truth serum," the other witch whispered with a huge smile. "It's working."

The prospect of having a reliable truth serum in her arsenal had made the rest of Lizzie's evening more bearable. She wasn't ready to return home and face Honoré but felt slightly less vulnerable. She hadn't figured out how the serum could help her situation yet, but she felt stronger knowing she could use it.

After the coven meeting, Lizzie had dreaded going home and had wandered the streets again before circling back to the auberge and taking refuge in the safety of her friend's attic.

At dawn, she headed back home, wondering what would await her. Honoré was an early riser, and she assumed he'd already be at work. She could slip into their quarters and start her chores without confrontation.

But she had no such luck.

Honoré was sipping coffee in the kitchen and reading a document. His cold gaze briefly rose to glance at her with disinterested silence.

Lizzie stood there, unsure whether to say something or remain silent. But what was there to say? Should she apologize? But for what? For interrupting?

Apologizing would mean acknowledging what had happened.

Honoré stood, leaving his dirty dishes on the table for her to pick up.

Lizzie braced herself for his ire.

He stood there for a moment, looking away.

"Don't be late for work." His tone was glacial and lashed at her heart.

He said nothing more before leaving. Lizzie wondered if a heated confrontation wouldn't have been preferable to his cruel indifference.

Did he not love her at all?

Or was this a cry for help?

He must be embarrassed, Lizzie reasoned.

Honoré never wanted to appear weak. In his position, he couldn't afford to appear weak.

And his world would crumble if a secret of that magnitude about him came to light. Lizzie understood this.

But surely he should know that she'd never betray him. The thought of him perceiving her as disloyal was painful, especially considering everything she had done for him. How could he doubt her?

A chilling thought wormed into Lizzie's mind: What would become of her if he distrusted her now?

CHAPTER TWENTY-SIX

Montréal, present day

"We go pray on Tuesday mornings," said Chuck
Leyner, one of the two seniors in the chapel at the
time of Eileen Robin's death. He seemed at ease being inter-
rogated and admitting he hadn't been on the best terms with
the victim. So far, nothing had suggested he might have had
anything to do with her demise.

"*We* being you and Lucien Villemure?" Tom asked,
sitting across from the man in a quiet corner of the residence's
dining room. Alex and Elenora were also at the table while
Serena was on her way. They also expected Yukiko, Juniper,
and Wren to show up soon.

When the team had arrived at Black Chapel that morning, Miss Pouliot told them that Mr. Leyner and Lucien
Villemure were likely lounging in the dining room. Sure
enough, they'd found the two seniors at a table in the upscale
room, which was nearly empty post-breakfast. Tom had asked
to speak to them separately, and Mr. Leyner volunteered to

move a few tables down and go first. While they talked with him, Lucien Villemure nursed a cup of tea and pretended to browse the morning's paper.

"Yes, Lulu and I," Mr. Leyner confirmed, lifting his chin in his friend's direction. "We've been doing this for years. At first, it was because he needed help to go around in his wheelchair when he got it. He's an old pro now, but the tradition stuck. Also, you have to find ways to kill time, you know? There isn't much going on around here on Tuesdays."

Serena approached the table with a cup of coffee, greeting Elenora, Tom, and Alex with a nod. She slid into the seat next to Mr. Leyner.

"This is our colleague Serena Winston," Tom introduced her.

Chuck Leyner gave her an appreciative once-over. "My, my, aren't you a sight for cataract-riddled eyes," he said, cranking up the charm in a cheesy manner.

Serena returned his playfulness, touching his arm and gazing into his eyes. "Those cloudy baby blues are a sight unto themselves."

Elenora noticed her friend's maneuver, recognizing the witch's own kind of once-over to assess the senior for a demonic or supernatural presence.

Alex, however, didn't seem to get the memo and quietly scowled at Serena's flirtatiousness, as if he judged it inappropriate.

Elenora found his reaction amusing. Was he worried Serena would come across as unprofessional? Even if so, his scowl seemed overkill.

Or maybe he thought she was shopping for a sugar daddy. But wildly independent Serena? As if.

Could it be a hint of jealousy, then? Despite them getting along like cats and dogs?

Hmm.

Serena gave Elenora an insistent look. She then glanced pointedly at her hand still on Mr. Leyner's arm and back at Elenora before giving a subtle head shake. She had gotten nothing from him. That was both good and bad news—they weren't in the presence of evil, but they weren't getting closer to it, either.

Mr. Leyner winked at Serena. "You can look at my baby blues anytime, darling."

Alex stood up abruptly, his chair screeching against the floor tiles. As he left the table, he grabbed his mug and muttered about needing more coffee.

Tom stood up, too, and handed Mr. Leyner his card. "Thank you for your cooperation, sir. Please let us know if you think of anything."

"What d'you figure happened? Management doesn't want to tell us nothing," the senior lamented.

"That's because they don't know," Tom replied kindly.

"But what about you?"

"It's too early to tell. But we will inform everyone in time."

"Do you think it's a serial killer? We have locks on our doors, but they're flimsy and decorative at best. Should I get an alarm system for my studio?"

Lucien Villemure's words echoed his friend's, down to the question about installing an alarm system in his apartment.

Serena repeated her schtick but dialed down her flirtatiousness to match Mr. Villemure's energy. He appeared less playful, more down-to-earth than his chum, and she opted for the friendly route once she learned of his past in the Air Force. She made engaging conversation with him, mentioning an uncle—real or imaginary—who had served in the military while she assessed the senior discreetly. Like Chuck Leyner, he proved free of demons. At least of the supernatural kind.

Tom thanked him for his time, and the team prepared to leave and join Yukiko, Juniper, and Wren, who were waiting for them near the entrance to the room, but then Mr. Villemure stopped them.

"Wait," he said hesitantly, concern marring his serious face.

Elenora sat back down. "What is it, sir?"

The others remained standing and let her take the lead.

The senior took a deep breath, looking unsure. "There's something I haven't told you." His eyes traveled to his friend, who had stayed at the other table. Mr. Leyner shook his head at him.

Lucien Villemure returned his attention to Elenora. "I don't mean to be dishonest by omission. That's not who I am."

"Are you worried we will jump to a conclusion about something you might tell us?"

He nodded. "It looks bad, but I assure you I have nothing to do with Eileen's death. I swear."

"Okay."

"I didn't come forward because..." He took another deep

breath. "We thought it wasn't pertinent and could muddle your investigation."

He looked away, nervous.

"Speaking with detectives can be unnerving—even for those beyond reproach," Elenora said. "And everyone's been on edge since the incident. What happened was horrific beyond words, and we all want answers. But I assure you we are not looking to blame the first person who might appear suspicious. We understand some things can be deceiving, and we always do our due diligence. We want the truth and to prevent other tragedies."

He nodded again, seeming closer to confessing whatever was eating him.

"Did you know the victim?" she asked.

"I knew Eileen well." He shot his friend another look. "I mean, I've known her very well for years before I moved here. We were briefly married." He almost choked on the words. "But we divorced soon after."

Elenora saw Tom and Alex shift at her periphery, no doubt as surprised as her that there had been a Mr. Robin number four.

"Who asked for the divorce?"

"I did."

"May I ask what made you want a divorce?"

Aside from the obvious.

His eyes searched Elenora's, as if trying to determine whether to trust her.

"I reckon she was trying to poison me."

Poisoning. Of course.

And Mr. Villemure was right: this didn't look great. But Elenora maintained a sympathetic expression to keep him talking. She felt Alex make a move toward the table and saw Tom bringing a hand up to stop him. Her colleague was champing at the bit to question the senior.

"What gave you that impression?" she asked Mr. Villemure.

"Soon after we tied the knot, my health started declining. My doctor was puzzled and chalked it up to aging. But my son's also a doctor, and he kept insisting on regular blood and urine tests. He's the one who figured out I was slowly being poisoned with arsenic."

Tom shot Alex a look.

Alex reached for his cell and started texting, probably relaying the information to Renaud.

"Why do you think she wanted you dead?" Tom asked Mr. Villemure.

"I'm well-off. She had an expensive lifestyle. Do you see why I was hesitant to share this? Again, I assure you I had nothing to do with her death. I was in the chapel when she died, and I always did my best to stay away from her. I wouldn't have touched her with a ten-foot pole. You can ask any of the staff. They'll corroborate. That woman was a menace."

"Did you confront her about the arsenic?" Tom sat back in the seat he had occupied earlier. Alex and Serena remained standing.

Lucien shook his head vehemently. "I know better than to provoke an insane person who's trying to kill me. And it was hard to prove, anyway. Apparently, there are traces of arsenic in all sorts of foods. She could have argued that I ate a lot of those. My argument wouldn't have held water."

"Could it have been that—a fluke? The food?" Alex asked.

"I'll never know for sure, but her behavior suggested it was deliberate. Before we married, I was always in top shape, and my eating habits barely changed, and I was doing most of the cooking. And in hindsight, I realized she had coerced me into marrying her. It wasn't obvious back then. I mean, she'd always been pushy and controlling, but in such a sweet way during our first year. But her real intentions became clear once I caught on to the fact she was after my bank account and trying to kill me."

"And she was okay getting a divorce?"

"No, not at first, despite the generous prenup and an additional payment I offered her. I just wanted out. But then, thank God, she found her next fool and couldn't sign the papers fast enough."

"How did she act toward you here, at the residence?" Tom asked.

"She snubbed me, acting all wounded. It suited me just fine that she avoided me."

"Were you afraid she'd try to retaliate?"

"I watched my back and my food, for sure. But she seemed too busy going after fresh meat to bother with me, now that I'd never be her cash cow ever again."

"How long have you been living here?" Alex asked.

"About five years."

"I imagined you weren't thrilled when she moved onto your turf."

Mr. Villemure sighed. "Of course, I wasn't thrilled. As if there aren't enough senior residences around the island. It had to be this one. My home. But what could I do? She was a paying customer. She had as much right to live here as I did."

"Did you wish she'd go away?"

"You mean, did I wish her dead?"

"Sure."

Mr. Villemure mulled over his answer. "I often had uncharitable thoughts about her, but I would never have acted on them, and I mostly kept them to myself. I tried not to speak ill of her. You have no idea how often I tasted blood from biting my tongue."

"Who knew about your past relationship with her?" Tom asked.

"Just Chuck. Unless he told someone, but I doubt it. He's good people, and he knew I had confided in him."

"It's good to have someone with whom to commiserate," Elenora agreed.

"Yeah. And to warn others to be careful. It was hard to see her charm other guys and not say anything when I knew what she was like. Chuck would carefully hint at others to watch their backs while making sure they couldn't trace his gentle warnings to me. The last thing I needed was to be in Eileen's crosshairs again."

"Did you report any of this to authorities?" Tom asked.

"Before the divorce, I didn't see the use—and again, I didn't think I had much of a case. But in recent months, with her here, it crossed my mind a few times. I think I would have said something if she'd started going after me. But I'm too old for that drama, and I prayed she wouldn't."

CHAPTER TWENTY-SEVEN

The talk with Lucien Villemure resulted in more bafflement than answers. He'd been married to the victim, who had presumably wanted him dead. He'd also admitted to feeling animosity toward her until her death. And last, but far from least, when Eileen Robin perished in a puzzling blaze, Mr. Villemure had been in the chapel near the location of Elenora's fiery vision.

It was hard to believe he was innocent.

But Elenora's gut leaned that way. And Tom, too, had a hunch the senior was telling the truth.

The team headed to the chapel in thoughtful silence. When they arrived, a man in his thirties was leaning against the wall by the door, scrolling on his phone.

"Hey there, Moss," Serena said to him.

He glanced at her, his head barely moving. "Hey." His gaze traveled to Tom, and he proffered a hand to him. "I'm Moss, as Serena astutely pointed out," he said dryly. His voice was poised, his expression a poker player's dream, his gaze sharp.

Tom shook his hand. "Tom. Thank you for your help, Moss."

So *this* was the new warlock?

Not what Elenora had expected. The word "warlock" reminded her of Joseph Gill, the cruel departed necromancer against whom she had the displeasure of fighting. Moss wore khaki pants and had an impressive head of wavy brown hair with copper highlights. He looked more like a young STEM professional than a "warlock."

Then again, the same could be said of Elenora, the milquetoast social worker mom. Who would believe she was a powerful psychic medium in the making just by looking at her?

Moss shook Alex's hand, then Elenora's. His grip was firm and...tingly? A wave of warm prickles traveled over Elenora's palm. The warlock's gaze snapped to hers with curiosity as he, too, seemed intrigued by their peculiar handshake.

"Interesting," he mumbled before letting go of her hand.

"What's interesting?" Serena asked.

"I don't know. That's why it's interesting." Moss searched Elenora's eyes, as if they held an answer. "Probably just static."

Probably just static.

A weird kind of static.

While he gave nothing away, Elenora suspected he didn't believe it was just static. Serena, however, accepted his answer and gestured at the chapel. "Still quiet in there?"

"As far as I can tell," he confirmed.

"Is Victorine still on for the next shift?"

"She is. Should be here within the hour."

"Good. You still on for tonight?"

Moss nodded.

"Great. Why don't you get some rest then? I'll stay until she shows."

He nodded again and gave them a restrained hand wave as he left, his questioning gaze lingering on Elenora. Was there meaning behind this strange interaction, or was it a personality quirk?

Tom opened the chapel door and invited the OPO gals to go in first. Serena led Yukiko and Wren to the infamous spot while Juniper went around the room, looking for supernatural activity at the atomic level.

"It was about here, right?" Serena asked Elenora, pointing to the spot where she was standing.

"I think so," the psychic replied.

"It does," Alex confirmed too. He pointed out a gouge along the side of the nearest bench. "It was next to this gash. This little bugger kept me up last night. I can't believe they fixed the floor flawlessly but couldn't bother to address this."

Elenora smiled. Typical Alex.

"Clearly the stuff of nightmares," Serena teased him.

He glared at her.

She laughed.

Counting the rows of benches, Tom caught up to them. "The twelfth row. Where Lucien Villemure was sitting."

"Right over the renovated spot, and where Ele's vision happened," Alex remarked.

The group stared at the floor.

"What the hell happened here?" Serena mused.

"Let's find some answers." Tom turned to Yukiko. "Shall we try our mystery woman?"

"I'll start setting up," Yukiko replied with her usual laid-back enthusiasm.

Despite hours of effort, Claire-Lune had failed to uncover the identity of the victims of the 1673 fire, including the woman from Elenora's vision. The fiery stranger remained an enigma.

"It's the oddest thing," she'd told Tom and Elenora through the car's speakers before their arrival at Black Chapel. "I can feel her. I know she's out there, in the ether, but it's as if her existence has been redacted. I bet there's a spell preventing anyone from finding out about her."

Claire-Lune wasn't used to being on the receiving end of an information ban, and it seemed to get her goat.

Hopefully, Yukiko's séance would circumvent whatever was guarding the woman's identity and bring them answers. The seasoned medium retrieved five candles from her bag and handed them to Wren, Juniper, and Serena, who arranged them in as big a circle as the aisle would allow.

"Should we do the circle thing?" Alex asked. In the past, he, Elenora, and Tom had joined the medium and the witches in a circle to assist with a summons.

"That would be helpful."

"I'll join, but I'll need to focus on monitoring the room," Juniper said. "I found nothing so far, but who knows what prodding a dead pyromaniac will do."

"I confirm the fire-retardant spell is still holding up," Serena declared, and Wren nodded in agreement.

"Excellent," Tom said.

As they gathered in a circle, Elenora hesitated before joining. "What if I trigger the vision again?"

"Would you like to check before we start?" Yukiko asked.

"Or you can sit it out if that makes you feel more comfortable."

"Let me check, and then I'll join if I'm not entranced."

Elenora took Serena's proffered hand and prepared herself to revisit the vision. Maybe she'd get more details this time, even if the pull she'd felt the day before was absent. She hoped she wouldn't experience being on fire again, though. That part had been traumatic.

Receptively, she stepped over the spot. When nothing happened, she walked around, searching. She quickly concluded that a repeat vision wasn't in the cards. Shaking her head, she joined the circle.

Yukiko lit the candles with a silver stick lighter. "Would someone kill the lights, please?"

With a flick of her wrist, Serena plunged the room into semi-darkness. Outside, the sky was overcast, and a faint, multicolored light filtered inside from the stained glass windows, creating a reverent mood.

"Spirit in this room, I respectfully summon you. Please show yourself," Yukiko said in a soft yet firm voice.

Elenora stared at the flame on a candle while they waited for an answer. The fire burned brightly and barely moved. Silence hung in the air. She noticed the mild tinnitus she'd heard on her previous visit to the chapel.

Yukiko repeated her summons with the same even voice.

And then, after nothing happened, she said it a third time.

"There might be nobody home," the medium concluded. Her gaze traveled to Tom for instruction.

"Thank you for trying," he said. "Let's see if Ms. Robin feels chatty this time."

Serena extinguished the candles with a snap of her fingers. "If she's not too busy burning in hell."

"Stranger things have happened," Wren pointed out.

"You're right. Never mind my pessimism."

"It's part of your charm."

The witches helped Yukiko put the candles back in her bag.

"Don't you worry they might cause a fire in there? Why don't we just carry them in our hands?"

"First, I snuffed them with a fire-repelling spell, so they won't reignite," Serena explained. "And second, wouldn't a parade of law-enforcement folks holding candles raise concerns around here? Especially after a resident's flaming death?"

Alex grunted his agreement as they filed out of the chapel.

"You coming, Junie?" Wren called to Juniper, who was lingering in the room. The healing witch wore an impressive frown.

"What is it?" Tom asked her.

"I'm not picking up on the camera feed."

"And that's unusual?" Tom closed the door to restore their privacy in the chapel.

"The camera has a wireless feed. I always pick up on the airwaves, to some degree, as they broadcast. I have yet to encounter a device sophisticated enough to bypass my senses or my magic. In fact, I don't think that would even be possible."

"Serena disabled the feed," Alex pointed out. "Could that be why?"

"Actually, I tampered with the feed, but it's still technically broadcasting," Serena said.

"Claire-Lune thinks something might be interfering with whatever's going on in this room. Maybe there's a cloaking spell at play?" Wren suggested.

"Do you sense a spell?" Serena asked her.

"No. But I'm far from infallible."

"You think it's like the security spell around the house on Maple?" Alex asked.

Elenora remembered the hidden, complex magical ward Joseph Gill had put around the old mansion. Upon Wren's encouragement, the psychic had succeeded in capturing the deadly, dark-magic incantation at its core. Serena had then downloaded it, allowing Wren to decode it and create a counterspell to subdue it. A magnificent team effort.

"Anything in the air seems off to you, Elenora?" Juniper asked.

"I don't think so, but let me check again." When Elenora had previously assessed the atmosphere in the room, it seemed normal. She closed her eyes and focused on the air.

It wasn't heavy.

It was...

Unremarkable.

The dull, distant ringing still in the background was the only thing noticeable.

Hmm.

"The air seems fine to me, but I'm having tinnitus."

Wren, Juniper, and Serena exchanged meaningful glances.

"Let's try to capture that sucker." Serena reached for the tablet in her messenger bag.

"What sucker? The ringing in my ears?"

The three witches nodded empathetically.

"It's the little things." Serena winked at Elenora and eagerly reached for her arm. "May I?"

"Go nuts."

Serena worked on recording the noise only her friend could hear while the others held their breath.

Would Elenora's tinnitus translate into an incantation?

Did it hold a key to the case?

Serena hit play on her tablet. A garbled sound file with predominant static came out of the speaker.

"Maybe it's encrypted," Wren said, her enthusiasm intact. "I'll analyze it."

Who knew the annoying little noise in Elenora's head could be of actual help and bring such excitement.

CHAPTER TWENTY-EIGHT

As Elenora set foot in the entertainment lounge, a bright shimmering greeted her. Over the burnt chair, the specter of Eileen Robin materialized in a flash, arms crossed and glowering at the psychic. "What took you so long?"

Elenora gasped in surprise. After her failed summons of the day before, she had not expected the spirit to show—and without prompting, no less.

"Have you people figured out what happened to me yet, or are you just good for bumbling around?" the specter added aggressively.

"Um... Serena!" Elenora gestured at the chair, urging her friend to do her thing.

The witch looked up from her phone. "What's up?"

"Your revealing spell!"

The witch stared at her friend, incredulous. "She's here? The old hag's here? She's not in hell?"

Eileen Robin scoffed at the insult. "This ain't no way to talk to your elders, young skank!"

Serena threw her spell at the chair in the middle of that

last sentence, just fast enough for everyone to see and hear the ghost calling her a young skank.

The witch snort-laughed at the insult. "*You*, of all people, are calling me a skank? That's richer than all your marks combined."

Eileen huffed with boundless indignation. She floated to Serena at warp speed and got in her face. "You want to take this outside? Hmm? You want to take this outside?" She tried to shove her, but her hands went through Serena, who just smirked back.

"I'd love to take this outside, bitch."

The spirit pursed her lips and tried pushing the witch again. She screeched in frustration.

"Yo! Ladies!" Alex shouted, his voice rumbling.

The two women snapped out of their heated confrontation to look at him.

Yukiko looped her arm with Serena's and coaxed her away from the upset departed senior.

Tom approached Ms. Robin calmly. "Sounds like we got off on the wrong foot here. Ms. Robin, I'm Detective Tom Madigan, and this is—"

"I know who you are," she interrupted him glacially.

"We're on the same team," he said, unfazed by her rudeness. "We all want to figure out what happened to you."

"You don't know yet?" Her tone was accusing.

"We don't."

"Do you have suspects, at least?"

"We don't. Do you have any ideas who might have wanted you dead?"

"How should I know? I'm supposed to do your job for you now?"

"What about your late husbands? Did you kill them?" Alex's directness took her aback.

"What?" She scoffed. "They ratted me out? Did they complain I was mean, too? Is that why they think I killed them? Whiny pussies."

"Ms. Robin," Tom asked her gently, "would anyone in their entourage think you had anything to do with their death?"

She mulled over his question. "I don't think so. None of them had much family or friends."

"Do you think Lucien Villemure might have been involved in your death?"

"That cowardly idiot? Please."

"What about the other residents of Black Chapel? Would any of them want you dead?"

The specter laughed and then started rattling off the names of every resident of Black Chapel.

Alex raised his hand to stop her. "We get the point."

"Do you have other questions? Your incompetence is tiring."

"I do," Elenora said. "I tried to summon you yesterday. Did you not hear me?"

"I did."

"Then why didn't you answer me?"

Ms. Robin shrugged. "I didn't feel like talking."

Hmm.

So, a spirit's moodiness was enough to throw a wrench in a summons—in Elenora's amateur one, anyway.

Serena gave the ghost a blank look. "You ignored my friend's attempt at helping *your* case because you didn't feel like talking? Are you for real?"

Anger flashed in Ms. Robin's eyes. "I died in the most humiliating way in a room full of enemies! Excuse me for being upset! And that outfit was brand new!"

Tom switched gears to cut the conflict short. "Ms. Robin, your daughter is arriving in town later this week."

Eileen Robin turned her hard stare on him at the mention of her daughter. "So? Your job is to look for my killer, not determine if I'm a good mother," she said sharply.

"How would you describe your relationship with her?" Elenora couldn't resist asking and faced the ghost's annoyed stare, too.

"She waited for me to croak before visiting. That should tell you enough." The specter sniffed.

Serena snorted. "I wonder why."

"I don't."

"Is there anything you'd like your daughter to know?" Elenora asked before she thought better of it. Serena shook her head and shot her a *don't go there* look. But it was too late.

Eileen offered Elenora a dubious expression. "What do you mean? You'd give her a message on my behalf?"

"Well..."

Crap.

Way to paint yourself into a corner.

"Don't waste your time, honey. She doesn't believe in magic crystals and whatnot. And she spent her entire life avoiding me. I don't see why she'd care to hear from me now."

The spirit's words were harsh but also wounded. Maybe the tough exterior was partly a façade.

"I won't tell your daughter anything then," Elenora said, relieved she was off the hook. But she also felt she couldn't just let it go. As they say, *Don't go to bed angry*. Maybe the same applied to death. Troubled relationships complicated grief for the living. Elenora imagined it could also complicate the afterlife of this prickly deceased woman—who wasn't in hell, surprisingly—and maybe her poor daughter's life, too.

But what were Eileen Robin's options? She seemed determined to protect her reputation as a heartless villain to the bitter end. Perhaps she felt there was no room for vulnerability in front of others.

But what will happen when she's all alone with her thoughts forever—wherever she might be?

"Maybe consider visiting her in her dreams. You can never go wrong with trying to make amends. At least you won't regret not trying."

Eileen Robin harrumphed at Elenora's suggestion.

Fine. She could suit herself.

But then Elenora couldn't resist one last nudge. "Eternity is a long time for regrets."

CHAPTER TWENTY-NINE

While she analyzed Diandra's latest version of the truth serum, Lizzie tried to pretend nothing was wrong—not even the offending bed in the infirmary that mocked her. The tight knot squeezing her stomach reminded her she wasn't fooling herself, but at least the pretense seemed to have worked with everyone she'd encountered so far.

A familiar man appeared in the room.

Dujardin.

Lizzie bristled at his presence. A prisoner shouldn't be allowed to roam freely around the penitentiary, let alone *this* prisoner.

The reason he was allowed to roam made her seethe.

The betrayal pierced her heart.

She was terrified of the uncertainty this dreadful situation caused for her and her baby.

The unwelcome visitor stood next to her in unnerving

silence. Lizzie refused to acknowledge his presence. Maybe if she ignored him long enough, he would go away.

Act as if he has no power over you.

She realized she was holding her breath and forced herself to breathe normally.

Don't let him know he's getting to you.

Dujardin's stare weighed heavily on her. She knew he was staring, no doubt willing her to look at him.

She dug in her heels.

He chuckled. "No need to feel awkward. I certainly don't."

The execrable character was laughing at her distress and delighted in doing so. She couldn't believe his cruelty.

Since ignoring the intruder was not working, Lizzie reverted to pretending everything was fine. She looked him straight in the eye and feigned being unaffected. "Mr. Dujardin. What brings you here? Would you like me to inspect your wounds?"

Maybe rub salt into them?

He studied her mockingly, no doubt planning his next move.

Shaking inside, Lizzie struggled to keep her composure.

"Why not," he finally replied, amused. Still amused.

Vile caitiff.

Lizzie mindlessly gestured toward the bed for Dujardin to go, a motion she'd made a thousand times before. But the meaning wasn't lost on her.

Nor on him.

"How would you like me, Lizzie?" he teased her, assuming a lewd position on the bed.

Her fake smile faltered. Her mind spun, desperate to shut him up. To make him pay.

"Let's look at those wounds, shall we?" She yanked a bandage off.

The volume of Dujardin's sharp inhalation rivaled the satisfying ripping sound. Redness flared around the wound where the spruce sap had bound the dressing to the skin. Lizzie looked forward to doing the same with the other bandages. However, Dujardin seemed unfazed. If anything, his smirk suggested he reveled in the pain she'd inflicted on him.

Why was Lizzie not surprised?

She inspected the wound, which was healing nicely. For once, she wished she could reverse her good care and make the gash fester again.

Dujardin retaliated with his own form of violence. "You seem to think I didn't mean for you to find me in bed with him. You are adorable."

His declaration stunned her. What did he mean?

"It was only a matter of time," he added. "I encouraged the fool to get bolder to ensure you would find us."

Not only was this despicable man twisting the knife in her heart, but he dared call Honoré a fool?

She grabbed a bandage on his forearm and yanked on it forcefully, ripping a patch of hair.

Dujardin swallowed a yelp.

After a few deep breaths, he asked, "Are you not the least bit curious?"

He's baiting you. Ignore him.

"Your beloved Honoré has been burning with desire for

me for years. You do not know how much he wanted this. *Wants* this."

Lizzie's ears rang. What was he saying? That Honoré had been lusting after him? How ridiculous!

That couldn't be.

Don't listen to him. He's a liar. He's a snake. Focus on his wounds.

"Do you love him?" she blurted out and regretted her impulsive question instantly. Why did she speak and with a trembling voice, no less? Why was she letting him get under her skin and have the upper hand? It was exactly what he wanted.

He snickered. "Love him? Women are so naïve."

Lizzie's hands balled into fists.

"If it's any consolation, my dear, you are not the only one who's naïve," Dujardin went on.

She wanted to shove his mocking words down his throat and trap them in there with a silencing spell. A permanent silencing spell.

She ripped another bandage.

How could anyone call her shrewd husband naïve? He was always steps ahead of everybody else.

"Every desire—everything—has a price," Dujardin said darkly.

What is he talking about?

"You will soon wonder how you can buy my silence."

Had Dujardin seduced Honoré so he could blackmail him? Was that it? If so, he wouldn't be the first criminal to try bringing her powerful husband to his knees.

Except Antonin Dujardin has already done that literally, the nasty little voice in Lizzie's head reminded her.

Dujardin snickered. "I admit I can't understand why you would want to protect him after what you saw—you are fascinating. He betrayed you. He doesn't love you. And he will be exposed. I will make sure of it."

Panic rose inside Lizzie.

A glimmer of evil shone in the miscreant's eyes. "I knew you would understand."

Whatever his dishonorable plan was, she couldn't let him win. She *wouldn't* let him win.

"What if I tell him?" she said coolly.

The mere thought of telling Honoré about Dujardin's sinister intent to blackmail him made Lizzie feel faint, but she would muster the courage to make him listen. If that was the way to foil this snake's wicked scheme, then so be it.

"You would tell him?" Another smirk appeared on his lips, this one even more derisive. "You would tell him I let him seduce me after years of him lusting after me so that I could do...what?"

"I will tell him you plan to betray him. Blackmail him. He will react unkindly to that. He will let no one take advantage of him or make him look like a fool. Especially not a *prisoner*," she retorted with disdain.

Her words didn't hit Dujardin the way she wished. His broad, taunting smile didn't waver one bit.

"You sincerely think he would believe you? The jealous wife who found out his darkest secret? The jealous wife without proof of my designs making blind accusations? You don't think he would send you—a witch—away to hush you much faster than he would turn on the object of his desire?"

Lizzie felt her blood go cold. Unfortunately for her, the

deceptive man was perceptive. Her husband could and would send her away if he perceived her as a threat.

Even if she told him the truth.

Even if she told him she was with child.

Lizzie returned to her desk to brace herself. To process the threat looming over her.

Not only was Dujardin threatening to destroy Honoré, but he was also threatening to destroy her life—everything she had worked so hard to get after enduring so many hardships. He wouldn't hesitate to expose her as a witch.

The room spun, and Lizzie gripped the table, struggling to ground her consciousness. Now was not the time to faint.

"Why are you doing this?" she asked without looking at him. "Why do you want to destroy him? What has he done to you? He's a kind man!"

"He is, is he not?"

"What do you want?"

When Dujardin didn't answer, she chanced a look at him. His eyes shone with sadistic amusement.

"What can I give you to cease this perverse game?" she added, her voice quivering.

"Nothing. Absolutely nothing, my dear child." He lazily rose from the bed and approached her, encroaching on her personal space.

"Let things be," he whispered. "You are no match for me."

CHAPTER THIRTY

Montréal, present day

Black Chapel's basement had been revamped to match the residence's luxury theme. Modern sconces shed light on mahogany doors, behind which former prison cells now had a new life as storage lockers. However, the thick, dark gray stone walls lining the narrow corridors and the wood beams supporting the ceiling gave the space an air of gravitas that anchored the atmosphere in its past. No amount of paint could erase the building's sordid history.

"I can't believe there are no spirits down here," Juniper said as they helped Yukiko pack up her candles. The medium had attempted a general summons, but no ghost answered.

Elenora recalled Eileen Robin's flaky attitude and moody refusal to answer her. "Maybe there are, but they're ignoring the summons for whatever reason."

"Well, if that's the case, there's not much we can do about it," Serena said.

Maybe so, but Elenora had coaxed people into talking

before. Spirits used to be people—*were* people? This might work. "What if we convince them?"

"What do you propose?" Yukiko asked, intrigued.

"Maybe if we give them a reason to speak to us, they will show themselves."

"We should elaborate on the summons?"

Elenora nodded. This made sense to her. "Yeah. We tell them why we'd like to talk to them. Everyone likes to be informed."

"You gotta admit, the summons sounds a little impersonal," Serena agreed. "If I didn't feel compelled to talk to you, I doubt you'd win me over with a boilerplate statement."

Yukiko considered the idea and asked Elenora, "Would you like to try it?"

"Sure."

Elenora scanned the corridor for a shimmering. "Spirit in this basement, I respectfully summon you. Please show yourself. We come in peace. We only want to ask you a few questions. There was a fire in the chapel in 1673 that claimed eight lives—several men and a woman. If you were here at the time and recall this event, would you please answer me?"

Elenora turned her mental dial slowly, pivoting to scrutinize both sides of the hallway.

No one answered her.

Dang.

Maybe Eileen Robin had been an exception. Or maybe Elenora's limited abilities and experience were insufficient.

The psychic turned to Yukiko to ask her to set up her candles but then noticed a shimmering at the end of the corridor. A thrilling sense of satisfaction delighted the psychic as it grew. She could get used to this.

"You see something?" Alex whispered.

"At the end of the hall. But it's just starting." Elenora held up her hand at Serena so the witch wouldn't be hasty with her revealing spell. They had never tried to reveal a ghost from a shimmer—only once they had manifested themselves to the psychic. Better not jump the gun and scare away a potential witness.

Elenora headed for the shimmering when another popped in front of her. She jerked back in surprise.

"What's going on?" Serena asked.

"I think there are two of them."

Another surge of satisfaction.

The shimmering closest to Elenora swirled and pulsed, almost growing into a form but then dispersed.

Oh, no!

"Kind spirit, please don't go! Let's talk. I promise to listen."

The spectral form of an emaciated man emerged. His gaze was vague. He looked broken.

"Hello, sir," Elenora told him in a kind voice to catch his attention. She gave Serena a discreet wave to proceed.

The witch threw the revealing spell at him. "Hello, there," she said, confirming she could see him.

"My name is Elenora, and these are my colleagues. May I ask who you are?"

The sickly ghost turned his unfocused gaze on Elenora. He didn't answer her question.

"Sir?"

His gaze sharpened slightly, and he blinked at her.

"What's your name?"

The departed man considered her question with confusion. Could ghosts be feverish? He looked unwell.

"Ge... Ge... Ge," he struggled before giving up and roamed the hallway, looking lost.

"Wow. That went nowhere fast," Serena said.

"His name is George," a voice called from where the other shimmering had been. There stood another spirit—a colossal man. He floated closer to the group. "He lost his mind. I doubt he can help you."

As if to further drive the point home, George stared at the wall, unresponsive.

"Was he tortured?" Tom asked the spirit who had his wits. Serena's revealing spell on George must have affected the other ghost, too, since Tom could see him.

The man nodded. "Whipped."

"I'm sorry to hear. That was a cruel practice. I'm Detective Tom Madigan. To whom do I have the pleasure?"

"Paul Mason." Curious, the specter studied Tom before surveying the group. "What would you like to know about the fire in the chapel?"

"Were you there?" Alex asked him.

"Not in the room, but I heard about it."

"What did you hear?"

"I heard that—" The specter stopped in mid-sentence and made a strangled noise. He frowned. "I heard that—" His second attempt at voicing what he'd seen yielded the same disconcerting result.

"What's going on?" Alex whispered to Juniper, next to him.

"My guess is a spell is preventing him from talking."

"Like a gag spell?"

"Yeah."

Paul Mason's ghost stared at Alex and Juniper in disbelief. "A spell?"

"That's a possibility," Wren answered, thoughtful.

"Somebody doesn't want anyone to know what happened," Tom said.

"Could be related to the interference in the chapel." Serena started texting.

"Why?" the puzzled inmate asked.

"We are trying to figure this out," Tom said. "Would you please try to explain what you know using other words?"

The man attempted to mouth words. Snippets of syllables were all he achieved.

"How about this, then?" Tom said before the burly specter grew even more annoyed. "As my colleague stated, we suspect eight people died, burned alive, including a woman. Can you confirm this?"

Elenora noticed a hint of sadness in Mr. Mason's eyes at the mention of a woman. His lips parted again, but no sound came out.

"Did you know the woman who died?" she tried.

"I..." he struggled to form words, frustrated.

"Can you nod or shake your head to confirm or deny the question?" Tom asked.

The inmate's head stilled. He grunted, as if physically fighting to move his head. His nostrils flared.

"The spell is strong," Wren said.

"I knew everyone in the chapel," Paul Mason blurted out. His answer frustrated him even more. "Sh—"

"So, that's a yes." Serena smiled.

"Every time I try to explain, the words die on my tongue!" the ghost complained.

"Mr. Mason, do you remember seeing women at the prison?" Elenora reasoned that if a spell prevented him from speaking about what had happened inside the chapel, maybe he was free to discuss matters outside of it and the tragic event.

Tom gave Elenora a nod of appreciation for asking the question.

Paul Mason's spirit looked at her. "Female prisoners?"

"Prisoners. Workers. Any women you can think of," Tom said.

"I don't recall seeing women prisoners during my time, but they kept me in the basement, away from most people."

Dang.

"But Lizzie, the prison nurse, visited me when I was ill."

"Do you remember Lizzie ever wearing a green dress?" Alex asked.

The question seemed to jog a fond memory. With a goofy smile, the spirit nodded. "Green looked great on her."

"Zenia specializes in intricate spells and curses," Claire-Lune said on the video call on Tom's laptop. "She's away on a study sabbatical in Eastern Europe, but she agreed to look at what we got."

In a different window, Wren nodded. Tom and Elenora were back in their makeshift office in their dining room with Alex. Pierre hovered over their shoulders with the baby. The witches were taking the call from the OPO headquarters.

After they'd found out about Lizzie, the prison nurse, Wren, Juniper, Serena, and Elenora had worked on the silencing spell crippling Paul Mason's specter. From the airwaves affecting him, they produced a file that sounded like the garbled static broadcasting in the chapel. It seemed like the impeding magic had indeed spread beyond the walls of the room of worship.

Wren's analysis of both captures of airways had confirmed a concealment spell shrouding the garbled audio, but her progress had gone no further. Juniper had suggested they bring their colleague Zenia on board to help.

"She thinks we might be dealing with a curse," Wren told everyone on the video call.

"That doesn't sound good." Alex's expression turned somber.

"It doesn't, but if it is a curse, that might be better than a spell," Claire-Lune replied. "Curses are usually specific, tailored to one person or their lineage. Hence, they tend to be more contained. So, best-case scenario, it might only target Eileen Robin's ancestors and descendants."

"Her daughter," Tom said. "How can we protect her?"

"Keep her away from Black Chapel for now. That would be a good start."

"I'll ask her to postpone her trip to Montréal until we know more," Alex said.

"That would be wise."

"So, someone could have put a curse on Eileen Robin's lineage in the chapel centuries ago," Tom mused. "Someone who would've had a beef with one of her ancestors? And then, the victim moved to Black Chapel. Talk about a wild coincidence."

"It sounds far-fetched, but it's possible. I will look into her family tree," Claire-Lune said. "If I can retrace the source of the dispute, we may be able to lift the curse, and then Ms. Robin's family will be safe."

Tom nodded.

"When Serena texted me about the gag spell in the basement," Claire-Lune added, "I started digging into the local witch and warlock population in 1673. We have some of its history here at the OPO, but a lot of it is buried, very covert and protected. But I found something shocking."

"Oh?" Serena said.

"The Ville-Marie coven—our very own sisterhood—was born before the fire in the chapel. When I researched Paul Mason, I found an account he gave shortly after the incident. Unfortunately, that information was magically sealed, but something in the signature of the concealment spell led me to a name in a grimoire in our archives: Agnès Dumoulin. She's mostly a ghost, so to speak, but she appeared to have been one of the original witches of our coven."

Audible gasps came from Serena, Wren, and Juniper.

"You think she would also have concealed a deadly curse?" Wren asked with dismay. "Why?"

"Because she felt someone's lineage deserved to suffer?" Alex suggested. "Why does anyone kill?"

"But our coven's mission has always been to do good in the world. To fight evil. Not to take part in vigilante justice."

"Damn right," Serena said defensively.

"Maybe there's a good explanation," Elenora volunteered.

"Let's hope there is," Claire-Lune agreed. "Anyway, let's keep digging. Maybe Zenia will have a breakthrough. I'll search for the prison nurse and see if she's our burning woman in the chapel."

"Thank you, Claire-Lune. And everyone," Tom said.

"Oh! Wait. Don't hang up!" she squeaked. "Elenora, I have ethereal mug shots for you to look at. That might help identify the Jesuit priest you saw in the bus shelter. So, whenever's a good time for you to pass by the OPO, let me know."

"Ethereal mug shots?" Alex gave the witch a quizzical look.

"It's my fancy term for images of suspects tethered to the OPO archives that I'll cast for Elenora like holograms. It's easier and faster for me to show them to her this way."

"Okay, wow." Alex's mind looked officially blown.

Tom chuckled. "Wow, indeed. I'd love to see that. Can I tag along?"

"Why not? You guys can also check out our daycare while you're here," Claire-Lune said with a wry smile.

CHAPTER THIRTY-ONE

E lenora was both eager and apprehensive to see Claire-Lune's holographic mug shots. As she brushed her teeth before bed, her mind swirled with questions.

Would she recognize the creepy stranger? And if so, who would he turn out to be?

What was his connection to the little twerp?

And more importantly, what the hell did these two want from her, and why couldn't they just leave her alone?

Seeing her reflection in the mirror, Elenora caught herself—she should not think about the two bullies while in front of a reflective surface. She couldn't risk summoning them into her bathroom like she almost had with Barlow's murderous spirit.

She forced herself to think of something else. The memory of Paul Mason's ghost popped into her head.

Hmm. Not that, either.

Even if he had seemed like a decent guy, he'd been behind bars for a reason. And she didn't need another ghost in her house, anyway.

Think of something else.

George.

Yukiko had helped him cross over before they left Black Chapel's basement. She had also offered to guide Paul Mason, but he suggested sticking around in case the team decoded the spell. Then, he could contribute his insights on the fire in the chapel. That had been noble of him.

But even if he's noble, I still don't want him in our house.

Elenora exited her bathroom and forced her mind back to George. She hoped the broken spirit was now in a better place. In a better frame of mind, too. The look of him brought her sadness. Victims of abuse always got to her.

Think of something else.

We're almost out of bread.

She slipped between the covers and started a mental grocery list. With every item, she pictured herself traveling down the aisle to where it was. She did this until the store in her mind took on a dreamlike quality. The lighting dimmed, and the shelves disappeared, leaving products to float around. They vanished, and Elenora found herself in an outdoor parking lot filled with cars.

In the distance, a man was unlocking the driver's door of a vehicle.

He opened the door.

And burst into flames.

Elenora woke up with a start.

Next to her, Tom was awake and on the phone, his expression grim. He glanced at her.

"Elenora's awake," he said to his interlocutor. "Let me put you on speaker." While he enabled the cell's speaker, he told his wife, "Serena said her protection spell on the residence got triggered. She thinks there's been another victim. She's on her way there to investigate."

Serena's voice jumped in. "Yeah, and I'm hoping the spell slowed down the fire enough for an intervention. Moss said the sprinklers didn't go off."

"That's because the victim was in the parking lot," Elenora replied.

"You saw what happened?" Tom and Serena asked in unison.

Elenora told them about her premonition. Tom hopped out of bed and started getting dressed.

"It must be the residence's parking lot then, or it wouldn't have triggered my spell," Serena pointed out. "Let me get Moss on the line. He's searching inside the building—no wonder he got nothing."

A few seconds later, Moss came on the line. "I still got nothing, Serena. No paranormal activity, as far as I can tell." His voice was level, but his footfalls told them he was moving quickly.

"Check the parking lot."

"Behind the building?"

"Yeah. Elenora had a premonition. She's on the line."

"Hi, Moss," Elenora said to confirm her presence.

"Hey. Did you see the victim?" It sounded like he was jogging now, even though his breathing remained normal. The dude must have been a serious runner.

Elenora hadn't gotten a clear look at the victim, but she could take an educated guess and didn't like the answer. It pained her it was someone she had met. Not that she didn't feel empathy for total strangers who met an untimely demise.

It was just that knowing someone—even if only briefly—struck closer to home.

"I'm not one hundred percent sure, but I think it was the guard from yesterday. Eric Decker."

"Jesus!" Serena exclaimed.

"I hope it's not because he spoke to us."

"You think he might have said something the curse didn't like?" Tom asked, uneasy.

If disseminating information was at the heart of the curse, could the deadly spell go after them next?

"That's not usually how they work," Serena answered. "But that's the thing about them—especially the deadly ones—until you figure them out, you don't know the driving force. That said, maybe Mr. Decker's related to Eileen Robin and conveniently didn't mention it. He was acting sketchy."

"He did seem nervous. But we get that a lot. Maybe he forgot to pay for a parking ticket," Tom replied.

"Okay, I'm in the parking lot. What do I look for?" Moss asked.

"Look for a car with the driver's door opened," Elenora said.

"Okay."

"Moss, did you see anyone leave the building?" Serena asked.

"No one near the chapel's exit, but there was a shift change at midnight. A guard would make sense."

Elenora glanced at the clock on her bedside table. It was 12:13 a.m.

"And how many residents still drive or even own a car in town?" Tom pointed out.

"Elenora, was it a blue Thunderbird?" Moss asked.

She knew little about cars, but a muscle car sounded right. "If the driver's door is open, I'd say yes."

"Looks like it is. I'm getting closer."

"See if you can find ashes and collect them," Tom said.

"'kay. But it's windy enough to dehorn a demon out here."

"Then throw a containment spell at whatever's left!" Serena screeched.

"Already done," Moss said before adding, "I caught a bit. But other than that, there's no sign of a fire. And I'm not sensing anything weird around the car."

"A security camera might have caught something. I'm heading there." Tom finished putting on his shirt.

"Tom, wait!" Serena said. "How about you stay put until Moss, Günther, and I do some recon first?"

Tom considered the request.

Elenora watched him with imploring eyes. She'd much rather he stayed home for now instead of rushing to a potential supernatural death trap.

He sighed and unbuttoned his shirt.

CHAPTER THIRTY-TWO

Ville-Marie, 1673

Lizzie was leaving her quarters for an evening walk to get some much-needed air when the scream of agony came from the end of the hall.

Had the horrible sound come from the blue room? Had it been Antonin Dujardin? She headed to the guest room to investigate.

The ear-splitting wail resounded again. It did seem to come from the blue room. Lizzie picked up her pace. Dread overwhelmed her as she vividly recollected her last conversation with Dujardin.

"Certainly, you wouldn't be stupid enough to poison me," the evil prisoner had taunted Lizzie the night before when she gave him medicine to swallow. "Should anything happen to me, Honoré would see through the machinations of his jealous wife."

He wasn't wrong. Lizzie had entertained the thought of getting rid of him several times, and she knew the timing would look bad. She would be an obvious suspect, and she couldn't afford Honoré's wrath and risk being punished and thrown out. All night, she had mulled over inconspicuous ways to retaliate against Dujardin so he no longer posed a threat to her husband, her, and her unborn child. But she had found no solution.

Until her mind had considered the truth serum.

After all, it was the truth she was after. To reveal Dujardin's intention to blackmail Honoré. If her husband heard about the nefarious plan himself from the mouth with the silver tongue, Lizzie's problem would solve itself without her looking like a vengeful, jealous wife. And even if the criminal tried to expose her, her secret would be safe—how could Honoré believe him at this point?

By early morning, she had decided to slip a few drops of the truth serum into Dujardin's stew at dinner. The flavorful meal would conceal the faint taste of the serum. She would then test its efficacy on the traitor and see if she could make him divulge why he wanted to blackmail her husband. She'd increase the dose gradually until she knew the truth could be revealed in Honoré's presence. Patience wasn't a virtue for Lizzie, but she was willing to make an exception in this case. Even if she kept silent like he wanted her to, she couldn't shake the feeling that he would inflict more suffering on her. And find great satisfaction in doing so, too.

Hence the need to act.

Another scream of agony echoed as Lizzie and a guard arrived at the blue room's door. She flung it open and faced a new nightmare.

Dujardin contorted in pain on his bed, drenched in sweat

and white as a ghost. His dinner tray and dishes were scattered on the floor.

What happened?

Lizzie had given him a negligible dose of the serum to start. It couldn't be what was causing his distress. It had to be a coincidence.

As she drew closer to the inmate to examine him, his feverish eyes latched onto hers, and he recoiled.

"Stay away from me, witch," he hissed.

Fortunately, the guard had already left the room—to fetch Dr. Barthes perhaps—and didn't hear the accusation.

"Where is the pain?" She forced herself to remain calm.

"You poisoned me!" he spat.

"I most certainly did not." That was the truth. She had not given him poison.

Unless he was reacting to something in the serum.

Lizzie's worry grew. A bad reaction to an ingredient was always a possibility. Why hadn't she accounted for that?

"What did you do to me?" Dujardin whined.

"Nothing," she lied. She wasn't about to admit anything to him—even if a smidgen of guilt was blooming in her conscience.

"Why do you want to blackmail Honoré?" she asked. If the scoundrel was dying, now might be her only chance to get the truth out of him.

His eyes narrowed at her before widening with understanding. "Because Honoré has—"

"What did you do?" Dr. Barthes's voice thundered as he entered the room with Honoré in tow. The doctor grabbed Lizzie by the arm and pulled her away from Dujardin.

"I didn't—" Lizzie tried to defend herself.

"She poisoned me," the viper rasped.

Honoré's face turned ashen.

"What did you give him, vile woman?" the doctor barked.

"Nothing special! He has a fever," she explained to the two men.

"She's a witch!" Dujardin said before screaming in pain again.

Dr. Barthes and Honoré turned brutal stares on Lizzie.

She shook her head vehemently. "He's delirious!" she insisted. Her skin felt hot.

"I saw her do unnatural things," the traitor whined.

Dr. Barthes's gaze traveled over Lizzie's shoulder. "Take her," he ordered a guard behind her.

Two hands grabbed Lizzie's arms. "No! He's lying!"

"Lock her up!" Dr. Barthes said.

"Burn her," Dujardin said in a strangled voice.

"Tell him the truth!" Lizzie commanded Dujardin. That's it—why hadn't she asked him to confess earlier?

She stared at him expectantly.

But instead of explaining his deceit, the inmate launched himself into a coughing fit.

Lizzie's heart sank. Her fate was sealed.

Dr. Barthes made an impatient gesture to the guard. "What are you waiting for?"

The guard pulled Lizzie toward the door, and she dug in her heels.

"No, wait! Please! Honoré, please!" she pleaded. "You know me! He's lying to silence the truth! He plans to black-mail you!"

Lizzie's husband lifted a hand at the guard to stop him.

Lizzie exhaled a breath of relief. Honoré would listen to her. To reason.

He leveled a chilling gaze at her, leaned close, and whispered in her ear. "You better pray he doesn't die, or I will light the fire under the stake myself."

⚜

"Whoever's out there, listening, please don't let him die," Lizzie prayed, despite a visceral desire to revolt.

At least, don't let him die until Honoré learns the truth and forgives me.

A series of loud bangs against the chapel's barricaded door told her the inevitable had finally arrived. She knew a mob on the other side of the door was coming for her. They'd drag her out of the chapel, where Lizzie had found refuge, heartbroken, betrayed, and scared out of her wits.

A spell. She needed to cast a spell on the door to slow them down and keep herself out of danger for as long as possible—ideally, until her husband came to his senses and called them off.

From her kneeling position in front of the altar, she struggled to stand up and stumbled to the door, terrified.

Please let me secure a spell on the door before they break it down.

The door shook with each blow.

"Open the door, Lizzie! You cannot hide!" Dr. Barthes shouted.

Lizzie's skin crawled. It was horrific enough to think her demise was near, that her past had finally caught up with her, but that it was the doctor himself—an insufferable man who hated her—leading the charge against her was unbearable.

She had to fight back.

Her mind revved. What could she possibly do? If she used magic on them, she'd only prove she was a witch, and they would kill her.

A loud crack made Lizzie squeal, her attention snapping back to the door as a hatchet blade appeared through it.

The door!

Lizzie's mind swirled, searching for a spell to keep the door in place. She thought hard, but all that popped into her head was Oliva's useless spell to remove lumps in flour.

She wanted to scream.

The blade of a second hatchet made it through the door as the first one disappeared, only to reappear, increasing the gash.

Come on, think! Think!

Thunk! Another blade. A fatal blow. A whole plank of wood was ripped out of the door, revealing the faces of angry men lit by torches.

Lizzie raced back toward the altar. Her gaze surveyed the room frantically for an exit despite knowing there was none.

She should have hidden somewhere else. It had been foolish to think the chapel would be a real sanctuary.

She heard the door crash behind her, and her heart plummeted.

She turned to face her executors. Dr. Barthes. Father de la Dauversière. Guards—all of them—and a handful of soldiers. They eyed her warily. The word of her being a witch had traveled fast.

Behind them, Honoré watched the scene unfold with

unnerving stoicism.

"Now, my child," Father de la Dauversière said to Lizzie in a syrupy tone. "There is no need to put up a fight. You are only making this harder. Surrender yourself."

Lizzie took a step back and hit a bench.

I will fight to the death before I surrender.

She made a broad sweeping gesture to keep the men at bay, and it worked. Cowering with fear, most of them took several steps back.

She turned to Honoré. "Please forgive me, my love. Antonin Dujardin wants to hurt you. To destroy you. Please believe me. I wanted him to tell you the truth before it was too late."

"It is too late now." There was nothing but ice in Honoré's eyes. "Surrender yourself, Lizzie."

She fell to her knees. "Please, Honoré, forgive me. I beg you. Please have mercy. I implore you!"

He sneered at her before ordering the guards and soldiers, "Bring her outside."

The men exchanged looks, hesitant to act.

"Honoré, please!"

He turned his back on her, ready to leave.

"I am with child!"

The warden stopped in his tracks as a collective gasp traveled around the sacred room. He glanced back at his wife with a mixture of anger and pain in his eyes.

"I am carrying your child. Our child." Lizzie held her breath, praying her announcement would sway him toward leniency.

Reverse her death sentence.

Time stood still as Honoré stared at her fiercely, considering her words.

"Sir, you cannot accept an unnatural child," Dr. Barthes said, adding fuel to the fire.

Honoré's eyes hardened.

"I warned you, Lizzie," the warden said before heading for the door, leaving his wife to fend for herself.

Lizzie's heart broke even more.

Father de la Dauversière was the first to dare approach her with his torch and a crucifix brandished at her. She scrambled backward down the aisle, her mind racing again for a way out.

"Surrender yourself, my child. You will get a fair trial," the clergyman lied.

As if Lizzie was naïve enough to believe him.

The moment they overpowered her and locked her up in the basement, they would either throw away the key or set her on fire in the public square. Make an example of her.

There would be no trial.

"She doesn't deserve a trial," Dr. Barthes spat. "I have seen her do witchcraft with my own eyes."

The blatant lie made Lizzie's ears ring. She had never used witchcraft in his presence. She knew that for a fact. He was seizing the opportunity to get rid of her.

She looked him square in the eye. The glimmer of malice confirmed her suspicions and made her see red. He would pay for this. She would make sure he would pay for this. For everything he had done to her.

"Take her before she uses witchcraft against us," the doctor said. His words spurred a few guards and soldiers, who jumped on Lizzie and grabbed her.

She fought back against their hold. More men came to

subdue her. She fought them harder, bucking and kicking like a spooked horse.

"She is possessed!" the priest declared, shoving his crucifix in Lizzie's face. His panicked voice rose through the chaos and fed it.

One man threw his torch at Lizzie, igniting her dress. The fire progressed quickly.

I'm going to burn alive!

Lizzie fought harder to free herself. She would die if she didn't get out of her clothes in time.

And my daughter will die, too.

A daughter...

She was having a daughter?

Lizzie let out a guttural scream as sheer agony ripped through her. They were taking from her what she had always wanted most. Blinded by rage, she thrashed violently against the men restraining her.

Threatened by the flames and the hysterical witch, the men let her go and stepped away, staring stupidly at the fire.

"Help me!" she wailed.

"Leave her! The witch deserves her fate," Dr. Barthes said with cruel glee.

"You will pay for this!" Lizzie shouted at him.

As will Antonin Dujardin.

With great effort, Lizzie removed her apron and cast a spell on the flames. If she couldn't extinguish them, maybe she could at least slow down their progression.

Her spell failed, and the fire moved to another layer of her garments, getting closer to her body. The heat increased against her skin as she struggled to shed her clothes.

"Help me!" she yelled to the crowd of men watching her.

"Please help me! Anyone! Have mercy on me!"

There were guilty looks exchanged, but none of the men so much as moved a muscle to intervene. Cowards! They were all cowards.

And persecutors.

They would all pay for her death and her daughter's.

Her dear, beloved daughter she would never get to know.

Intense heat seared Lizzie's skin, but the pain was nothing compared to the agony strangling her heart and her soul and her burning desire to exact revenge. Set the entire world on fire.

The smoke thickened around her, filling her lungs. She felt light-headed, and the memory of her mother burning at the stake flooded her mind.

As did the words of the curse her mother had pronounced back then as the flames consumed her.

And the devastating effect of those words on the abhorrent perpetrators responsible for her death, watching her burn alive.

Lizzie started reciting the words—at first through a string of coughs and then with lethal conviction.

"*Persecutores, vōs exsecror. Ardete!*"

One guard caught on fire. His cry of surprise quickly turned to horror and agony.

"*Persecutores, vōs exsecror. Ardete!*"

Five more men, including Father de la Dauversière, ignited. They howled with pain and terror.

A sense of triumph and vindication welled up inside Lizzie. They deserved to suffer the same fate as hers, the same unfair pain they'd inflicted on her.

Especially Dr. Barthes.

Lizzie's gaze searched for him through the smoke and found him near the door. The coward was trying to flee. As if sensing her attention on him, he turned, and his eyes met Lizzie's.

"*Persecutores, vōs exsecror. Ardete!*"

Lizzie's skin seared, and smoke saturated her lungs, but she stared her longtime nemesis in the eye, delighting in the pompous man's fear, disbelief, and agony as he, too, caught on fire.

You will never hurt me again.

But the sweetness of revenge didn't last. As Barthes and the other men perished before Lizzie, so did her delight, leaving an unwelcome bitter taste and a growing sense of guilt in its wake.

You are killing them.

The realization made her feel faint.

This makes you a killer.

The ugly truth made her heart and soul ache as much as her burning flesh.

What have I done? She wondered as her consciousness began to fade.

I'll never know my daughter because of them.

A pang of grief stoked her fury.

They did this! They should suffer for this!

While there was truth to her argument, Lizzie's moral compass refused to clear her conscience. There would be no relief for her. No justice. She was condemned to carry everlasting guilt and rancor.

She couldn't win.

Filled with rage and resentment at the cruel injustice of her demise, the witch's consciousness slipped away for good.

CHAPTER THIRTY-THREE

Montréal, present day

"I might have found our warlocks," Tom said as Elenora passed by the dining room on her way to the kitchen for coffee. Her husband crackled with enthusiastic energy despite his lack of sleep. After learning of the new victim in the parking lot of Black Chapel and Serena insisting he stay home, Tom had convinced Elenora to get back to bed. She had heard him creep down the stairs, probably to comb through what they had so far on the case once again.

"Warlocks? Plural?" Elenora stopped—she didn't like the sound of that.

"Yes. I have a theory."

"I'm all ears."

"First, you need coffee," he replied, a teasing smile on his lips.

Elenora knew that look. He was reveling in the suspense.

"Coffee takes time to make," she countered, the suspense killing her.

"It's brewing. I heard you going around, so I started a fresh pot."

"Mammmaaaaaaaa!" Aubrey greeted her from her playpen, hoisting herself to a standing position and waving her arms wildly to get picked up.

"Good morning, sweetie." Elenora lifted her daughter from the playpen. "Have you heard from Serena?" she asked Tom, who had snuck into the kitchen to prepare her a mug of coffee.

"Yes, but nothing conclusive on her end yet. She and Moss and Günther are still throwing magic around and running analyses. She got us the security footage of the parking lot and other pertinent locations inside the residence. The details of the incident are hard to see, but Eric Decker is indeed the victim."

"How did security and Miss Pouliot take the news?" Elenora grabbed a cardboard book on the credenza and sat beside Tom's chair with Aubrey.

He waltzed back into the room with a steaming mug.

"With my blessing and Chief Costa's, Serena's going full OPO on the case to ensure our safety and the residents'. Using her wonderful power of magical suggestion, she might have been vague about what happened in the parking lot to Miss Pouliot and the staff."

"And when Mr. Decker doesn't show up to work later today...?" Elenora took a sip of coffee and savored the warm liquid's internal hug.

"He's calling in sick. For the time being."

"Of course he is. And I gather I'll soon be asking his ghost if he knows who killed him?"

"Maybe, but that might not be necessary."

"Okay, you're killing me. I don't need more suspense in my life. Who are the warlocks?"

"As they say, 'Careful what you pray for,' right?" Tom sounded as cryptic as his earlier smile.

"I think it's usually, 'Careful what you *wish* for,' but sure."

"Oh, this might change your mind." Tom swiveled his laptop so she could see the screen better, though the video player was blank.

"What am I looking for?" Elenora asked.

"First, you need context. Claire-Lune texted me that Zenia, the curse expert, deciphered the files and found words that sounded like a curse. Don't read this out loud."

He showed her a text on his phone: *Persecutores, vōs exsecror. Ardete!*

"Um, the Latin I never took is a little rusty," Elenora said.

"It means something like 'Persecutors, I curse you. Burn!'"

"Hmm. I wonder if the word 'curse' gave it away."

Tom chuckled. "Yeah, that might have tipped her off."

"Can the witches reverse this curse now that they know the wording?"

"They will try, of course, but Zenia thinks it's linked to the person who cast it. That person might be the only one able to reverse it."

Elenora thought of the woman in her vision—this Lizzie woman, perhaps?—who had been long dead. Getting her to reverse the curse would undoubtedly pose a challenge.

"Let me get this straight: the woman on fire originated the curse and... Wait. You said warlocks? Where do they figure in this?"

"Okay, look at this." Tom played a video file showing a male senior rummaging through a well-stocked fridge in the residence's corporate kitchen. He retrieved a piece of cake with evident joy. Tom pointed at the timestamp, which showed 12:09. "Mr. Decker's shift just ended, and he's on his way out."

The guard walked in on the man. He took the cake from him and bit into it, taunting the irate senior. The resident shot daggers at Decker and gave him an earful as the guard left the room with the cake, suppressing a smile while the senior scowled at his retreating back.

"Are these your warlocks?" Elenora asked. If the clip had convinced Tom that the two men had magic, his logic was as clear as mud to her. "What am I missing?"

"Hold on."

Tom brought up a different clip. "This happened four minutes later, right before Eric Decker went up in flames." At 12:13, the images showed the seething senior shuffling down a hallway with a walker. He suddenly halted, cocked his head, and narrowed his eyes, as if something had caught his attention. Confused, he appeared to mumble something to himself.

"Wanna guess what he's saying?" Tom's eyes shone with excitement. Since the video had no sound, he must have read the man's lips and found something significant.

"Is it in Latin?" Elenora guessed.

He gave her a wide smile.

"He spoke the curse?"

Tom nodded.

Hmm. What was going on? Was the older man related to the woman in her vision?

She tried to put the pieces together. "So, this guy might be a descendant of the woman on fire and have magical abilities, and he killed Eileen Robin with her curse? And because he wasn't on our witness list, we didn't speak to him, so we didn't pick up on his abilities. Is that it?"

"That's one theory," Tom said diplomatically, which meant this was not what he was thinking.

"You don't think he has magical powers, yet you think he might be a warlock? I'm really confused."

Tom smiled. "I don't know what's up with this guy, but I think he's not the only one. When I figured out what he was saying, I didn't just make a connection with what Claire-Lune told me. I also remembered seeing those words being spoken. Which I had mistaken for a prayer."

Tom pulled up another clip. "I've zoomed in so you can see better."

Elenora leaned closer to the laptop screen to examine the reframed clip and saw Lucien Villemure and Chuck Leyner in the chapel at the time of Eileen Robin's death. Mr. Leyner napped while his companion had his eyes closed, lost in thought or prayer. Now that she saw his expression up close, Mr. Villemure looked irritated. He had a more noticeable frown, and a scowl curled his lips. His eyes flew open, and he cocked his head in confusion, much like the senior with the cake, and he mouthed words.

"*Persecutores, vōs,*" Tom said, the two words matching the senior's moving lips. "You get the picture."

Lucien Villemure repeated the words with knitting brows, as if trying to make sense of them.

Huh.

"Does he strike you as a crafty warlock in full power of his craft?" Tom asked her.

"It looks like he doesn't understand what he's saying."

"My thoughts exactly."

"What do you suppose is going on?"

"No idea. I texted Claire-Lune and Serena about it, and I'm waiting to hear their thoughts. Why don't you finish your coffee, grab a bite, and get ready if you feel like tagging along? I'm itching to have a chat with two gentlemen."

CHAPTER THIRTY-FOUR

"What altercation?" Mr. Matthew Miller asked, bewildered.

Tom studied him briefly before answering, "He took food away from you, and that upset you."

"Oh, that." The resident rolled his eyes. "I wouldn't call that an altercation. I often sneak into the kitchen at night. He catches me half the time, and I get pissed off at him." He shrugged.

"But last night really bothered you..."

"Damn right, it did! It was the last piece of Black Forest cake! Fernando rarely makes it. It's my favorite, and I didn't get any because of that meddling bastard."

Alex pointed at the refrigerator in the senior's kitchenette. "Couldn't you have gotten it earlier and kept it in your fridge?"

Mr. Miller shook his head. "My fridge is monitored. I have diabetes. His Black Forest cake is a dietary offense worthy of capital punishment."

"Is diabetes why Eric Decker was on your case about the cake?" Tom asked.

He shrugged. "He can't mind his own business. Has to bust my balls over something that's none of his business. He has power trips."

Tom retrieved a piece of paper from the inside pocket of his jacket and unfolded it. "Sir, let me show you a few words written in Latin."

"Read them in your head—not out loud," Serena insisted, inching closer to Mr. Miller.

Elenora suspected it was so she could clasp her hand over his mouth should he ignore her instruction. Tom had been careful not to repeat the curse at their home to avoid worsening the situation. The psychic could only imagine how much worse it would be to say the words on the premises of Black Chapel.

The resident took the paper, squinted at it, and mumbled, "I don't have my reading glasses." He moved the paper away from his face and then closer, trying to find the best distance to decipher the words. "Latin, you say?"

"Yes."

"Why? Nobody speaks Latin. It's a dead language." He shoved the paper at Tom. "This is gibberish. Means nothing to me."

Elenora touched his arm to get his attention and asked him in a patient voice, "Sir, as you neared your room last night, you stopped and looked around as if you'd heard something. What was it?"

He blinked at her while recollecting. "Yeah, I don't know. That was gibberish, too."

"You heard gibberish? Can you tell us where it came from?" Tom asked.

"From my damn hearing aids. They're new. They're supposed to be good. But the garbage I pick up, you wouldn't believe. If I ever want peace of mind, I'm gonna have to chuck 'em, I swear."

Tom, Alex, Elenora, and Serena exchanged glances.

"They're Bluetooth enabled?" Serena asked.

"Yes."

"Just to confirm, you heard gibberish through your hearing aids last night," Tom said.

"Yes."

"And you repeated the gibberish out loud."

"Yes. I tried to make sense of it. It was puzzling. And aggressive. If some invisible woman's threatening me, I'd like to know."

The team exchanged more glances.

"Were you thinking about Eric Decker when you said those words?" Serena asked.

Mr. Miller considered the question before answering. "Maybe? I was still all lathered up. I suppose he was still on my mind."

"Do you have older hearing aids you could wear that don't have Bluetooth?"

"Yeah, but why would I want to do that? They suck too."

"We'd like to analyze your current pair." Tom offered his hand to the senior, prompting him to surrender the small hearing devices.

Mr. Miller glanced at the detective's hand, unsure. He pointed at his ears. "You want them now?"

"Yes, please."

"They're expensive."

"They're dangerous," Serena jumped in, short on patience. "Remember Eileen Robin?"

The man's eyes widened. "Her hearing aids caught on fire?"

"I didn't say that. But you never know."

The man scrambled to remove the devices from his ears, as if his life depended on it.

Lucien Villemure confirmed he had also heard a woman's peculiar words in the chapel through his hearing aids and felt compelled to repeat them aloud. He admitted to thinking about his ex-wife angrily at the time. She'd been harassing a new guy he was befriending, and he'd been beside himself. He wished she would leave his new friend alone and get what she deserved.

"I'm not proud of this, but Eileen could really rile you up, you know?" Mr. Villemure said, looking contrite. "She was a master manipulator, and it was so unfair, the toxic things she kept doing to people."

"We understand," Tom said.

"Who's the woman who spoke in my ears, and what did she mean? Is she a suspect in Eileen's death?"

"We're working on this. In the meantime, may we please have your hearing aids and ask you not to repeat anything in Latin out loud or even in your head should something like this ever occur again?"

"I have the weirdest request you might ever hear in your life. I can't explain the details, but I would appreciate your cooperation. Lives are at stake," Tom said to Miss Pouliot before asking that all residents wearing Bluetooth-enabled hearing aids surrender them temporarily.

After their chat with Mr. Villemure and Mr. Miller, Serena had told her sister her theory that repeating the curse while angry had channeled it and directed it at the object of the person's anger. Claire-Lune expanded on her twin's speculation and posited that Mr. Villemure's location in the chapel and his intense negative feelings and thoughts about his ex could have reactivated the curse for good. She agreed they should remove the hearing aids from the equation until they could lift the curse.

The residence director blinked at Tom, processing his unorthodox demand. "You think those hearing aids are a fire hazard?"

Tom hesitated.

"In a way, yes," Serena answered on his behalf.

"We will give the hearing aids back as soon as possible. I wouldn't ask if it wasn't important," Tom said.

Miss Pouliot scrambled before agreeing. "Okay."

"Effective now, please."

She nodded. "I'll inform the staff."

Serena glanced up from her cell phone and whispered to Elenora. "Loonie has news and a potential plan. She'd like us to swing by the OPO."

CHAPTER THIRTY-FIVE

"Make sure to include your imaginary friends. Nobody likes to feel left out," a woman's voice floated out of a room down the hall.

Claire-Lune needed to wrap something up before meeting with them, so Serena had jumped on the occasion with glee to "show them something" while they waited for her sister to be ready. The fiery witch had led Elenora, Tom, and Alex to a wing of the OPO's headquarters unknown to Elenora, but the psychic didn't need to be one to know where they were going.

Serena stopped by the door from which the friendly voice had come and hailed someone with her hand.

A woman in her sixties with a mane of white hair came to greet them. "You must be Elenora and Tom. I'm Monica. I was looking forward to meeting you. Please come in and have a look." She noticed Alex standing a few paces away from the group. "You're welcome, too, sir."

They followed her into a large, bright space with warm brick walls and soft jazz playing. If it weren't for the young children and a handful of educators, this place could easily be mistaken for a trendy café or a lounge within Black Chapel. Like the senior residence, the OPO's Montréal branch was in a historical building that had been richly updated with modern means.

"Oh. Wow," Tom whispered behind Elenora. "A few notches above the station's daycare as far as the décor is concerned."

"Yes, but that's cosmetic. Don't let shiny objects sway you," she whispered back. She meant that and was determined to do her due diligence, but something about the room and its pleasant atmosphere felt right. And for the first time since Serena had brought up the over-the-top idea of Aubrey attending a daycare for supernaturally gifted kids, Elenora could picture her daughter here.

The children were engrossed in activities. Many sat at tables doing crafts or puzzles, while others were huddled around board games. There was also a reading corner with cozy window seats, beanbags, and egg chairs hanging from the ceiling. Everyone and everything seemed so...normal.

A sense of calm filled Elenora, a calmness she had yearned for ever since she and Tom had begun pondering the daycare question.

"We're doing free play," Monica explained, "which is why everyone's mellow. We also do more physical activities. We often go outside to play. But our current cohort thrives on unstructured play, so we adapt to match their needs."

Tom rubbed the back of his neck, a sheepish look on his face. "I know this will sound stereotypical, but I expected to see magic going on."

"We have that, too. And the kids can explore their magic

with our educators whenever they want to. But we don't push them to grow into their abilities. Learning about magic and personal gifts is paramount, of course, but for an environment conducive to learning, we first need to provide a safe place for them to be themselves. One where they can discover who they are and gain confidence and a caring attitude toward others so they grow into well-adjusted individuals—who will embrace their gift in time and understand the responsibilities that come with having special powers. And then we guide them whenever they show readiness."

At a corner table, a serious-looking boy made a pair of scissors levitate in front of him. Without missing a beat, a male teacher chatting with a girl extended a hand toward the boy, and the scissors gently returned to the table. "Not sharp objects, Leo," the man said kindly to the boy. "Not yet, okay?"

The boy nodded and turned to an orange blob of modeling compound on his table.

"As you can see, we are also proactive in avoiding accidents. Several of my colleagues have divination skills. They're very attuned to the kids and their abilities and usually see things coming."

This was music to Elenora's ears. Part of her reluctance regarding the OPO's daycare might have been a subconscious fear that another child's uncontrolled powers could hurt her daughter. The OPO had thought of this, and its educators were on top of it. It made sense that they would be.

"Let me show you our toddler corner, where Aubrey would be at first." Monica led them to a glass door that opened to another well-lit room. The smaller kids were busy doing different age-appropriate activities. There were play structures and a story time in progress. The teacher reading the book had a prairie dog on her lap, who turned the pages for her.

"That's my colleague Sasha, and Pickle, her familiar. Pickle's always a big hit with the little ones."

Alex shook his head with raised brows, as if he'd seen it all now.

"What's over there?" Tom pointed at a wall of windows with darkened spaces behind them. Some had cribs or beds and rocking chairs. "Napping rooms?"

"Yes," Monica confirmed. "Depending on the age and needs of the child, we have individual rooms and quiet areas."

Elenora surveyed the spaces, her good feelings persisting. Again, she could see her little girl here.

She wanted her to come here.

If Aubrey turned out to be different, she'd be welcome and well taken care of at the OPO daycare while Elenora helped her colleagues save the world.

"How does a child get in? Are there tests for them to qualify?" she asked Monica.

Serena gave Elenora a side hug. "I told you. Aubrey's already in."

"What Serena said. We already know your daughter, Elenora. We would be delighted to welcome her."

"But we don't know that she's gifted," Elenora protested. "I wouldn't want to abuse the system."

"I think it's pretty safe to assume she's gifted," Claire-Lune chimed in behind them.

"And at the very worst," Serena said, "even if she's not, her mother is. And the OPO encourages diversity, anyway."

"You don't have to decide now," Monica told Elenora and Tom. "Take all the time you need."

———— ❧ ————

"Our gal is Lizzie Delacroix, née Dumoulin. Agnès Dumoulin's sister. The Black Chapel prison's nurse. Warden Honoré Delacroix's wife. And a card-carrying member of the Ville-Marie coven. At least, until things went south and sideways for her." With her index finger, Claire-Lune trailed magic in a pattern over a keypad next to an ancient birdcage elevator—the only way to the archives in the basement. The elevator starkly contrasted with the other ultramodern ones in the building.

As the motor clanked and chugged to bring up the cage, Alex studied the intricate designs of the wrought-iron door. "This is a beaut."

"Isn't it?" Claire-Lune concurred. "I'm glad they kept it instead of modernizing it. It goes great with the bibliosmia in the basement."

"The what?"

"The old paper smell," Serena answered.

"Huh," Alex said, pensive. "That's a word, or you two are pulling my leg?"

"No, that's a word." Claire-Lune slid open the double retractable grid doors of the elevator.

"There's a word for everything," Serena said as the five of them squeezed into the small space like sardines.

"Wait. What's the weight limit on this thing?" Alex's arm shot out to prevent the doors from closing while he searched for the information inside the cage.

"It's magically enhanced to hold an infinite amount of weight. The donuts I ate this week won't make a difference," Claire-Lune replied.

"You had donuts?" Serena asked her sister, envious. "You didn't tell me you had donuts. Was I around?" She pressed a button labeled "RTG" with her finger, producing blue and yellow sparks. There were about twenty other buttons with intriguing three-letter codes.

"You were at Black Chapel when Harvey brought donuts his wife made."

"Dammit. I always miss the good stuff."

"What does RTG mean?" Tom asked.

Claire-Lune looked at him. "It actually means nothing. It's a bogus acronym meant to confuse an intruder. All the other buttons lock the elevator down and notify security."

Tom laughed. "Clever."

The security around the OPO building was already top-notch. Elenora figured the additional layer of protection on the old elevator must mean the basement held extraordinary information and priceless items.

"Are we going down there for things you found on this Lizzie woman?" Alex asked Claire-Lune.

"Not quite. This is a quick detour to show Elenora the mug shots before we see Jeb to figure out our next move with our dear Lizzie."

Jeb was the OPO's attorney and liaison with the Gray Court. Laid back on the surface, the T-shirt-wearing, jasmine-candle-loving descendant of Osiris was not to be underestimated. His soul had reincarnated enough times to have picked up a few tricks and gained much wisdom.

The turtle-paced elevator cage reached the basement, and Serena moved the grid doors aside. Hints of musky florals and vanilla hit Elenora's nose, flooding her with memories of old bookstores. The basement looked stunning and inviting with its dark gray stone walls, fancy sconces, and rich wood accents—well-preserved history mingling with high technology. While the OPO basement also bore similarities to Black Chapel's, its atmosphere was the opposite of the old prison cellar. Here, instead of a lingering aura of oppression, one could feel an enduring vibe of freedom, creativity, and ingenuity put to the use of the greater good.

"You think Jeb can help?" Tom asked Claire-Lune.

"I asked him to check the hell registry to see if Mrs. Delacroix was on it," she replied, leading them down a corridor that gave the impression they were going to a wine tasting.

"And she's on it," Tom volunteered.

"She's on it."

"The reason the séance didn't reach her," Elenora deduced.

"Correct."

They passed an open area lined with old-fashioned cauldrons in separate hearths. Some had a fire crackling underneath them.

Noticing Alex's quizzical expression, Serena said, "That's a lab."

"So, we're in a dead-end," Tom mused out loud. "If we can't reach Mrs. Delacroix because she's in hell, we can't ask her to reverse the curse." He gave Claire-Lune a questioning look to see if he was right.

"Being in hell complicates things. Considerably. But we could try a few things, like creating a counterspell, but that might take some time."

"We're short on time. The curse might claim another

victim at any moment if it finds another way to reach some-one," Tom pointed out.

"True."

"What about appealing to the Gray Court?" Alex made a face as he spoke the words. Elenora understood why. It was hard to be a fan of a powerful, crooked, and cruel supernatural entity that held the fate of souls in their dirty hands under the guise of justice.

"Jeb thinks the Gray Court would be a long shot," Claire-Lune replied. "But... Maybe... Um..." She glanced guiltily at her twin sister.

"What?" Serena asked, unsure she wanted to know.

Claire-Lune raised an eyebrow.

Realization dawned on Serena. "Surely, you don't mean..."

Claire-Lune's guiltier expression confirmed Serena had guessed right.

"No. Come on!" Serena let out a wailing groan. "Can't we try something else first?"

"Like what? We're out of options. And this is nothing to you in the grand scheme of things."

Serena let out a sigh of exasperation that rivaled a teenager told to clean their room.

"Okay, what the hell are we missing?" Alex said, annoyed at the sisters' covert conversation.

"We might have a shot if she bargains with Thelonious," Claire-Lune replied.

Thelonious was an odd-duck emissary of Satan who worked for the Gray Court. The eerie custodian could transport people from hell to their realm of existence for judicial purposes.

Serena grimaced with disgust. "Somebody shoot me."

"Why would she have to bargain with that asshole? Didn't Jeb just call him the last time?" Alex asked.

"The circumstances were different last time because it was a win-win for him," Claire-Lune explained. "Since Lizzie Delacroix is already in hell and her curse is wreaking havoc on our side, there's nothing in it for the Gray Court. So, this time would be a favor. And Thelonious made it clear he'd only accept currency from Serena the next time we needed a favor."

Elenora gave Serena a panicked look. "Why? What happened?"

"He tricked me into having coffee with him. Once! And because I wasn't nasty to him the whole time, now he thinks we should date. Ugh."

"You think he might coerce you into dating him in return for access to Lizzie Delacroix?" The idea seemed to appall Tom as much as Elenora. And judging by Alex's scowl, he wasn't keen on the idea either. Elenora knew Serena could defend herself, but it felt wrong to have her deal with a slimy potential stalker to advance a case.

"Don't make that face," Serena said to her. "Thelonious is a major pain in the ass, but he's harmless. To me, anyway." She sighed and told everyone, "I'll do it."

"Are you sure?" Tom was still concerned.

"That's a shot we need to take." Serena gestured at the door they were approaching. "All right, Loonie. Get this show on the road."

They entered a monochromatic archive room with wall-to-wall shelves holding identical brown cardboard boxes. Claire-Lune approached a large table with such a box and removed its cover. She carefully retrieved a pile of weathered papers.

Tom leaned in to examine the top sheet, which displayed elegant cursive writing. "Are these files on the suspects?"

"They are records that mention the suspects. They were all men of God who dabbled in the supernatural in various capacities, even if it was a remote interest in the occult. The information in these documents, and sometimes the handwriting itself, allowed me to tap into the past, generate a likeness of these men, and build a catalog to show Elenora. Reena, lights?"

The lights turned off, plunging the room into near darkness. A faint glow from the doorway remained until Serena closed the door. By then, Claire-Lune was projecting the image of a man with magic from one hand while her other rested on a sheet of paper. The hologram-like effect was stunning. Light pixels coming from the witch gave life to the stranger. His posture was stiff, and his cassock complemented his stern expression.

"Contestant number one," she said. "Elenora, is this our winner?"

Elenora didn't recognize the clergyman, but she studied him to give the process a fair shot. She didn't have a clear recollection of her bully, but her gut told her this wasn't the stranger she'd seen in the bus shelter's reflection. "I don't think so."

Papers rustled, and then, like a slide show, the mug shot made way for another one. "How about him?"

Another man in clerical attire, but this one had a neutral expression.

Hmm.

"If only he looked more menacing, like the other guy," Elenora said, uncertain.

"Ask, and ye shall receive." Claire-Lune wiggled her fingers at the man's face, and his features hardened.

"Creep," Alex mumbled disdainfully under his breath.

"Yeah, a creep for sure," Serena agreed.

While the man's creepiness was palpable, Elenora wasn't convinced it was him. She shook her head. "I don't think so."

"We can always go back to him—or any of them." Claire-Lune brought up the next suspect, another creepy dude.

Elenora shook her head again at him and then at the following five suspects.

The next one made her gasp.

"You recognize this man, Ele?" Tom asked, hopeful.

The man's stare pinned Elenora in place, filling her with a paralyzing sense of dread. There was something sick and dead in his eyes, a promise of something horrific. Alarm bells went off in her mind.

He was coming for her.

She felt weak in the knees.

"Ele?" Tom appeared before her, obstructing her view of the stranger and interrupting the overwhelming effect his mere image had on her. "Are you okay? Look at me."

Elenora made herself focus on Tom and reminded herself she was in a room with friends who had her back. She was safe.

"Who's this fucker, and is he still alive?" Alex's voice rumbled low as he asked Claire-Lune. His murderous tone hinted that the stranger's days were numbered if he was still alive.

"Father Crispin Bovet, and he's lucky to be dead," she

replied. "Little is known about him, except that he was a Jesuit priest interested in the occult. He drowned in a lake in Heritage, a remote gold-rush town in the Abitibi region in 1902."

"In Abitibi? In 1902?" Tom repeated, as if this would help him connect some dots.

"Yeah. Does any of this ring a bell?" Claire-Lune asked.

Elenora and Tom both shook their heads.

"The last name? You have no connections to that area?"

"Not that I know of," Elenora said. The Abitibi region was way up north and out of the way. People traveled there mostly when they had a reason to or a deep need for wilderness.

Serena approached the hologram and stared it in the eye. "So, he's one of the two creeps harassing you?"

Elenora nodded, and the witch drilled an even harder stare into the projected mug shot, as if she could virtually kick his ass. "What the hell do you want, bozo? Why are you after her?"

Elenora studied the man. *Father Bovet.* What could he possibly want from her?

And why was she such a creep magnet?

"I'll see what else I can find about him," Claire-Lune said. "This will sound like inane advice, but try to avoid him in the meantime."

CHAPTER THIRTY-SIX

"Yeah, no. Sorry, toots. No can do." Thelonious inspected his fingernails with a bored expression.

The team had migrated to Jeb's office so the attorney could request the hell custodian's presence. In this cozy, candlelit room, the team had once established a supernatural connection with the Gray Court to save their friend Rolland when he'd been possessed.

"You totes can do," Serena retorted, unfazed.

"You're right. I totally can." He gave her his trademark bright, used-car-salesman smile. Elenora's skin crawled.

"But you choose not to. May I ask why?"

"You may."

Serena took in a deep, calming breath to avoid throttling him. "Why?"

"Because." He shrugged before raising an eyebrow seductively. "Unless you have a proposition I can't refuse."

She groaned. "You're such an ass."

He grinned wider at her.

Jeb calmly observed their negotiation from behind his desk, his expression hard to decipher. Once upon a time, he and Serena had been an item, and their current relationship was complex.

"Fine. Bring us Lizzie Delacroix, and I'll do coffee," Serena told Thelonious, not bothering to suppress a noticeable shudder.

"Dinner."

"Coffee." She held her ground, looking determined not to give him an inch.

"Okay. Coffee..."

A slight smile curled the corners of Serena's lips.

"...with chocolate fondue," he added with a glint of mischief in his eyes, erasing her smile.

"Fondue takes forever," she grumbled.

"Take it or leave it," he shrugged again.

Serena shot her sister an annoyed glare. Claire-Lune answered her with an exasperated *It's just coffee!* expression.

Serena let out a huge sigh before telling Thelonious, "Fine."

A split second later, a female ghost materialized in the room. Her skin and dress bore severe burn marks. She seemed disoriented at first but then realized she was in the presence of strangers. She sprung back several feet, her eyes wild, her posture guarded. Ready to strike back like a feral animal being cornered.

"Mrs. Delacroix," Claire-Lune said in a soothing tone. "My name is Claire-Lune. My sister and I belong to the Ville-Marie coven—your coven. We are piecing together the horrible events that happened to you—"

"What do you know of what happened to me? Of my pain?" Lizzie snarled.

"We know a mob of men set you on fire in a chapel," Claire-Lune replied.

"Is that all you know?" Lizzie's sharp gaze shone with distrust.

Claire-Lune studied the specter, likely to give her the answer she wanted to hear and avoid further antagonizing her. "Will you please tell us what we should know?"

Lizzie sniffed. "If I have to explain, then you'll never understand."

"We understand you put a curse on the men," Tom tried diplomatically. "And it has recently killed two innocent people."

"If the curse affected them, they weren't innocent," she replied sharply. "They deserved it. They all deserved it."

"They had nothing to do with your grievances," Claire-Lune pointed out firmly. "It is not our role as witches—especially from the Ville-Marie coven—to dole out justice or punishment."

Lizzie bristled at Claire-Lune's rebuke and stared her down before ordering Thelonious, "Bring me back, minion."

He snorted. "You'd rather go back to hell than have this discussion? Wow. Somebody has a thin skin."

Uncertainty flashed in the eyes of the irate spirit, but she maintained her uncompromising stance and gave him a sharp nod.

The tall custodian from hell unfolded himself from the plush seat from which he had watched the show.

Serena warned him, "You bring her back now, and the coffee and fondue are gonna be to go."

Amused, he sat back and told Lizzie. "Looks like we're gonna be here a while."

"Mrs. Delacroix, I can only imagine how horrific it was for you to be burned alive," Tom said. "This should never happen to anyone. Ever. I am sorry you have suffered... Others are suffering now. If they deserve it, as you say, then they will pay the consequences—"

"By going to hell?" Lizzie asked snootily.

"I imagine."

She crossed her arms over her chest. "Then what's the difference between them going to hell and me sending them there a little earlier if that's where they are meant to go? Hmm?"

"It's not up to you to send them there," Serena reminded the specter.

"Was it up to the people who hunted me to send me there? When I didn't deserve to be hunted?" Each of Lizzie's words dripped with bitterness.

"It's *your* curse that sent you there," Serena reminded her.

Claire-Lune shook her head at her and mouthed *Not helping*.

"They pushed me into a corner. I stood up for myself when no one else did," Lizzie argued vehemently.

Elenora understood where the wounded specter came from. If she had been hunted, it was no wonder that she was angry and mistrustful. And by the looks of it, her time in hell hadn't been conducive to recovering from her trauma and making peace with her past—fear and rage still drove her.

Living in hell has to be the antithesis of therapy.

How could they get through to her in her heightened state of fight or flight?

"Did you know your sister, Agnès, hid your curse?" Claire-Lune asked her softly, her eyes watching for Lizzie's reaction.

The mention of her sister got the specter's attention. "Agnès..." Her breath hitched, and she blanched. "Did they get her too? Please tell me they didn't get her!"

"I don't know what happened to her, but I can—"

"Of course they went after her!" Lizzie's voice rose, becoming more frantic with each word. "Of course they did! Why wouldn't they?"

The specter fell to her knees, her breathing erratic. Elenora crouched next to her. "We don't know this for sure." She laid a hand on the woman's shoulder—it felt semi-solid.

Lizzie recoiled at the touch. "How could they not? They thought I was a witch. Logically, my sister would be one too!" She looked around, her gaze unfocused, as if Elenora weren't there. Lost in her agitation. "They're going to pay for this! I will make sure that they pay for this! They will all pay for this!"

Elenora struggled to find a way to appease the ghost, clearly in a state of crisis.

Lizzie stilled as a realization dawned on her. Her gaze grew wilder, and she smiled to herself. "If they think the current curse is bad..." she muttered to herself with sick enthusiasm.

Claire-Lune and Serena exchanged concerned looks.

"Thelonious, please bring her back," Claire-Lune asked Satan's emissary.

He looked at her lazily. "I'm not in charge."

"*Persecutores...*" Lizzie mumbled, searching for words. She nodded to herself. "*Persecutores et posteris tuis...*"

"Yeah. Bring her back," Serena commanded him.

"*Persecutores,*" Lizzie said confidently as tension shot up in the room.

"Bring her back now!" Serena shouted.

"'kay, babe. I'll call you. Wear something sexy." Thelonious winked at Serena while Lizzie chanted, "*Vōs et posteris tuis ex—*"

The custodian and the specter vanished.

After a moment of dumbfounded silence, Serena said, "Don't mind me while I go barf." She turned an accusing glare on her sister. "Remind me why I agreed to this."

"Your heart of gold made you agree to this," Elenora said to her friend. "Thank you."

Serena sighed, but her gaze softened.

"Want me to show up at the restaurant and glare at him the whole time?" Alex offered gruffly.

Speaking of hearts of gold.

The detective's offer took Serena aback. She looked somewhat pleased with his concern for her well-being. "Thanks for having my back, Alex, but that won't be necessary. I could handle Thelonious while under sedation and taking a test for Mensa. It just won't be my favorite thing."

Alex nodded despite looking unconvinced. "Okay. But say so if you change your mind."

"Was Mrs. Delacroix trying to change her curse?" Tom asked Claire-Lune, reminding the group their attempt at eliminating the curse had failed spectacularly.

"She was trying to broaden it. Include the descendants," the witch replied.

"Just what we need," Alex said. "If only we could crank up the heat to make her cooperate."

"She's been burning in the flames of hell for over three hundred years. I doubt any intimidation tactics would make her shake in her mules," Serena said dryly.

"So, we're back to square one," Tom said.

"More like minus fifty," Alex retorted grimly.

CHAPTER THIRTY-SEVEN

As Aubrey's bedtime neared, Elenora rocked her in the baby's room, her mind mulling over their impasse with Lizzie Delacroix.

If only there was a foolproof way to reason with the specter—and pronto. Things were precariously stable at Black Chapel, with the hearing aids out of play and Moss monitoring the premises. But what if something else triggered the curse, and it claimed another life? The team had to act fast.

If only they had something to act on.

Everyone was racking their brains for a solution.

On their way home from the OPO, Tom and Elenora had brainstormed ways to make progress and kept returning to the fallen witch as the key. If only they could bring her back to reason with her, but her return would likely allow her to cast her "improved" version of the curse, making everything drastically worse. Bringing her back felt like they'd have just a few seconds to disarm a bomb before it blew up in their face.

Elenora hummed to Aubrey as she rocked her, the

humming soothing the daughter as much as it helped the mother think.

If only Lizzie Delacroix would listen to them and give them a chance to plead their case. They sure hadn't gone through to her, and nothing showed that she'd ever be receptive to them in her damaged state of mind. Maybe her psychological scars were too deep for her to listen to reason.

Elenora remembered the spirit's reaction to the mention of her sister, her horror at the thought of Agnès suffering the same fate as hers. She cared deeply about her.

Agnès.

Had Lizzie ever listened to her?

Elenora stopped rocking. Would Lizzie listen to her now if that were an option?

What if they summoned Agnès in Jeb's office and brought Lizzie back again? Would that be enough to make the angry specter hear them out?

The idea enthused Elenora. Aubrey started babbling, prompting her to resume rocking. She couldn't wait to share her idea with Tom.

Maybe they should summon Agnès to assess the feasibility of this plan first and see how cooperative she would be. At worst, the Nouvelle-France witch might give them insights into how to deal with Lizzie. How to make her traumatized sister change her mind and consider rescinding the curse.

Elenora wondered if she could summon Agnès Dumoulin by herself. How convenient it would be to have a preliminary chat with a departed person at will and gather information. Save everyone time.

Hmm.

That'd be nifty. Maybe mastering her summoning technique would get her there someday. But for now, even though she knew Agnès Dumoulin's name, she'd probably need Yukiko's help since they didn't know where the witch had died.

"Maaammmmaaaaaaaa." Aubrey wriggled and pointed across the room.

Elenora looked up to see shimmering near the closet door, and her heart nearly stopped. She drew her daughter against her before realizing it might be Mr. Leclerc. She relaxed.

But then Willem hissed at the shimmering.

And Aubrey became even more agitated.

Elenora's mind began racing. What was going on? Were both the baby and the cat sensitive to this supernatural presence? And if so, who was it?

A skirt-wearing silhouette slowly materialized, and Elenora's heart nearly stopped again.

Not Mary! Please, not Mary!

Was Mary Gallagher about to visit her in her daughter's room, of all places? In all of her gruesome glory?

Would Aubrey see her?

Elenora wanted to scream a firm "No!" to prevent the spirit from appearing and invading their privacy, but she was too stunned to speak. Fortunately, she had the wits to cover her daughter's eyes to avoid scarring her for life.

"Peepapoo?" Aubrey asked.

The shimmering silhouette solidified into an unknown female specter with her head in the right place.

Not Mary. Thank God.

But Elenora's relief was brief. While Mary Gallagher was the opposite of presentable with her severed head on her hip, she had no reason to hurt Aubrey. This woman, however—who knew what her intentions were.

"Tom?" Elenora called despite knowing he was likely still in the shower and wouldn't hear her.

"I am not a threat." The female specter must have noticed Elenora's panic in her voice. She was an old lady with a gentle demeanor. Maybe wise, even. She reminded Elenora of Angéline.

"I didn't mean to scare you. I had a feeling you wanted to talk to me," the spectral stranger added.

Aubrey squealed at her, inviting her to glide closer and kneel at eye level with the baby. "You are adorable. I remember when my daughter was your age. A long, long time ago."

Elenora scrambled to cope with how her daughter seemed to react to the ghost. Or maybe her reaction was to Willem? The cat had trailed behind the apparition and now stood before them, staring up at the woman, his tail swishing back and forth over the floor.

"I am Agnès Dumoulin. Please do not fear me."

"Mrs. Dumoulin? How did you know I wished to speak with you?"

The ghost smiled at Elenora and studied her face affectionately, like one would a long-lost friend. "Like you, I have psychic abilities." Sadness flashed in her eyes, and she corrected herself. "I have *some* psychic abilities. I don't see everything coming."

"Like what happened to your sister, Lizzie?"

The specter nodded. "I dearly wish I had foreseen what happened to her and been able to prevent her horrible demise."

"And the curse?"

Agnès sighed. "And the curse. You must think she was an awful person. But please believe me, what she did—the curse—was out of character. Too many betrayals and heartaches had a devastating effect on her."

Elenora nodded—she had figured as much. "I understand. She is still very shaken."

"You saw her?" Hope emanated from the ghost's surprised face.

Elenora explained the situation to her, from her premonition of Eileen Robin's death to the frustrating encounter with Lizzie.

Agnès sighed again while shaking her head. "Always so stubborn and impulsive, that one. I am sorry she refused to cooperate."

"Can you undo the curse?" Elenora asked. Even though the OPO witches had tried and concluded that only the curse's originator could rescind it, it didn't hurt to ask. After all, Agnès Dumoulin had hidden the ugly spell. She might be familiar enough with its mechanics to undo it.

"Alas. I'm afraid that, given the circumstances, only she can undo it."

"What do you mean?"

"She pronounced a killing curse in a place of worship while a priest attempted to exorcise her as she burned to death. It's complicated."

"I appreciate that it's complicated, but innocent people are dying. If we let the curse be, it might keep happening," Elenora said before it occurred to her that maybe the witch had hidden the curse to protect it and keep it in place. The realization made her nervous. Perhaps the woman's intentions weren't as friendly as she appeared. If she was anything like her sister...

"Tom?" she called again.

"What's troubling you?" Agnès asked. She seemed kind and innocuous, but what if it was all an act? What if asking her to talk to her sister unleashed something worse?

But getting Agnès on board seemed like their only hope.

Dammit. Why did everything have to be so complicated?

"What's up?" Tom appeared in the doorway, toweling his hair.

Relieved, Elenora stood up to hand him the baby. "Can you please get Serena in a video call on your phone, stat? I'm having a lovely chat with Mrs. Agnès Dumoulin, Mrs. Delacroix's sister." She gestured to where the specter stood.

A look of understanding crossed Tom's face, and he remained calm. He took Aubrey in one arm and pulled his phone out of his pants pocket with his free hand. "How lovely. I cannot see you, Mrs. Dumoulin, but welcome to our home."

Agnès put a hand over her heart, as if touched. "Thank you. That's Tom, correct? I gather he's your husband?" she asked Elenora.

"Indeed. And he is calling our friend Serena, a member of your coven." She realized the witch might not understand how Tom was "calling" their friend with a hunk of metal, but it seemed unimportant. Agnès looked happy to be there. Keeping her in a positive mood was a good thing.

Serena answered the video call, and Tom filled her in. She, too, hid her surprise and rolled with it. Elenora's anxiety melted. Now that her friend was there, she could intervene if the ghost became hostile to them.

"Mrs. Dumoulin, it's such an honor," Serena said. "May I cast a revealing spell on you so that my friend Tom and I have the pleasure of seeing you?"

Agnès's eyes widened at Elenora. "She can do that?"

"She can," Elenora confirmed.

"By all means!" The specter hardly contained her excitement.

"She agrees," Elenora relayed the answer.

Elenora wondered if her friend not being in the room would hinder her revealing spell, but as Serena murmured the words, Agnès appeared to her and Tom.

"I'm curious why you concealed the curse," Serena said to Agnès.

Leave it to her to drop this bomb without ceremony. Elenora braced herself for the ghost's reply and for her good humor to shift under the veiled accusation.

"To protect the coven. In Europe, many hunted us, including some of our own, if you can believe it. Any of them could have come to the colonies, and I couldn't risk them discovering the curse and using its existence against us."

Serena nodded with understanding.

Knowing the spell concealment had been done with good intentions was a great relief. There was hope that Agnès could be on their side.

"If we connected you with your sister, would you try to convince her to undo her curse?" Elenora asked the ghost.

"Of course."

"Do you think she'd listen to you?"

CHAPTER THIRTY-EIGHT

"Dinner with coffee and chocolate fondue. Final offer," Serena spat.

Once again, the team was bartering with Thelonious in Jeb's office.

The hell custodian leered at the witch, his usual disturbing smile plastered on his face. "Oh, my dear, dear Serena... We both know I'm gonna require more than dinner for this new favor."

His smile broadened.

Elenora's skin crawled.

Serena fumed. "I'd say over my dead body, but I'm not going there," she muttered.

He chuckled. "Stop fighting it, love. It's only a matter of time."

"That's enough, asshole," Alex interjected before turning to Jeb. "Can we ask the Gray Court to send us a different clown?"

Elenora thought of Stefan, the cruel, stick-in-the-mud clerk they'd dealt with at the Gray Court when Rolland needed help to exorcise the serial killer possessing him. She doubted one of Satan's little helpers would assign them someone nice and helpful.

"Good luck with that. Everyone's on vacation." Thelonious smirked.

Alex snorted. "Yeah, right."

"Unfortunately, he's not wrong," Jeb said.

"Could we maybe explore another agreement, then?" Tom suggested.

Serena made a panicked face at him and shook her head, urging him not to go there.

"I doubt you have anything I want," Thelonious said, also shooting down that possibility.

"Then, would you please consider helping us for the sake of helping us?" Elenora blurted out and regretted speaking when the custodian turned his derisive expression on her.

"You mean out of the kindness of the heart I don't have?"

"Men with hearts are attractive. Just sayin'," Serena quipped.

The devil's emissary gave her a dry look before returning his attention to Elenora. "I don't do charity."

Then, something must have occurred to him because his mocking expression changed, and he looked at her differently. He became serious and took her in, as if noticing her for the first time. If Elenora thought his smiling self was disturbing, there was no word for his somber mood. After scrutinizing her for what seemed like an eternity, he declared, "Actually, there *is* something *you* could do for me. Laura, is it?"

"Elenora," everyone but Elenora corrected him.

"And there's absolutely *nothing* that she can do for you!" Serena barked in protest.

Thelonious ignored her and told the psychic. "There's this slippery guy who's been eluding me for too long. He's not honoring his pact, and he's a loose cannon."

Serena snorted. "Here's a fun idea: tell your boss to stop making shady deals with scuzzy losers. Problem solved."

He gave the witch a blank stare and then switched back to a businesslike expression when he looked at Elenora again. "Anyway. I don't like being toyed with. I want you to bring him to me."

Elenora blinked at him. Why would a powerful being from hell think that she, of all people, could help him catch an evil person he had trouble catching?

"Me? Why?"

Serena wedged herself between Thelonious and Elenora and looked her in the eye. "Please disengage. And no matter what, do *not* give him a blank check!"

"Shouldn't we at least hear why he thinks I can help, especially when he can't?" Elenora asked her quietly.

Serena whispered loudly, "He probably can't because his powers are limited on this plane. He's like a glorious bus driver between our realm and his, ferrying losers."

"I heard that," Thelonious said.

"I'd be disappointed if you hadn't," Serena said to him over her shoulder before telling Elenora, "It's not your job to do his job."

"You're right, Reena," Claire-Lune jumped in, "but Elenora has a point. Thelon, why do you think Elenora can help you? Maybe someone else on our crew can help."

Elenora became hopeful there might be a solution that didn't involve her.

The custodian contemplated her for another agonizing moment. "I doubt someone other than her can help."

"Why?" Alex asked gruffly, crossing his arms over his chest.

"Because I have a strong feeling he has an interest in her." *That* didn't sound good.

"That's it? You want to put her in harm's way because you have a *feeling*?" Serena exploded at the custodian.

"Who are we talking about?" Claire-Lune asked him calmly.

Thelonious stared at Elenora as he enunciated each syllable of his answer. "Crispin Bovet."

Aware he was trying to read her, she tried to control her reaction, but she inhaled a little too sharply.

"I see the name rings a bell." His smirk widened.

"What do you know about him?" Serena asked coldly.

"You think you're in a position to make more demands?"

"Nuh-uh. Not a demand. I'm asking so we can help *you*, dumbass."

Thelonious stared at her and said nothing.

"You want Elenora to catch this guy for you because he might be interested in her? That sounds like a dangerous—and very tall—order. Actually, like an unfair deal," Jeb said.

Thelonious must have known that Jeb was cunning and not to be messed with because he pondered his statement carefully before replying. "Then, I'd like to know why she reacted to his name."

"If we give you an answer—one answer—you will fetch Lizzie and leave Elenora alone?" Claire-Lune asked.

"One answer in good faith, and I will fetch Lizzie," he agreed.

"And leave Elenora alone," Serena emphasized.

"And leave Elenora alone," he said before adding, "For now."

Serena groaned.

Claire-Lune raised a questioning eyebrow at Elenora. "May I tell him why you reacted to the name?"

The psychic nodded.

Claire-Lune turned to Thelonious. "Father Crispin Bovet's reflection appeared to her in the plexiglass panel of a bus shelter. He did not speak to her. We just discovered his identity. We don't know what he wants from her, and we have no theories yet. But she felt threatened by him, so we intend to find out what he wants and make sure he leaves her alone."

While this was true, Elenora expected the Gray Court minion to question Claire-Lune's answer. Instead, he gave her a nod, like he trusted her.

"Anything you can tell us that will help us stop him should we get the chance?" Claire-Lune asked him.

"I'm just a bus driver," he retorted cheekily.

She gave him a pointed look that invited him to cut his bullshit. "And he's a common enemy. You have everything to gain from cooperating."

"Fine. He was a priest in Heritage during the gold rush, but you probably already know that. He sold his soul to prolong his existence on earth and later drowned himself in the town's lake."

"That doesn't make sense," Alex said. "If he wanted to live longer, why kill himself?"

Thelonious shrugged and beamed him his car-salesman smile. "That kind of logic is above my clown pay grade."

Alex glared at him.

"He must have found a loophole," Jeb mumbled thoughtfully.

"Anyway. That's all I know." Thelonious vanished and reappeared almost instantly with Lizzie in tow. She looked even more annoyed than before, scowling so hard it might leave a mark.

"I am not changing my—" the spirit growled as Serena threw a silencing spell at her, shutting her up. Wren had customized a spell to silence Lizzie and prevent her from making her curse even nastier.

Under the reassuring watch of Yukiko—who was in the room as a backup—Elenora's thoughts turned to Agnès as she endeavored to summon her. The friendly Nouvelle-France witch had told the psychic that she'd be on standby, waiting for her call.

"Agnès Dumoulin, I respectfully summon you. Please show yourself." Elenora brought up her mental dial overlay to tune into Agnès's frequency. The witch's eagerness to partake must have sped up the process—shimmering appeared by Jeb's desk and morphed into a fleshed-out apparition in record time.

If only all ghosts were this easy.

Lizzie was shocked to see her sister. "Agnès?"

Agnès floated to her with open arms, and they hugged each other tightly.

But then Lizzie pulled back, and her face became a mask of quiet rage. "I cannot forgive what they did to me. To us. If you are here to convince me otherwise..." she warned her sister.

"What happened to you, Lizzie, was horrific and unforgivable," Agnès agreed.

Tears appeared in Lizzie's eyes. "Honoré turned on me."

Agnès took her hands. "I know. But he regretted it bitterly."

Lizzie stared at her incredulously. "What do you mean?"

"He told me himself. And then his actions showed me he meant it. I lived a long life thanks to him. As did your niece and her daughters."

Lizzie shook her head in disbelief. "But how? Didn't my curse get to him?"

"Yes and no. The curse did affect him briefly and burned him. But he was already repenting when it happened. I suspect his remorse protected him and repelled the curse. I also think this proves his remorse was sincere."

Lizzie stared at her sister with a stunned expression. "Honoré was remorseful? My *husband* was remorseful? And he saved you and Portia?"

Agnès nodded. "Right after your death, he quickly came to his senses and knew we were in danger. He covertly helped us escape to a remote settlement despite putting himself in danger by doing so. I will forever be in his debt."

Lizzie considered her sister's words with conflicting emotions. "He did what was right," she conceded. "But he still betrayed me. And this does not excuse what Antonin Dujardin and the others did to me. I lost my own unborn daughter because of them. I cannot forgive them. The unfairness. We never asked to be hunted and live in constant fear.

You had to exile yourself to survive! You nearly lost everything again. Why aren't you angry?"

"Because they were fools. The world is full of fools. But the world is also full of good people. We can't make everyone pay for the sins of these fools."

"The curse only affects those who deserve to pay," Lizzie retorted.

"Are you certain? Are you telling me that, for once in your life, you had absolute control over a spell?" Agnès skewered her sister with a knowing look. Her words hit the target —Lizzie looked away. Agnès added, "From what I hear, it sounds like the curse triggers easily these days."

Lizzie changed the subject. "What happened to Dujardin? Did my curse get him?"

"It did."

A satisfied smirk played on Lizzie's lips. "I hope it burned him to a crisp. Do tell, and don't spare any details."

Thelonious snickered. "Oh yeah. There was a nice char on that posh asshole."

"He's in hell?" Lizzie asked him expectantly.

"Where else would that fan of Machiavelli be?" He chuckled to himself. "He tried to sweet-talk and blackmail my colleagues—thinks he can manipulate his way out of hell. Amateur."

"Thelonious..." Claire-Lune cocked a warning brow at him to mind his own business.

The custodian put his hands up in surrender and then mimicked driving with an invisible steering wheel. "I'll stick to driving."

"Lizzie, this is not who you are," Agnès told her sister.

"You are a healing witch. You don't destroy or revel in destruction—you mend."

"I *was* a healing witch. That ended when they scorched my world and took everything from me." Lizzie's bitter voice choked. "They murdered my precious daughter. How am I supposed to forgive?"

"It is your choice to forgive or not—and maybe you don't. Frankly, I don't know if I could forgive them or if they even deserve to be forgiven. But your curse is greater than forgiveness, than what they did to you. To us. A handful of hateful men are the culprits. They paid your price. The two souls who recently died from your words didn't deserve to get caught in someone else's revenge, and neither would future victims."

Lizzie began to shake.

Agnès went on, "I can believe you didn't foresee your spell ever being unleashed again. But it has happened, and unless you revoke it, it will destroy more lives. And this time, if you let it happen, you will be no better than Antonin Dujardin himself and those responsible for your death. Their deaths will be on you and your conscience for all of eternity."

"But it is Maman's curse for persecutors. If it fits, then they deserve it," Lizzie mumbled, digging her heels despite looking less sure of herself.

Agnès shook her head. "My dear sister, it is not for you to judge. You, of all people, should know this. We spent years running away from persecution because they feared us and judged us unfairly. And besides," she pointed out at Serena and Claire-Lune, "these fine women are our legacy. Your selfish curse is working against them. If you were in their shoes, you would be outraged. Your soul might be damned, but do you want them to remember you as an ancestor who disgraced their sisterhood and turned her back on them?"

Lizzie stared at her feet, a look of shame on her face.

"You worked hard to become who you are, Lizzie," Agnès said. "You earned the respect and love of your fellow witches in the Ville-Marie coven at its beginnings. And rightfully so. You worked hard, and you've always had a heart of gold. Grief and hurt tarnished it, but it doesn't have to be this way. You can't erase the damage done, but you can prevent further damage. Do you think it was easy for Honoré to do the right thing? Don't throw everything away because of hurt and misplaced pride."

She opened her arms to Lizzie and whispered, "I love you."

Lizzie hesitated before accepting her sister's embrace. And then she did and broke down in sobs. "I don't know how to reverse the curse."

CHAPTER THIRTY-NINE

Standing in the very spot in the chapel where she had cast her deadly curse and perished, Lizzie's ghost shook uncontrollably from sheer terror and panic.

Once she had agreed to undo her curse, the team had gone to Black Chapel with Wren and Juniper in tow. Elenora had summoned Agnès again while Yukiko watched on with a smile. Thelonious had refused to set foot in the holy room and had brought Lizzie back to it from the safety of the doorway. He waited there, pretending to be scrolling on his phone, but Elenora had caught him spying on them with interest.

Noticing Lizzie's distress, Elenora put a comforting arm around the terrified specter's semi-solid shoulders. She vividly remembered walking in the witch's shoes in the vision —the debilitating sadness and anger, the horror of burning alive.

Lizzie endured this unspeakable experience firsthand, and she's forced to relive it.

Elenora felt a surge of sympathy for her.

"You are safe. You are not alone," she told the specter.

"She's right. We're here for you, and no one can hurt you anymore. Breathe," said Agnès.

Lizzie let out a sob before inhaling deeply.

"I'm proud of you," Agnès added.

"You are brave to come back here and do the right thing," Elenora said. "Hopefully, this will bring you some closure, too."

A spark of hope flashed in Lizzie's eyes, the prospect appealing to her. "Let's end this," she said feebly, her voice carrying centuries of exhaustion. "What do I say?"

Wren had figured out a counterspell and was thrilled to pass it on to the strong-willed witch. She came forward and held up a piece of paper with neat handwriting in front of Lizzie. "Here."

Lizzie read the words and then turned a worried face to her sister. "What if I mess up? What if I make it worse?"

"You won't. This counterspell is strong and foolproof," Agnès said before smiling at Wren. "Wren is a wise and powerful witch." Her gaze traveled to the other women in the room. "You all are. I am proud and touched to see what our coven has become. You are magnificent descendants."

"We have magnificent ancestors," Claire-Lune returned the compliment to Agnès. She then looked at Lizzie, her expression remaining kind.

"I am sorry for the harm I have caused," Lizzie mumbled, averting her eyes. "I wish I were a magnificent ancestor instead of a disgrace."

"We all make mistakes," Serena said. "I, for one, am glad that you recognized your fault and have the strength of character to rectify it. I will not forget this."

Lizzie looked at Serena, grateful. "Thank you." She took a cleansing breath and focused on Wren's paper, memorizing the counterspell. She then glanced at everyone in the room, concerned and hesitant.

"We have your back, Lizzie," Serena declared. She linked arms with Elenora and then Yukiko. Her fellow witches followed suit, and they formed a circle around Lizzie and Agnès.

Lizzie's expression brightened, touched by their show of solidarity. Elenora felt equally moved. While she wasn't a witch from the Ville-Marie coven, she felt like she belonged with them. These women were the sisters she'd never had. A sentiment of security and purpose swelled inside her, along with a loving embrace around her heart.

Agnès beamed a wide smile. "This is wonderful."

This is *wonderful.*

A tear rolled down Lizzie's cheek, and she smiled. "It is, and I'm ready."

The witches stepped back to give her a wider berth. Yukiko placed two candles before the ghost. Claire-Lune and Juniper lit them with a snap of fingers.

Lizzie eyed the flames with apprehension.

"You can do this," Wren encouraged her softly.

"I agree," Agnès added. "My dear sister, you are a survivor. You are formidable. You can do this."

Lizzie steeled herself. With newfound determination, she pointed her hands at the flames and spoke the words of Wren's counterspell.

"*Persecutores poenas sunt. Maledictio, revertere ad me, et in aethere dispare.*"

The flames atop the candles flickered. Lizzie repeated the

words with more conviction, and the flames burned higher and brighter. Sparks flew from the fire to her hands, startling her.

Elenora's heart fluttered—was the witch about to catch fire again?

Serena put a calming hand on her shoulder and mouthed *It's normal* to her.

"You are doing great. Keep going," Agnès encouraged her sister.

Lizzie repeated the words. The flames flared. Ribbons of fire flowed to her hands, and her palms absorbed them.

"*Persecutores poenas sunt. Maledictio, revertere ad me, et in aethere dispare!*"

A shower of sparks shot from her hands like fireworks.

"Holy hell!" Alex said with awe.

The sparks became clouds of smoke and floated through the room.

"Crap! The sprinklers—" Tom groaned.

"Took care of them," Serena said.

The smoke dissipated, and the room returned to normal.

Agnès hugged her sister. "You did it!"

"Did I?" Lizzie looked around the chapel, dazed and unsure.

"I think so," Wren concurred.

"We'll sweep the room to make sure, but it looks like it," Claire-Lune said.

Taking her words as their cue, Juniper, Serena, and Wren went around the chapel, scanning the room with their distinct abilities to ensure the curse was truly gone.

"They will be so relieved," Miss Pouliot said after Tom told her the affected seniors could get their hearing aids back. The team had stopped by the director's office on their way out to let her know.

"I'm sure they will be. And I'll be in touch regarding the case." Tom had remained vague about the investigation. They would likely settle on the "faulty cell phone scenario." But first, they'd reexamine all the options with Günther and the OPO before giving the Black Chapel director an official statement.

As they made their way to the exit, Elenora felt a tingling sensation in her neck, like when she had left the Black Chapel attic. She turned to identify the cause of this reaction but saw nothing in the lobby. Was she imagining things again?

She took a few steps forward, and warm chills replaced the tingles.

Maybe it wasn't her imagination.

"Wanna get to the bottom of this?" Serena asked, guessing what was going on.

"Might as well."

The witch poked her head inside the director's office. "Miss Pouliot? My friend lost an earring the other day and thinks it might have been here. Do you mind if we retrace our steps and look for it?"

Elenora suppressed a smile, impressed with her friend's quick thinking. With the director's blessing and the team following her, the psychic let the warm chills guide her up the stairs to the top floor.

To the utility closet leading to the attic.

Alex headed for the stubborn door.

"Fore!" Serena warned before blasting the door open without ceremony, making Alex jerk back as it swung in front of him.

"*Fore* applies to golf!" he snapped at her.

Serena shrugged and started up the stairs. "A warning's a warning."

As the attic came into view, Elenora spotted a shimmering near the rafters. Her gut churned with dread as she realized what she was about to see.

Sure enough, the form of an imposing man dangling from a rope tied to a wood beam appeared in front of her.

Following her line of sight, Serena threw magic at the man, revealing him to them.

Alex recoiled with repulsion. "Dammit! I knew it!"

The hanging specter was hard to look at. The burned marks on his skin didn't improve the ghastly picture.

"Warden Delacroix?" Elenora presumed.

He stared at her, stunned. "You can see me? And you know who I am? Did Lizzie tell you about me?" He waited for her answers with urgent expectation, as if he'd been waiting for this moment for several lifetimes.

"Yes, we can see you. And Lizzie and Agnès told us about you."

His face lit up with hope. "You've seen her?"

"We have."

"How is she?"

"At peace. She rescinded her curse."

Relief washed over his damaged face. "She was a kind soul. Did she get into heaven?"

"She...moved on," Elenora replied diplomatically. She wasn't about to tell him that his wife had gone back to hell, even if Thelonious said he'd bring her to a *milder* realm because of her repentant actions—whatever *milder* meant in this case. Equally cryptic was his declaration that he might have some work for her, right before he vanished with her. They'd probably never know what that was about. The important part was that Lizzie had seemed at peace before leaving with the custodian.

Warden Delacroix's ghost nodded, his disappointment visible. "Then I presume you won't see her again. But if you do... Please tell her I am sorry I betrayed her. That I failed to protect her." His voice was gruff, and every word seemed painful for him to say. His tortured expression told Elenora he yearned to say more but couldn't bring himself to.

Maybe a man not used to admitting he was wrong or handling his emotions.

She wondered if he'd ever managed to tell Lizzie that he cared for her—that he loved her—since that seemed to be the case. She also wondered if his wife's demise and his guilt were the reason he was dangling from a rope.

Elenora offered him a sympathetic smile. "Sir, if I ever have the chance, I will pass on the message. But you might be comforted to know that Agnès told her you saved her and her daughter. Lizzie knows you regretted what you did."

The specter closed his eyes and let out a heart-wrenching wail of relief.

CHAPTER FORTY

Before leaving Black Chapel—and with Tom's blessing—Serena cast a light memory-soothing spell on the building to ease the residents' fears and restore a sense of safety. They would be left with a vague recollection of what had happened to Eileen Robin.

And then, later in the week, the "unrelated" death of Mr. Eric Decker would be announced.

Life would go back to normal.

Mostly.

Father Crispin Bovet lurked somewhere in the shadows, supposedly *interested* in Elenora. This mysterious threat was unsettling. But now that they knew who he was, Wren tailored a spell to alert the OPO if he ever appeared to Elenora again. The spell would slow him down and give the witches a shot at a magical riposte. While this plan was temporary and far from perfect, it was a good start in the right direction, and it reassured Elenora and Tom. It allowed the psychic to return to the mundane routine of her daily life and recover from the emotional roller coaster the Black Chapel case had been for her.

Doing a puzzle with Aubrey on the living room floor to the soundtrack of Romain's hammering in the powder room, Elenora mused about her role in figuring out Eileen Robin's bizarre death. Without her, the OPO would have eventually figured out the curse and a way to get to Lizzie. But who knew how many more casualties the deadly spell would have caused. Elenora's ability to sense and record the curse and bring Agnès on board had expedited the resolution of the situation.

Simply put, she had played a crucial role in preventing the deaths of innocent people.

She felt proud to be essential. But with great power came great responsibility. Their brush with the curse and Lizzie's chilling attitude had been a reminder of how devastating powers could be in the wrong hands. And how risky the business of solving paranormal crimes was. But in the end, the positive outcome—the happy ending—outweighed the crazy risks.

The witches' protective spells make a huge difference.

When Elenora worked regular cases with Tom, magical safety nets didn't exist, and the risks in civilian cases were just as real.

Am I trying to rationalize my decision to work for the OPO with rose-colored glasses now that the danger is gone?

Elenora snickered at herself. Maybe she was.

But so what if she was?

This felt right.

It felt like a calling.

And now, she knew she must embrace what she had

become. Use her gift for a purpose much larger than herself. Working for the OPO was in the cards.

Admitting this to herself and deciding to own her destiny brought her peace.

Her cell phone rang with an out-of-province number she didn't recognize. Probably a telemarketer. She considered not answering, but her gut made her push the answer button.

"Elenora Bello speaking."

Silence met her cheerful greeting. As she was about to hang up, a hesitant female voice asked, "You're Elenora?"

"I am. Who is this?"

"My name is Sylvie Robin. I'm Eileen's daughter. Detective Bélanger gave me your number."

Alex, right. He had been the one to talk to her. Maybe he thought she needed therapy and had recommended she speak to her. "My condolences, Ms. Robin. How may I help you?"

The woman dismissed Elenora's condolences and asked, "Is this a hoax?"

"I'm not following. What would be a hoax?" The conversation was taking a sharp turn into weirdsville. "How may I help you?"

After another hesitant silence, the woman inhaled loudly and said, "This is gonna sound crazy, but my mom told me to call you."

Ahhh! If prickly Eileen Robin had followed Elenora's advice and made contact with her daughter, the call finally made sense. Though the notion was as surprising as learning from Jeb that the nasty woman hadn't been on the hell registry like they'd thought. She had murdered none of her husbands, after all, and the underworld must have deemed her toxicity too vanilla to welcome her.

"Did she come to you in a dream?" Elenora asked the daughter.

"Yeah. Several dreams. In fact, she's been badgering me every single night to get in touch with you. I think she won't rest until she knows I spoke with you. Can you please make her stop? She's driving me crazy."

That sounded like Ms. Robin. Elenora suppressed a chuckle. "She wanted you to call me?"

"She said that was the only way for me to believe it was her for real. She's not wrong. She said you encouraged her to apologize to me."

"And did she?" This would also be surprising.

"Kind of. In her own way. She told me she wished things had been different. And that my life should improve now that she's gone. Except she's harassing me instead of leaving. She can't see the irony."

"From the little I know about your mother, she seemed complicated. But the fact she reached out to you tells me she cares. When I suggested she do this, she was adamant that she wouldn't."

A soft gasp came over the line. "You really did talk to her."

"I did."

A pause.

"After she died?"

"Yes."

Another pause.

"Is she going to be okay?" the woman asked with a tinge of concern.

"Now that she has reached out to you, I think she will be."

Sylvie Robin sighed—a mixed sigh of relief and frustration. "You know, I don't want to sound ungrateful. I appreciate her taking the first step. I recognize it must have been almost impossible for her. But, seriously, how do I make her stop?"

Elenora considered the question. She supposed she could try summoning Eileen and tell her Sylvie believed her, but Elenora might need to return to Black Chapel or ask Yukiko for help. Maybe there was a simpler way.

And then it occurred to her. "Tell her that when I met her, a woman named Serena called her a hag."

The daughter snorted. "I wonder why."

"Pass on that detail, and I bet she'll know you talked to me. If not, call me again."

This solution satisfied Ms. Robin's daughter, who thanked Elenora and hung up, leaving the psychic smiling. Elenora had assumed her advice to the curmudgeonly spirit had fallen on deaf ears. People never failed to surprise.

As Elenora reached for another puzzle for Aubrey, Romain passed by with his toolbox. The baby looked up at the contractor, smiled, and woofed at him.

He winked at her and barked back, making the baby giggle. Now that Elenora was paying attention, she noticed a canine quality in his response.

Hmm.

"Be back in a bit," he said to Elenora as he headed out the door.

Elenora nodded absently. Her daughter... What abilities did she have? Did she really sense that Romain was a shifter —if he was? Had she seen Agnès Dumoulin's ghost?

For once, Elenora mulled over the question without

panicking. In fact, her curiosity was growing. Exploring and embracing Aubrey's gift and destiny now seemed as inevitable as Elenora accepting her own.

And making sure that Aubrey would grow up to accept herself and thrive.

Elenora thought of the OPO daycare. They would guide and support them on this peculiar journey. This, too, felt right.

Daycare question solved.

CHAPTER FORTY-ONE

"Wish me luck," Elenora said to her cell phone, on speaker and propped up on a cinder block in Mary Gallagher's vacant lot. Happy to have settled the daycare question, the psychic was determined to tie up more loose ends in her life and had decided to meet Mary at everyone's earliest convenience to get the dreaded visit over with. To her delight, Tom, Yukiko, and Serena had managed to mobilize a few hours after her decision.

And now, here she was, in the eerie location, about to face the infamous ghost. Serena, Yukiko, and Tom watched and listened in from his and Elenora's car parked across the street.

The fall evening was already dark despite it being early. Aside from a steady flow of cars, the neighborhood was quiet. Since Elenora's summoning technique didn't require candles, it was thankfully discreet, and any passersby would only see a middle-aged woman in a vacant lot staring at the wall of a building bordering it. This scene was night and day compared to when she and Yukiko had held a séance there to coax Mary out of hiding.

Mary...

What did she want from Elenora?

Was she seeking revenge for her death? Would she ask the psychic to assist her in finding her murderer?

Elenora had done some research on Mary and found out that her alleged killer—her friend Susan Kennedy—had been brought to justice. Maybe the ghost didn't know that. It made sense that a spirit might have missed what happened after her beheading with an axe. Mary might also have missed the very odd demise of Michael Flanagan, a john she had brought to Susan's dwelling a few hours before Mary's death. Strangely, he drowned in a canal on the day Kennedy was initially scheduled to be hanged—though her death sentence had been changed to life imprisonment.

To this day, the circumstances around Mary's death remained murky. Michael Flanagan and Susan Kennedy's husband had been suspected initially but later cleared of wrongdoing. Susan insisted a mystery man had come over and killed Mary. Her claim sounded far-fetched, and the evidence against her was strong, but could she have been telling the truth when she said she was innocent? Maybe the ghost knew her friend hadn't killed her, knew the identity of her actual killer, and wanted justice.

But even if that were the case, the murderer was long dead, and little could be done to rectify the wrong at this point.

Unless one wished to involve the Gray Court.

I'm so not going there.

Hoping Mary wouldn't ask her for anything unreasonable, Elenora focused on her memory of the infamous specter's appearance while looking at where she had previously appeared to her and Yukiko.

Maybe she wants to move on.

After over a century of being stuck in a crappy space near a busy college campus in a neighborhood undergoing gentrification, the spirit deserved to move on if she wanted to. Elenora would need Yukiko's help for a crossing, so it was good that the medium was nearby.

"Mary Gallagher, I respectfully summon you. Please show yourself," she said gently, tweaking her overlaid mental radio dial. She smiled at the thin air before her, trying to make herself as non-threatening and welcoming as possible. "My name is Elenora. I come in peace."

A tiny warm chill briefly skimmed over her arm. Elenora smiled wider, thrilled that the technique might work on the skittish ghost.

"We have met before, right here. I think you wanted to talk to me."

A faint shimmer danced before her, as hesitant and ephemeral as the warm chill.

"Ms. Gallagher, my friend Rolland Carmichael says he played poker with you." During her prep, Elenora had wondered how to establish a rapport with the spirit. Rolland had met the woman a few times in the late 1800s. He hadn't socialized much with her, but maybe Mary would remember him.

A mass of warm chills wrapped around Elenora. Had she hit the bull's-eye? "Do you remember him?"

"Can one ever forget Rolland Carmichael?" a voice said as the shimmer brightened.

Was this really happening? Elation replaced the worries that had been pooling in Elenora's stomach.

The shimmering materialized into the same likeness of Mary Gallagher as previously manifested. The departed woman wore her heebie-jeebies-inducing blood-soaked dress and held her head against her hip.

Surprisingly, it wasn't the gore that caught Elenora's attention as she had feared, but Mary's wistful expression.

She smiled. "You do know him."

"I thought I had recognized him, that man with you. He's still as cheeky."

In the spring, before Elenora and Yukiko had attempted to summon Mary, Elenora had learned of the ghost's existence when she'd felt warm chills on her way to meeting Serena and Rolland at a nearby coffee shop. Her friends had recognized the location as a known haunted spot, and Rolland had even teased Mary loudly as they'd walked Elenora to her car.

The specter frowned. "Does he ever age?"

"He does now. It's a long story."

Back when he knew Mary, Rolland had been unpleasantly immortal before he was freed from Barlowe's spirit and the curse on him. He now lived a happy, normal life, thrilled to age like a normal person.

"Hmm." Mary's gaze surveyed the lot. "I gather he is not around."

"No, he's at home tonight." Elenora stopped herself, wondering how much of Rolland's private life she was at liberty to reveal and where the conversation was going. So far, it didn't sound like Mary was angling to enlist her to exact revenge on anyone. But maybe the spirit was stalling?

"We had some wild nights," Mary said, reminiscing fondly. Elenora was unsure how to interpret that—or if she even wanted to interpret that.

"I miss the camaraderie," the ghost added. "Does he still play poker?"

"He does. He still loves the game and tries to convince us to play with him, but—"

"You know better?" she snickered.

Rolland had always been quite the card shark.

"We are no match for him," Elenora admitted. Except for Serena, but even she had had to resort to magic once just to kick his ass and wipe the smirk off his face.

A glimmer of mischief appeared in the spirit's gaze. Her demeanor so far had been the opposite of their previous encounter, in which she had vanished before even saying a word. "I volunteer to challenge him. He owes me a hand or two..." Her expression turned hopeful. "I don't suppose you could arrange for this to happen, could you? Be an intermediary?"

The request threw Elenora off. "You would like to play poker with Rolland?"

"Yes. If it's not too much to ask." Then she added, "There's no hurry. I'm not going anywhere."

Hmm.

Mary's request was much more benign than expected but still posed a challenge. Elenora tried to assess its feasibility. Rolland would have to be on board, of course. Ideally, they would summon the ghost in a more private location than the lot. They might need Yukiko's help. Would Rolland perhaps agree to welcome Mary into his home? How would his girlfriend feel about this? Anna was exceptionally open-minded, but—

"Psst. Ele," Yukiko's whispered voice came from Elenora's cell. "Tell her we'll find a way and to expect a summon from you or me."

Upon hearing the disembodied voice, the ghost stiffened, and Elenora feared she would lose her. As she prepared to launch into an explanation to soothe Mary's concerns, the ghost curiously pointed at the cell. "Did the voice come from your little box? They seem to captivate everyone around here."

Elenora picked up the cell. "Yes, it's a phone without wires. The voice you just heard is my friend, the woman who was with me when we summoned you. With candles."

"Hmm. She seemed nice."

"She is. Is the poker game why you wanted to talk to me?"

"Yes, of course. Why else?"

"Well..." What to tell her? If Mary's true reason was indeed to reconnect with Rolland, Elenora certainly didn't want to suggest looking into her murder or anything else she couldn't deliver on.

"You thought I wanted to move on?" Mary suggested.

"It did occur to me. Do you want to? You've been trapped here for a long time."

Mary swatted at the air with her free arm in a pshaw gesture, which brought attention to her severed wrist and missing hand. Elenora had read about the limb but hadn't noticed its absence until now.

That's gonna complicate poker.

A wave of queasiness threatened to unfurl inside her, but the ghost spoke, redirecting her attention.

"I can be lonely sometimes, but there's no one waiting for me on the other side. My best friend betrayed me in the worst imaginable way, and I have no intention of speaking to my cheating husband ever again."

"You witnessed your own death?"

"No, I was sleeping when I was killed. But I heard enough of her lies and enough gossip about me."

"It must be hard to hear people talk about you," Elenora sympathized.

Mary shrugged and grinned. "I don't mind being a legend."

"Ele, you got company," Yukiko said from the cell. Elenora looked over her shoulder and saw a group of college students approaching with interest, probably wondering if she'd seen Mary.

The ghost flickered and waned. "I'll eagerly await your summons for a poker game."

Elenora: Guess who wants to play poker with you.

Elenora put her phone away. It amazed her how well her visit with Mary had gone. Why had she gotten so worked up over it? Fretting and obsessing over nothing. Again. So much unnecessary stress. Again.

Ugh.

She ought to stop doing that.

"How does she expect to play poker with only one hand?" she asked Tom while he drove them home.

"How does a ghost expect to play poker with the living at all?" he replied.

Whether or not Mary knew this, it would require a good dose of magic for her to play cards with Rolland. To be fair, the severed hand was a detail compared to that.

Elenora's phone chimed.

Rolland: Thelonious?

Elenora snorted. While Rolland had never met the satanic emissary, he'd heard plenty of rants about him from Serena, who loved to rage against him.

"What did he say?" Tom turned to her expectantly.

"I asked him to guess who would like to play poker with him, and he replied, 'Thelonious.'"

Tom snorted, too.

Rolland: I'll be happy to make him cry.

The text made Elenora snort again before she read it out loud.

Tom snorted again, too.

Elenora: I'd love to see that.

While she wasn't big on Schadenfreude, the opportunity of seeing Rolland humble the arrogant custodian would be something else.

Elenora: But no. It's Mary Gallagher herself. I think she'd like a rematch.

Little dots danced on the cell's screen. They stopped for a moment, started again, then stopped. It took a while before Rolland's reply appeared.

Rolland: I have no words.

Elenora: You're not alone.

Rolland: For real or are you joking?

Elenora: Not joking. But you don't have to agree if you're not comfortable.

Then again, it was Rolland she was talking to. If there was anyone on earth unfazed by the prospect of playing cards with a gory ghost, it was him. He was not only incredibly laid back and thrived on novelty, but he had also worked with the dead in a morgue—back when medicine used medieval tools and modern refrigeration wasn't a thing yet. And now, he assisted a doctor with a supernatural clientele. He lived a crazy life.

Rolland: I'm so in!

Elenora: I should tell her yes?

"Rolland's psyched to play poker with Mary," she said to Tom.

Tom chuckled. "Of course he is. Did you really think he'd say no?"

"No, but you never know."

"True. But he knows Mary."

"Yes, but he hasn't seen her in all of her gory glory."

"It sounds weird to say—and I don't mean this in a judgmental way—but don't you think he'll only be more fascinated?"

"Probably." Elenora looked down at her screen and smiled. Yeah, there would be fascination.

Rolland: Tell her to bring it on.

The dots danced again.

Rolland: When and where?

Elenora: Yukiko suggested we do a proper summon to up our chances, and Serena will put a revealing spell on her. So, this could happen anywhere, but a place close to the vacant lot might help.

Like Serena's condo, Rolland's place wasn't far from Mary's turf. Elenora hoped he might suggest hosting the game.

Rolland: Anna says you guys can all come over.

Yesss!

Elenora: If you don't mind, that'd be great. Let me check with Yukiko and Serena, and I'll get back to you. TY! You're a doll.

Rolland: I aim to please. Just so you know, the next few weeks are gonna be insane at work. But Mary's waited over a century for this, so what's a few more weeks, right?

Elenora: Totally.

CHAPTER FORTY-TWO

Elenora cursed her hunger as she padded down the stairs for yet another middle-of-the-night snack. As she reached the kitchen, she heard Mr. Leclerc talking to Willem. She smiled, ready to greet the kind ghost.

The kitchen was dark, but Mr. Leclerc's spectral glow gave away his location near the island. He was in deep conversation with...not the cat, but another man—a silver-haired stranger leaning against the counter, drinking wine.

Naked.

Elenora froze in the doorway, her brain struggling to figure out what she was looking at.

The two men turned to her. The stranger reached for a dish towel to cover himself with his free hand and took a nonchalant sip with the other.

Okay, this is a new one.

Mr. Leclerc looked at a loss for words. After opening and closing his mouth twice, he finally said, "I'm sorry we woke you up, Elenora."

The stranger chuckled. "You're only sorry because now

you have some explaining to do." He hid an amused smile behind another sip. He was lithe and probably in his thirties.

Mr. Leclerc turned a patient expression on him. "Willem, this concerns you as much as me."

"Willem?" Elenora repeated, dumbfounded. "Like the cat?"

The man put his glass on the counter and offered her a hand to shake. "That's right, Ele. I'm the weirdo you've been feeding cat food to."

Elenora blinked as she shook his hand mindlessly. "Our cat, Willem?"

"Do you have more than one cat?"

"Is there really a need for impertinence?" Mr. Leclerc gave the man a pointed look—though, like everything else about him, the reprimand was on the gentler side.

"You're right. I apologize," Willem said flippantly. "I rarely get to sass people with words."

"Elenora, my dear, this is indeed your cat, Willem. My longtime associate and friend. And—"

"A shifter?" Elenora said, still dumbfounded. "The cat?"

Hey, you've been rubbing elbows with witches, ghosts, and demons. Why is this far-fetched?

"Yes. A shifter. Just like your handyman, Woofboy," Willem said with a hint of disdain. "Didn't see that one coming, did you?"

No, but at least Woofboy *wears clothes in my house,* she wanted to retort.

Mr. Leclerc breathed in a long, patient breath. "Please don't mind his manners."

"What's wrong with my manners?" Willem raked a hand through his silver mane with feline grace. The long and lazy gesture struck Elenora. The cat man's mannerisms betrayed his nature. She also recognized his eyes, though the pupils were currently round instead of vertical slits.

"I have so many questions," Elenora mumbled.

"So do I," Tom said behind her, startling her. He had a gun trained on the naked stranger in his kitchen.

Willem snickered. "I'd love to say this is not what it looks like."

Tom frowned at the comment, unamused.

"We will be happy to answer your questions," Mr. Leclerc said.

"It's okay." Elenora motioned to Tom, silently instructing him to lower the gun.

His quizzical look asked her if she was sure about that.

She nodded emphatically. "Mr. Leclerc's spirit is happy to explain."

Tom lowered the weapon, his brows still knitting. "Mr. Leclerc? Willem's owner? He's here?"

Elenora remembered he couldn't see the ghost. Only an aloof stranger in his birthday suit. "Yes. And this is Willem."

"Our cat?"

"Willem told me your friend Serena has a spell to make spirits appear to civilians," Mr. Leclerc said to Elenora. "I need to go, but let's reconvene soon, and maybe she'll help so your husband can hear my answers firsthand?"

"That's a good idea." Elenora turned to Tom. "Mr. Leclerc proposes we ask Serena to make him appear for you when he explains what's going on."

"Farewell for now, Elenora." Mr. Leclerc's glow began to fade.

"Wait! How do I get in touch? A summons?"

"That, or tell Willem. We'll talk soon. You take care, my dear."

"You take care too, Mr. Leclerc," she said to the vanishing specter. She looked for Willem, not seeing him until her gaze dropped to the floor. He had transformed back into his feline form, his usual unnerving stare on her. Flicking his tail, he strutted to the patio door and pawed at it to be let out.

"Wise choice." Tom couldn't open the door for him fast enough. He locked it the second the cat was outside and tested the lock.

Elenora shared his relief that Willem was gone. She needed time to process having a shifter dude in her house. *If* they kept the cat. That was a big if. Who the hell would choose to keep a shifter as a pet?

A naked stranger who seemed obsessed with her baby daughter?

A shiver traveled down Elenora's spine. Hell no! They were *not* keeping the damn cat.

"I know that look." Tom slid an arm around her waist. "Let's go back to bed. The problem will still be there in the morning. I can promise you that."

She didn't argue and went back upstairs with him.

To think she had trouble sleeping before.

THANK YOU FOR READING!

Elenora, the gang, and the little boy at the bottom of the river will return.

If you enjoyed this book, please consider leaving a review. They are always appreciated.

For book news and reader perks, sign up for my newsletter: http://www.jacinthedessureault.com/newsletter/

A THOUSAND THANKS

Thank you, family and friends, for your support and words of encouragement, especially in this time of grief.

And thank you, Nadene and Gloria, for your feedback and much-appreciated enthusiasm.

ABOUT THE AUTHOR

Jacinthe Dessureault writes paranormal mysteries and humorous fiction. She is a big fan of lemon meringue pie and the silly antics of Jackson, her family's adorable lop bun. She lives in Montréal, Canada.

For more information: www.jacinthedessureault.com.

HER BOOKS

Elenora Bello Paranormal Mysteries
Shade of Evil (short story prequel)
A Sinister Gift
Trapped Souls
Dark Ashes

Humorous Fiction
Igloo High (young adult)

9 781999 443177